EDEN WAITS

*A novel based on the true story of
Michigan's utopian community,
Hiawatha Colony*

MARYKA BIAGGIO

Milford House Press
Mechanicsburg, Pennsylvania

MILFORD HOUSE

an imprint of Sunbury Press, Inc.
Mechanicsburg, PA USA

For information about special discounts for bulk purchases, please contact Sunbury Press Orders Dept. at (855) 338-8359 or orders@sunburypress.com.

To request one of our authors for speaking engagements or book signings, please contact Sunbury Press Publicity Dept. at publicity@sunburypress.com.

ISBN: 978-1-62006-354-5 (Trade paperback)

Library of Congress Control Number:

FIRST MILFORD HOUSE PRESS EDITION: August 2019

Product of the United States of America
0 1 1 2 3 5 8 13 21 34 55

Set in Bookman Old Style
Designed by Chris Fenwick
Cover by Chris Fenwick
Edited by Chris Fenwick
Cover Photo by Brenda Weber Sangraw (used with permission)

Continue the Enlightenment

Dedicated to my lovely mother, Phyllis T. Biaggio, Aunt Dolores M. Hawthorne, Uncle Gerald M. Weber, and all the other descendants of Abraham and Elizabeth Byers. May their memory live on.

THE CAST OF CHARACTERS
(in alphabetical order by first name)

Abraham Byers. Itinerant preacher and founder of the Hiawatha Colony. Married Henrietta Lee in the early 1850s and had five children. After Henrietta died in 1861, he married Elizabeth Ann Kepler in Indiana and they had four sons.

Alberta Noel. Wife of Gideon Noel, first President of Hiawatha Colony.

Alice Highland. Wife of Gus Highland, the first Vice President of Hiawatha Colony.

Alva Kepler. One of the original landowners of the Byers' Settlement. Husband of Ann Kepler.

Ann Kepler. Wife of Alva Kepler and one of the original landowners of the Byers' Settlement.

Artin Quick. Manager for the Chicago Lumbering Company in Manistique.

Beech Byers. First son of Abraham and Elizabeth Byers. He proved up 80 homesteaded acres in the Byers' Settlement and worked in the lumber mill in Manistique.

Charles Bernardo. Member of the colony and associate of colony officers.

Claude Faust. The first elected Secretary of the Hiawatha Village Association.

Clifton Huey. Youngest son of Sarah and Eli Huey.

David Byers. Abraham and Elizabeth Byers' youngest son.

Edgar Huey. Eldest son of Elizabeth Byers' sister, Sarah, and Sarah's husband, Eli.

Eli Huey. Disabled husband of Sarah Kepler Huey and Civil War veteran.

Elizabeth Kepler Byers. Wife of Abraham Byers, the matriarch of the Byers' Settlement. She served as doctor, midwife, and nurse to the other settlers and neighboring residents.

Elonzo Byers. Abraham's oldest son by his first wife and one of the original claimants in the Hiawatha homestead.

Elvila Kepler. Abraham Byers' niece. She and her husband, John, who was Elizabeth Kepler Byers' half-brother, were among the original 1882 claimants of the homesteaded lots in the Byers' Settlement.

Emil Forberg. Member of the colony and associate of colony officers.

Emily Rose. Joined the Byers' Settlement in its early years with her husband and remained as colony member.

Essie Wright. Moved with her family to Hiawatha Colony in 1894.

Florence Byers. Married Beech Byers around 1888. They had two children, Goldie and Artie.

Francis Mills. Son of Walter Thomas Mills, elected to officer position in the colony.

Frank Dodge. Justice of the Peace and neighbor of Alva and John Kepler families.

Fred Scadden. Officer of the Manistique Bank.

Gideon Noel. First elected president of the Hiawatha Village Association.

Gus Highland. Employee of Chicago Lumbering Company Mill in Manistique who later joined the colony.

Harvey Booth. Son of Abraham Byers' sister. A close companion of Abraham Byers, he joined him on preaching forays as assistant preacher.

Ida Smith. Member of the colony in charge of the sewing department.

John Henry Randall. Active member of the Greenback Party who organized a march of unemployed men on Washington, D.C., in 1894. He and his family joined Hiawatha Colony later that year.

John Kepler. Elizabeth Kepler Byers' half-brother. His wife, Elvila, was Abraham Byers' niece. He was one of the original 1882 claimants of the Hiawatha Settlement homesteaded lots.

Jonas Wright. Wagon driver and colony member.

Joseph Booth. Son of Harvey Booth, he lived in the Byers' Settlement.

Josephine Byers Lobdell. Daughter of Abraham and his first wife; married to Ira Lobdell.

Lenniel Byers. Abraham and Elizabeth's third son.

Link Byers. One of Abraham Byers' sons by his first wife.

Lottie Randall. Daughter of John and Charlotte Randall.

Lucinda Clark. Wealthy widow from Peoria. She made a financial contribution to the Hiawatha Village Association upon joining the colony.

Mary Mills. Walter Thomas Mills' first wife. She accompanied him on his first visit to the settlement.

Nettie Mills. An aunt of Walter Mills.

Pearl Huey. Daughter of Sarah and Eli Huey and niece of Elizabeth Byers.

Sarah Kepler Huey. Elizabeth Byers' younger sister and wife of Eli Huey. She and her husband, Eli, had five children.

Walter Thomas Mills. Well-known orator and progressive political activist of the late nineteenth and early twentieth centuries. In 1894 he published **The Product-Sharing Village**, an important influence on Abraham Byers.

A MAN OF THE PEOPLE

JULY 1892

"Dear Lord in Heaven, how could he be so heartless?" Abraham Byers switched the wagon reins to his left hand and faced his son. "Are you telling me Artin Quick refused to take Gus to the doctor?"

"We didn't even look for him." The wagon heaved over a bump in the rough dirt road, jostling Beech. "It happened fast, blood was spurting everywhere."

"You let Quick off the hook. Just what you shouldn't have done." Abraham, a wiry man of sixty-three, hoped he'd seen the last of grinding poverty when he moved his family to Michigan's Upper Peninsula. But now desperation nipped at his own relations, who depended on the Lumbering Company for their wages.

"Don't you lecture me." Beech scrunched up one side of his lean face, glaring at his father. "I couldn't just stand by and watch Gus bleed to death. I wrapped up his hand and took him to the doctor myself."

Abraham thumped a palm to his knee. "It's not right for Quick to dock your pay."

"That's what I told him. He just kept saying, 'company policy, company policy you can't absent yourself without notice. You know the rules.'"

"Company policy is to discard the maimed. How many more will end up like Joshua?" Abraham was referring to his great-nephew, whose leg had been crushed at the mill, rendering him fit only for tending the settlement's livestock and hauling goods by wagon.

Beech stared ahead at the road tunneling into thickening woods. "Don't start on that again."

"Artin Quick needs a lesson in common decency."

"And you're not the one to deliver it. You'd just get me fired."

The prospect of denouncing Artin Quick sorely tempted Abraham. This wasn't the first time Quick had set Abraham's blood to boiling. "I can't stand by and let even more be mangled. It's got to end."

"You'll stay out of it. I've worries without you adding to them."

"All they care about is raking in money for the owners."

"And all you care about is spouting off. That'll not help any of us."

The way Abraham saw it, his son was only one of many hurt by the Company's cruel ways. Some three dozen of his relations also depended on the Lumbering Company for work, to say nothing of all the men come to Manistique on the promise of decent wages. "I believe I can find a way to help you and the others."

Beech spun around toward his father. "What're you talking about?"

"I'm the settlement's preacher. I'll do what's right for all of us."

Beech locked eyes with his father. "And what's that?"

"Not sure. Have to figure some more." Someone had to fight the Lumbering Company and its cold-blooded ways. Otherwise, they'd squeeze the life out of every last worker and then turn around and bring in a fresh crop of hungry men. Why, his own son was already struggling to support his wife and two young ones on paltry pay.

Beech gripped his father's forearm. "Promise me you won't go riling 'em up."

"Don't you trust your own father to care for his own?"

"Not sure I do." Beech raised up his chin. "If you do anything that costs me my job, there'll be a mountain of trouble between us."

"All right, all right, no reason to bring that up." It was true, Abraham had failed in his fight against the Furnace Company's harsh ways. Still, a man ought to do some good in the world, not end up feeling helpless and poor of spirit. He swore when he moved his family north that he'd make up for what happened at the Furnace Company, and now, as God was his witness, he would. But he'd let his plans simmer and take one small step at a time. The Lumbering Company owners and managers were not to be trifled with. His every move must be sure-footed.

Abraham decided not to worry Beech about the scheme he was forming. He clapped a hand on his son's shoulder. "It'll be all right, Son."

Beech rubbed his brow. "I hope you're right."

"Now, let us enjoy this fine summer day." Abraham leaned back and said a prayer of thanks for the agreeable weather, beautiful land, and his good health—his straight back, strong arms, and steady legs. Still, at times he felt his sixty-three years, in muscles and joints that ached after cutting down trees, chopping wood, tending livestock, and mending wagons and implements. But he just slept it off and started over the next day. That was all a man could do: give his best to taking care of his wife and kin.

The two horses drawing their wagon swished their tails at deer flies, and the July sun bore down on Abraham's back. He opened his top shirt button and jangled the reins, urging the horses to pick up the pace. They had a long trip ahead from the edge of Manistique to their settlement in the woods of Hiawatha Township—twelve miles over the cut pine flats and rocky rollaways, past the slough and through the thick hardwood forests wedged between Lake Michigan and Lake Superior.

Abraham loved this land. Whenever the evils of the world stirred him to anger or impatience, its peacefulness calmed his soul. Almost every time he made this drive, he indulged in the memory of his first foray, ten years ago this summer. It was August of 1882, one of those perfect summer days filled with glowing heat and tepid breezes. He'd prevailed on his most trusted companion, Harvey Booth, his nephew and assistant preacher, to take up pack and blanket roll, travel by train to Michigan's Upper Peninsula, and venture out across its dirt and corduroy roads. The pre-emption law had opened land for homesteading, and he hoped to find parcels for himself and his many relations.

"Think of it, Harvey," Abraham mused as they rode through a stand of towering white pines. "We could leave off preaching on the streets of hardened cities."

Harvey, a sturdy forty-two-year-old widower, nodded. "It'd be a chance to start fresh."

"Yes, we could build a community of our brethren."

Several miles inland from the north shore of Lake Michigan they meandered on horseback through an expansive stand of beech, maple, and birch. Abraham straightened in his saddle and gazed at the plush forest floor and its jade-green brush, all stippled in golden hues. Perking up his ears, he said, "I feel the Lord's presence here, Harvey."

"Amen, Uncle. The sun shines like rays from Heaven through these treetops."

Abraham and Harvey steered their mares toward the fringe of a swamp lined with cedar, and Abraham pulled on the reins.

"Look," said Abraham, sliding out of his saddle and squatting down to scoop his hands into a clear, gurgling spring. He tasted the water—so pure and cold that its sweetness lingered long on his tongue—and splashed it on his sweaty face and mosquito-bitten neck. As he rose and turned a full circle, he divined, in the flicker of shimmering branches and the whisper of the breeze, the strains of angels' songs.

"This is it." He smiled up at Harvey. "This is our Eden."

From the fall of 1882 on through the summer of '83, the relations of Abraham Byers and his wife—eight Byers and Kepler families in all—proved up eight adjacent 160-acre parcels in Hiawatha Township. They logged pine and hardwood to build cabins and craft furnishings, cleared stumps to make meadows, and planted gardens and orchards. Even a few neighbors, drawn by the settlers' religious spirit and adherence to temperance, bought tracts from the homesteaders. They called it Byers' Settlement, and Abraham Byers proudly reigned as its patriarch.

Abraham turned the wagon up his drive. At the sight of his lean-limbed wife, Elizabeth, stepping out the door to greet them, he broke into a broad smile. Abraham had endured loneliness and privation after his first wife died of childbed fever, so he thanked the Lord every day for Elizabeth's thirty-some years of steady companionship.

"Hello, Mother," Abraham called to her. He brought the horses up short alongside the house and climbed down from the wagon.

Elizabeth scanned the empty bushel baskets in the wagon bed. "Looks like you sold all those huckleberries."

Beech hopped down, hitched up the pants sagging from his sinewy frame, and circled around in front of the horses. "You know Father," he said, giving his mother a peck on the cheek. "Could sell buttons to a button peddler."

"Berries is not what matters today," said Abraham, his mind abuzz with plans. He reached into the wagon bed and gathered his satchel and the filled-up tin kerosene can.

"Well," said Elizabeth, planting hands to her hips, "I hope they mattered enough for you to get a good price on them yesterday."

Beech smiled at his mother and tugged the lead horse's rein. "I'll unharness the horses."

"Don't you fret, Mother," said Abraham, taking Elizabeth's brusqueness in stride: He understood she had a household to manage, and that required money. He followed her into the house and plopped his satchel and the two-gallon can on the table. "I've got the money. And your kerosene, too."

Elizabeth closed the door behind Abraham. "How much the berries bring in?"

"Two dollars and twenty cents." Abraham pulled a crumpled bill and some change out of his pocket. He plunked the money down on the table. "Government's not printing enough green-backs."

"Doesn't make sense we can't get the same price as last year."

"The government could fix this if they wanted to."

"Price of flour's higher than ever," said Elizabeth. "Where's the money going?"

"Hmm," said Abraham, brushing his bone-white beard. "That's just what the farmers are asking."

"How we supposed to afford flour and lard and everything else?" Stepping up to the table, Elizabeth lifted a handful of water-covered huckleberries out of a bowl, picked out the stems, and dropped the berries into a hefty pot.

"We'll have to find a way. Sell more venison or trap more beaver." Abraham made a note to get all the traps in working order. He didn't have the heart to confess to Elizabeth: In recent years he'd relied more and more on Harvey's help setting traps and, even then, they'd ranged far and wide to collect a respectable number of pelts.

Elizabeth sighed and shook her head. "Beech have any news?"

"Gus Highland had an accident. Lost part of two fingers. Beech drove him to the doctor." Abraham shook his head in disgust. "Artin Quick docked him a day's wages for leaving without notice."

"Humph," Elizabeth grunted. "Up to their usual shenanigans. Gus going to be all right?"

"It's losing wages while he heals up that'll hurt." Abraham waited for Elizabeth to look up at him. "But the company just might get their comeuppance—and soon."

"How's that?"

Abraham stood beside the table, pulled the Populist Party circular out of his satchel, and held it up like a flag. He liked trying his ideas out on Elizabeth, not that she was the type to sympathize. But at least he could hear the rhythm of his spoken words, for he knew well the power of a convincing cadence. "The Populist Party has a platform. A new wind's blowing across the country."

"Platform? What's it mean to us?"

"I tell you, Mother, it's the most poetic and pure statement of God's vision for the common man you'll see outside the Scriptures. The preamble alone sets me to shivering."

Elizabeth looked up from her berries.

"Just listen to this." Abraham read: "Corruption dominates the ballot box, the legislatures, the Congress, and touches even the ermine of the bench. The newspapers are subsidized or muzzled, homes covered with mortgage, and land concentrated in the hands of the capitalists. Workmen are denied the right to organize, and public opinion silenced. From the womb of government injustice, we breed two classes—tramps and millionaires."

Abraham waved the paper before him. "I see change sweeping this land. With this platform James Weaver will take so many votes from the Democrats and Republicans, the whole country will take notice. Finally, there'll be someone to rein in the

Lumbering Company barons. And with God's blessing, I aim to join the fight against corruption and injustice."

Elizabeth plunged her hands into the watery bowl of berries. "Oh? How?"

Abraham pulled himself up to his full five-foot-three. "The Populist Party is wanting local organizers. I'll hold a convention here to support the party and elect the next president of the United States."

The slightest humph escaped Elizabeth's lips. She kept her eyes trained on her work. "Fine, as long as you still see to this household—and the settlement."

Abraham saw Beech emerging from the barn. He tucked the circular back in his satchel. What Beech didn't know he couldn't fret about. "Mother, this is the very way for me to do that."

Over the next month, Abraham traversed all corners of Schoolcraft County, selling subscriptions for *Populist Nation* and preaching politics on doorsteps and at the city's bandstand: "The fruits of the toil of millions are stolen to build colossal fortunes for a few, and the possessors of those fortunes endanger Liberty . . . We can't count on either the Democrats or Republicans to help our mill workers and brothers in the mines . . . It's the Populists we need."

It was trying work. Many shooed him off their doorsteps, but he prayed that those who listened would recount his words to their sons and brothers around the dinner table. Although he gathered crowds of only four to ten at the bandstand, he enjoined them to spread the message far and wide.

Editors at the Manistique *Weekly Tribune* published the occasional report on Abraham's speechifying: "Mr. Abraham Byers is so besotted with the Populist platform that it's hard to tell where their candidates leave off and Mr. Byers begins . . . Mr. Byers commences to think free speech is not allowed in Manistique. Indeed, free speech is alive and well, but our citizens sometimes insist on a certain voice being rested."

"They've got their own crow to pluck," Abraham told Elizabeth upon reading the paper's comments. Abraham felt it in his bones—now was the time for change, and he would be the Populist Party's instrument. Words to the contrary would not scare him off. "Of course, they wouldn't take to the Populist Party. The Lumbering Company owns all the newspapers, to say nothing of the rest of Manistique. But they'll not silence me."

A SETTLEMENT OF KIN

AUGUST 1892

Not many knew it, but it was Abraham's wife, Elizabeth Kepler Byers, who deserved most of the credit for founding Byers' Settlement. It was 1882 when she put the homesteading notion in Abraham's head. Her suggestion to up and move from their southwest Michigan farm seemed natural enough to her. She was nearing the forty-year mark, and she figured it'd be easier to up-root a household while she still had sons at home to pitch in with the organizing, selling, and packing. So she told Abraham, "I want more womenfolk near. Let's gather our kin close around us." When Abraham asked how she proposed doing that, she was ready with her answer: "Homestead some land for all of us. Look here," she said, pointing to an announcement in the *Van Buren County News*, "Pre-emption law opens up land for homesteading in the Upper Peninsula."

When Elizabeth said she wanted their kin closer she didn't mean only the four young boys she and Abraham had and the four stepchildren from Abraham's first marriage on top of those. No, she meant her siblings and half-siblings, too. For Elizabeth had tasted loss early—her first husband left her a Civil War widow after three months of marriage—and she cherished the closeness of kin as much as any woman who ever gave her all to a husband only to lose him.

In all their ten years living off this rugged land, Abraham never told anybody the settlement was her idea. But this mattered little to her, for she cared more about getting her way than shouting to the world that she knew how to get it.

And now, ten years later, Elizabeth and Abraham were settled in a sturdy frame house in the middle of a meadow, where pine-scented breezes wafted over knolls and stiff, dew-laden fescue sparkled in the sun. Yes, she this new life pleased her, though she admitted the harsh winters tested her and her rheumatism. But she'd gotten her way, and while Abraham was in town cajoling his fellow citizens to take up the Populist cause, Elizabeth looked after the citizens of the settlement in her own way.

Today Elizabeth stood at the kitchen table, her spright five-foot-two frame pivoting as she kneaded a two-loaf lump of dough. She glanced through the side window, which gave a clear view of the well and the settlers who visited it regularly. Abraham sat in his low-slung reading chair, sifting through the week's issues of the *Pioneer Tribune*.

"Well, look at that," said Elizabeth when she spotted Florence, the twenty-two-year-old wife of their eldest son, Beech, making her way to the well with a few others.

Elizabeth knew better than Abraham—or anyone else—about the goings-on in the Byers' Settlement. From their porch she could see any rider or wagon coming into or leaving their lands. Without really trying, Elizabeth had become the social center of the thousand-plus-acre settlement, the point where all the spokes of the wheel that counted for family and friends—sons and step-sons; brothers, sisters, and in-laws; nieces and nephews; and unrelated settlers—came together. She was the first one the other settlers thought of if they needed to borrow some lard or sugar or wished to air a grievance about a neighbor. They started out by studying her square face, with its broad forehead and thin lips. If her brow was relaxed and her green-blue eyes serene, then the conversation was sure to flow like a meadow stream, and she could be counted on to offer help. But if any hint of a scowl cramped her level forehead, well then, she'd be the one inquiring and discoursing.

Elizabeth looked through her kitchen window, studying the group tramping to the well.

Heading up the party was three-year-old Goldie, Florence and Beech's little girl, tugging at her mother's hand. Despite Goldie's urging, Florence kept a steady pace, her head held high and her long chestnut hair bunched loosely under her soft-brimmed cloth hat. Florence clutched her little boy Artie to her side, and his baby-plump legs dangled and jerked with the rock of her hips. Harvey Booth, Abraham's much-loved nephew, followed close behind Florence, toting two buckets and gazing ahead. Bringing up the rear was Harvey's son, Joseph.

Abraham leaned sideways for a view. "Don't know why you bother yourself about it."

"I tell you that Joseph is trouble." Elizabeth peered at twenty-year-old Joseph, who gripped a bucket in each hand and swung his arms in casual arcs. She couldn't say exactly what bothered her, other than something about Joseph's long-legged stride, the swoop of his abundant black hair, and the stiff way he held his head. It put her in mind of a brooding stallion. She fixed her attention fixed on the party, pausing from her kneading.

Florence stopped beside the well and hiked her son up on her hip. Her muslin-colored cotton dress rippled in the wind, and the brim of her bonnet buffeted her forehead. She pitched her head back, stood stock-still, and let the wind waft her hat brim up off her brow.

Harvey latched the bucket to the well hook, and Joseph wheeled down the windlass. Joseph's back was to Elizabeth, but she could tell that he looked in Florence's direction as he turned the crank with slow, sweeping motions. Studying Joseph, Elizabeth said, "He's prideful. That's what it is."

"He's just a lad. Harvey'll steer him right."

Elizabeth frowned with the skepticism of a seasoned schoolmarm. "Isn't it time he started at the mill?"

"Harvey needs him here. He's strong," said Abraham, relaxing back into his chair. "And good with the horses and wagon."

Elizabeth slapped the flank of her hand against the middle of the dough ball and folded it onto itself. "Just because that's what Harvey wants doesn't make it right."

"Harvey's a good father. He brought his children up to know godliness."

Elizabeth leveled her gaze at Abraham and waited to catch his eye. "Knowing and doing are two different things."

"Oh, Mother," said Abraham, closing his newspaper. "I don't want to hear any more of your complaints about Harvey."

"Not talking about Harvey. Joseph's been skulking around ever since our David and Lenniel left."

"Well, I expect he misses them. They were like brothers to him."

Did she need to spell everything out for her husband? He could be so exasperating. "Joseph thinks you should've convinced Harvey to let him go off for schooling, too."

"'A sound heart is the life of the flesh: but envy the rottenness of the bones.' Proverbs 14:30."

"Don't preach to me about it," Elizabeth said. "Joseph's the one needs sermonizing."

Abraham leaned over to grab his satchel.

Elizabeth picked up her mound of dough, flipped it over, and let it land with a thud. "And if Harvey'd let him work at the mill he'd have money for schooling. Wouldn't be passing the time with Florence."

"Just being neighborly," said Abraham. "It's hard on Florence having Beech gone so much."

Elizabeth just didn't trust Joseph. When he was a youngster, she could hardly coax a smile out of him, even when she offered him a piece of pie, as if he resented anybody doing him a good deed. "There's such a thing as being too neighborly."

Abraham tucked his pack of newspapers into his satchel and flapped it shut. "It's Florence I worry about. Too headstrong. Beech ought to take her in hand."

"It's not his way. And I expect he likes her spunk."

"Well, Mother," Abraham said, standing and shaking down his pant legs, "you may think a man wants spunk in a wife, but it only leads to problems."

"You don't mind my spunk when I'm chasing weasels out of the chicken coop in the middle of the night." Elizabeth's eyebrows arched up. She'd not tolerate Abraham's dismissive ways. "I'll remind you who keeps this house running while you're gallivanting all over the county."

"Yes, I'll leave you to it then and get to town." Abraham came up beside Elizabeth and kissed her forehead. "Need to get a letter to the editor submitted."

She could look Abraham level in the eye if she chose, him being only an inch taller, but she kept herself pitched forward over her kneading job. She plunged the heels of her hands into the dough. "Get a good price for those apples."

"Best I can," he said, taking up hat and satchel. "I'll be back with Beech tomorrow."

Elizabeth sighed as Abraham tromped out. No sense telling him she had enough chores to last all day and all night, and now she'd also have to find time to look in on her daughter-in-law.

After her bread had baked and cooled, Elizabeth bundled a loaf in a cloth and stepped out onto the path behind the house. She hurried across the sunbaked clearing toward the shade of the forest. Once on the dappled path, she slowed her pace, yielding to one of her few pleasures—an unhurried walk under the cool umbrella of waving boughs and fluttering leaves. The pine-needled forest floor cushioned her step as she considered the chickadees and finches chirruping and flitting at their food-gathering. They're just like us, she thought, gathering what they may, and she pictured her pantry: what supplies she'd already stored and what crops and pickings she'd yet to harvest and put up. With money low and prices up, she'd need to fill every inch of her shelves before winter.

In the clearing ahead, Elizabeth's granddaughter, Goldie, sat cross-legged beside her little brother in front of Beech and Florence's cabin.

"Nana," Goldie squealed, jumping up and bounding toward Elizabeth.

Elizabeth reached down to stroke Goldie's blond-haired head. "Such a big girl you're getting to be."

Florence appeared in the doorway. "Oh, Mother Elizabeth," she said, smiling. "Abraham gone to town?"

"Left this morning." Elizabeth walked up to Florence and handed her the loaf. "Brought you some bread."

Florence lifted the bundle to her nose and smelled it. "Mmm, bless you."

Elizabeth cooed at Artie and indulged Goldie's chatter for a few minutes— "I'm taking care of my baby brother, Nana," "Oh, what a good little helper you are"—before following Florence into the cabin.

Florence was much taller than Elizabeth, the same height as her husband, Beech, about five-and-a-half feet. Her intense, ocean-blue eyes were steady, and when she looked at someone she turned her face full on them. She carried herself with the poise of a heron—tall, still, and composed. With her well-proportioned figure and high-set cheekbones, anyone could see why Beech had taken to her. But even Beech's younger brothers were surprised when she consented to marry him and move all the way from Fort Wayne to the Upper Peninsula's backcountry. Elizabeth wouldn't have matched Florence up with Beech, either. She would have chosen a more practical woman. But she thought Beech deserved any wife he set his heart on and figured Florence would appreciate the country wilds after being cooped up in the apartment over her father's grocery and liquor store all her years. But Florence hadn't much taken to country life, at least not yet.

Elizabeth spotted a cluster of upended canning jars on the kitchen table. "What're you working at?"

"Canning up my green beans," said Florence, brushing her palms together as if to gather resolve. "Never have before, though."

"Well, I can help." Elizabeth opened her eyes wide to take in the room—its counter tidy except for a few dirty plates and cups, Beech's simple rocking chair in the corner, and the square kitchen table surrounded by three straight-backed chairs and the highchair Abraham had crafted after Goldie was born. The dark atmosphere of Beech's two-room cabin depressed Elizabeth, for she was accustomed to the light of her larger, well-windowed home. Florence kept the place neat enough and had even given it a touch of refinement, putting up scallop-edged white curtains on the two windows in the main room and keeping a finely stitched quilt from her grandmother on her and Beech's bed. But the sooty log walls and dank smell of the place always left Elizabeth feeling she needed to cheer up the cabin's inhabitants.

"Between the two of us," said Elizabeth, "should be able to make quick work of it."

Florence put Artie down for his nap and told Goldie, "Go pick some cowslips for Nana."

Elizabeth and Florence settled in side-by-side, Florence washing the beans and Elizabeth dipping them by the basketful into the blanching water.

"Just as well you waited till later in the day to do this," Elizabeth said to Florence. "Been hot these afternoons."

Florence put a lid on the processing pot to quicken its boil. "I wanted to finish before Beech gets home."

Elizabeth squeezed the last batch of blanched beans into jars. "How you and Beech doing?"

Florence glanced sideways at Elizabeth. "Beech been talking to you?"

"No, you know Beech—keeps things pretty much to himself. Got eyes of my own. You don't seem too happy these days."

"It's hard getting used to living here. Still learning country ways."

"Well, you can always ask me for help," Elizabeth said, pushing a row of the full jars across the table to Florence. She liked her daughter-in-law, even if Florence held herself back. She figured time and kindness would eventually win her over. Besides, she'd always wanted a daughter of her own. Might Florence be one to her—a younger woman seeking her counsel and, later, when she was old and bent over, showing her the gentleness only a woman can offer?

Florence rolled her shoulders out of their work-stoop. "I appreciate it."

"It's not easy when a wife has young'uns to watch after," said Elizabeth, brushing the back of her hand over her moist brow. "Been through that myself."

Florence plopped down into a chair on the other side of the table. "Beech don't understand how hard it is—him gone all week and me with the children and cabin to take care of."

"A man's got to earn wages." Elizabeth twisted a lid over the last jar of beans and sat down across the table corner from Florence. "He's just trying to provide for you and the children."

"I know. Just don't see why he's got to do it at the mill. Can't he log around here, like Harvey and Joseph?"

"You ask me, Joseph should work at the mill, too," said Elizabeth. "He'd be a bigger help to his father if he did."

"Harvey says it's dangerous not having a good cross-saw partner."

Elizabeth trained her gaze on Florence. "What Harvey and Joseph do has nothing to do with you and Beech."

Florence looked down at her folded hands. "I know. Just hard not having my husband near."

"You want my advice, take Beech like he is. Only way to be happy with a man is to see him for who he is. Can't be changing him." Beech was a good man, gentle as could be. If Elizabeth could accept Abraham, she figured Florence ought to see her way clear to appreciate the husband she had.

"I expect you're right," Florence said. Her voice had turned whispery, and Elizabeth couldn't tell whether her daughter-in-law was dubious of her advice or humbled by it.

"You're family now." Elizabeth reached out and patted Florence's folded hands. "And I want the best for you and Beech."

Florence looked up at Elizabeth. The corners of her mouth drooped, and her eyes misted.

Oh my, Elizabeth thought, that's a deep well of unhappiness. I hope there's enough love between them to salve that sorrow.

CAMPAIGN SEASON

SEPTEMBER 1892

Manistique's Township Hall throbbed with commotion and joviality. Over eighty men and a few women—lumber workers, schoolteachers, and citizens of modest means, all proud to call themselves Populists—milled about, stirred to fervor by the presidential campaign. Emboldened by the camaraderie of the crowd, they beamed with purpose as they joshed and bantered. With each new arrival, affable greetings sounded and conversing clusters widened to welcome the newcomers. Some of them even wheedled smiles out of stodgy Sheriff Jachor.

Amid the hum and gesticulation, Abraham gripped his gavel and rose from his seat at the long pine table on the hall's stage. Such a good turn-out, he thought, surveying the dozens of workers from the Lumbering Company Mill and the many others he recognized from his bandstand speaking and subscription gathering. And here he was leading the assembly. Pride welled up in him; quickly he batted it down. You're here to do the Lord's work for your fellows, he reminded himself, not to laud yourself. Still, mightn't a man take some satisfaction in making up for past missteps?

At Abraham's elbow sat his son, Beech, who'd consented to accompany him on the condition he wouldn't have to speak. On Abraham's other side sat Beech's co-worker from the mill, Gus Highland, all healed up from his accident. Several other mill workers huddled around the twenty-foot table, and a reporter from the *Pioneer Tribune* had wangled a seat there, too.

Abraham banged the gavel; its thud resounded above the hall's din. The crowd quieted, and all eyes turned to the head table.

"Welcome, brothers," Abraham called out. The three women sitting in the first row of benches nudged each other and glared at him, and he added, "And sisters."

"We are called together this evening like so many others across this great nation to consider the People's Party platform and whether we will endorse it and its presidential candidate, James K. Weaver. Do I have a motion for the platform?"

"Read it, Abe," Gus hollered. "One part at a time, so we can hear all of it."

"Shall I do that, gentlemen?" asked Abraham. "And ladies?"

Heads nodded and murmurs rose from the crowd. Abraham smiled and nodded at young Gus Highland; he couldn't help but wish his own son showed such pluck.

"Then I shall," declared Abraham, sweeping up the papers spread on the table before him. "We declare, first, that the union of the labor forces of the United States shall be permanent and perpetual."

"Aye, aye," yelled a smattering of men.

Gus called out, "A union of all labor! Who's to tell the mill managers?"

A loud cheer erupted from the lumber mill contingent.

A man sitting near Gus hollered at him, "You, Eight." (Gus's fellow workers had started calling him Eight since the saw accident that reduced his digits by two.)

Gus guffawed, and the man at his side jostled his shoulder.

One of the ladies, an elderly, hunched-over woman, rose to speak. "What says the platform about the woman's vote?"

"Dear lady," said Abraham, gripping his jacket lapel. "The platform says nothing, but the party leaders have spoken. They say the cause of the ladies is the cause of the people, and they will work for women to vote alongside men."

The woman swung from side to side and eyed the men in the hall. "Then I am for the party, and I ask all of you to work for the woman's vote."

The men sitting near her shifted in their seats.

Abraham, who knew well how to handle such women—he'd often debated Elizabeth about the suffragists' cause—nodded to her. "We are grateful for your support."

"Go on, Abe," urged Gus.

Abraham straightened up. At that moment he felt much taller than five-foot-three. "Second. Wealth belongs to him who creates it, and every dollar taken from industry without an equivalent is robbery. If any will not work, neither shall he eat."

The reporter, a lean-faced fellow in a rumpled suit, stood. "If I may ask, Mr. Byers, will you expound on that?"

As Abraham cleared his throat, the door burst open and four men in tailored suits strutted in and lined up against the back wall. Abraham knew two of them—Artin Quick, Lumbering Company manager, and Fred Scadden, owner of the Manistique Bank. Given the self-satisfied gapes of the other two, he suspected they were fellow businessmen. The crowd followed Abraham's eyes to the back of the room. Upon spotting the foursome many of them squirmed and jerked back around to the front, hunching their shoulders as if to hide their faces. Beech slouched in his chair and dropped his head. A hush fell over the hall.

Abraham faced the reporter, his head held high. "Why, this platform speaks for the common laborer. The people abhor those who profit on the backs of the worker: the usurers and mortgage lenders who take the fruits of their labor from them in high interest; the capitalists and monopolists who buy up the businesses that ought to serve the people and speculate on land they'll never dirty their hands working." Abraham cocked his head and studied the reporter. "Do you see now, brother, what it means?"

The reporter tapped his pencil against his pad, dropped to his seat, and wrote in staccato strokes.

The lumpy-nosed banker, Scadden, yelled, "Are you saying the mortgage lenders don't work because they have no dirt under their nails?"

Abraham's heart quickened and his words flowed fast. "Tell me why, sir, one man should make money from the work of another? Is it right for the so-called work of the mortgage lender to burden the honest farmer or lumber worker with so much debt that he cannot feed his family?"

Artin Quick, a stocky, fat-faced man, called out, "Sounds like anarchy you're preaching."

Finally, Abraham faced Artin Quick man to man; he had cataloged his cruelties; he had prepared a speech just for him. But no—this was not the time. And he must consider his son: Beech had begged him not to inflame his boss. Commanding himself to practice patience, he held up an open hand. "Anarchy has caused naught but strife and bloodshed since Cain slew Abel. It is only fairness, sir, and fair pay for our work that we ask for."

"You ought to be careful what you ask for. We don't need the likes of you troubling these good people," the banker said, his face blotched with redness. The crowd, hushed and sullen, studied Abraham.

Abraham felt the color rise in his cheeks. "Sir, these good people come to listen and air their views. It is you, not them, threatening strife."

"Why, you," the man beside Scadden yelled, raising a fist at Abraham.

"Whoa," hollered Sheriff Jachor, standing and looking first to Abraham and then Scadden. "I'll disband this whole meeting if you don't all settle down."

"No need for that, Sheriff," said Scadden, bouncing his head to signal his companions. They marched out, one after the other, stiff as a military detachment.

Putting down his papers, Abraham held his curled fingers in front of him and examined his nails. A smile gathered on his face, and he opened his palms and thrust his hands toward the crowd. "Are we ashamed of the dirt on our hands that shows we come by our wages honestly?"

"No, no," sounded a scattering of replies.

"Do we aim to stand up for the working man?"

"Yes, and amen," said many in the crowd.

"The platform, Abe," hollered Gus. "Give us the platform."

"Third," Abraham said, taking up his papers, "we believe that the time has come when the railroad corporations will either own the people or the people will own the railroads." He circled his gaze around the room. "Who shall own the railroads—the corporations or the people?"

"The people, the people," all chanted. Only the reporter refrained from joining the cheer.

Abraham waited for the chanting to find its end. "Let me enumerate our demands. Tell me if you agree. Enforcement of the eight-hour day and a penalty for those who break it?"

Arms shot up and yeas reverberated.

"No government aid to private corporations?"

"Yea and yes," the people hollered.

"A graduated income tax?"

Gus yelled, "Fair taxation for all," and a cheer rang out.

Abraham raised his voice above the clatter. "Neither shall land be monopolized for speculation. This is the platform of the Populist Party. These are the demands of the people." He dropped his papers to the table and held his arms out to the gathered. "Do I report that the Schoolcraft County Convention of the People supports the Party and its candidate for president?"

The crowd cheered. They sprang to their feet, thrust their fists skyward, and broke into chant, "the people, the people, the people."

The convention goers drifted out of the hall, with alacrity but not haste, as if to show anyone who may have been watching that they didn't fear lingering but rather chose to turn their thoughts to such simple pleasures as stripping off their work boots and playing a hand of cribbage. Abraham was the last to leave, sparing no words on the departing. Beech stood to the side, forbearance writ on his face and impatience jiggling his legs.

When they stepped out onto the cool, dark street, the hour was nine, too late to make the trip home. They'd spend the night at Beech's boarding house on the outskirts of Manistique and set out early the next day for the settlement.

"It was a success, a great success," said Abraham, climbing up onto the driver's seat. He kept his voice even, for he sensed Beech's lack of exuberance.

Beech settled alongside him. "Even with Quick and that banker there? Threatening like that?"

"If everyone in the hall spreads their enthusiasm to the rest of Manistique, and if populist citizens across the nation do the same, the election will be ours. And I expect you to pitch in."

"A lot of men from the mill are nervous," said Beech, turning to his father. "You saw. Only sixty out of five hundred showed up."

"You can at least encourage them to vote for their interests." Abraham brushed his hair off his brow, letting the night breeze cool his heated forehead. "If that's not too much to ask."

"I don't talk politics at the mill. And I've had enough for one night, too." Beech leaned back and propped his feet atop the dash rail.

Abraham sighed and leaned over the reins. Elizabeth had warned him off pushing his politics on Beech: "He's got his own troubles. Last thing he needs is your haranguing." Well, there'd come a time for Beech to cast his vote, and he figured his son wouldn't let him down at the ballot box.

Father and son sat side by side in silence. A quarter moon hung like a sleepy sentry over the horizon of treetops, casting a faint light on the road. The two-horse team knew this road well, but as the wagon trundled around a bend, the lead horse snorted. Abraham stretched out his neck and squinted. Something or somebody was in the road.

Beech jolted upright. "There's a man ahead. Just standing there."

Abraham could make him out now—a lone man, sixty feet ahead, his legs straddling the road's mid-section. He tugged the reins, stopping the horses, and called, "Hello, brother, what is it?"

The man, who wore his hat angled over his brow, strode toward them. As he came closer, Abraham could tell he had a big nose, in fact, the biggest nose he'd ever seen.

Beech gripped his father's arm and spoke in a low voice, "There's another off in the woods, to my right. It's trouble." Beech reached around to the bin behind the driver's bench, where they kept the rifle, and slipped his hand under the lid.

The man approaching the wagon called in a nasal voice, "Don't move. Let me see your hands."

Beech twisted back around.

"What do you want?" Abraham's guts clenched, but he inhaled and released a deep breath, summoning calm. He'd faced ruffians in Chicago; standing up to them usually fended them off. "We mean no fellow man any harm."

The man stopped ten feet in front of the horses. "We want what money you got and any other property on you. And don't touch your rifle, because we've got one aimed right at you."

"Will you break God's law, brother, and risk your soul?" asked Abraham. "The Good Book says thou shalt not steal."

Beech shoved an elbow into his father's arm. "Just give them what they want."

The man strode to Abraham's side of the wagon. His shoulders were wide and strapping, and he was tall—maybe six feet. Abraham reached into his pocket and pulled out a dollar bill and what change he had. Beech, too, dug into his pockets and handed his money to Abraham. With both hands, Abraham held the money out and said, "Times are hard, young man, and we all have our crosses to bear. But stealing from another's no way to make your way in the world."

As Abraham handed the money over, he tried to glimpse the man's face. But the man bowed his head, and Abraham could only see his dark, wide-brimmed hat and, under it, his oversized nose.

Without a word, the man grabbed the money from Abraham, shoved it into his pocket, and circled to the back of the wagon. He hopped onto the wagon bed. Abraham craned his head around. The man grabbed his satchel.

"Just papers in there. Leave me my satchel," said Abraham. "The only other thing we have of value is some nails. Take those instead."

The man jumped off the wagon with Abraham's satchel. Speaking in his peculiar nasal voice, he said, "Got a message for you, old man. Watch your ways." He bounded into the woods, toward the other man.

Abraham watched the two men dart among the trees and disappear into the dark forest. "They're gone, thank the Lord."

Beech twisted toward his father. "Better get back to town. Tell the sheriff."

"Tell him what?"

Beech widened his eyes. "That two men robbed us."

"Old Sheriff Jachor won't do anything." Abraham shook his head in disgust. "They took my satchel, my father's gift to me."

"To hell with your satchel. They had a rifle trained on us."

"Thieves." Abraham looked up at the sky. "I call on you, Almighty God. Pour out thine indignation upon them, and let thy wrathful anger take hold of them."

"They could've killed us."

"They're gone now." Abraham turned to face Beech and gleaned the fear in his eyes. "You all right?"

Beech flapped a hand in the air, as if outraged with disbelief. "No, we've just been robbed."

What, Abraham asked himself, were they after? And who had sent them? This was no random robbery. "Did you see the nose on that man? Must've been a disguise."

"That was the last of my week's pay. What am I going to tell Florence?"

"I'll give you some of the money I put away for hard times."

"And not tell the sheriff?"

"No." Abraham gripped and jiggled the reins. The horses started up, and the wagon lurched forward. He'd keep this matter hushed up. Let the villains wonder what he'd do about their treachery. "You'll say nothing of this to anybody—including your mother."

Beech jerked his head back. "How you going to explain your satchel being stolen?"

"I'll think of something. I'll not have your mother worrying about what the good Lord will see to."

"Don't be a fool. They told you to watch your ways."

"I had three subscriptions to *Populist Nation* in there. Good thing I remember the names."

"That's what you're worried about?"

"They were just trying to threaten me."

"Darn right. And you best take heed."

"I'll not buckle to the capitalists and profiteers." Abraham raised a fist. "They don't know me if they think they can scare me. And I'm only one of the Lord's warriors. Let them try to stop all of us."

"Think of Mother. Be careful for her at least."

"They've got my satchel," said Abraham. It was a gift from his father, who'd told him: You're destined to be more than a humble farmer, Son; you'll have need of this. "They shall not have the satisfaction of depriving me of my father's handiwork. I'll make another just like it."

"Don't you understand what just happened?"

"Of course I do. And I'm not surprised."

"If I was you, I'd watch my bluster. And you'd better not cause Mother any grief."

"Leave your mother out of this." Abraham turned full toward Beech. "I mean it."

Beech scowled and shook his head.

"I'll deal with this in my own way." And so, Abraham thought, the battle begins.

HUSBANDS AND WIVES

SEPTEMBER 1892

The next afternoon, Elizabeth sat on her sun-filled porch, knitting mittens for Goldie. Through the thin woods, she glimpsed the strut of horses' legs and whirl of spokes. Sure enough, it was Abraham driving the two-horse team, with Beech's chestnut mare loping behind. Beech sat beside his father, relaxing against the seat back. Peaceful Beech, she mused, he's more my son than Abraham's.

They had nearly lost Beech that first year of the settlement, when he was only seventeen. The pneumonia took hold of him in late winter, just about the time they began resorting to unseasoned wood. Elizabeth had to burn it to cook and keep everybody from freezing, especially Beech, but it never blazed hot. So, she employed every remedy she'd learned from her physician father. Perhaps she prized Beech more than their three younger sons because she'd almost lost him then. Or maybe she just took to his quiet, steady ways, since she was more at ease with him than their other sons, who were easily infected by their father's verve.

The strident pitch of Abraham's voice rode over the day's soft breezes.

"Full of talk again," she muttered, gathering her knitting.

September's rays lengthened over the land, and the tang of drying leaves scented the air. Easing up out of her chair, Elizabeth went inside to light the stove, for the house held only vestiges of the low sun's warmth.

Harnesses rustled and hooves clomped as the wagon passed by the side window. While she waited for Abraham and Beech to unhitch the wagon and settle the horses, she lit the neat pyramid of kindling in the stove and nursed the crackling fire.

"Hello, Mother. Such a time we had." Abraham stepped over the back-door threshold, swept off his hat, and unbuttoned his jacket.

"Oh?" said Elizabeth, knowing well he'd soon satisfy her curiosity. She'd learned that when the fervor took hold of Abraham, he'd go wherever it willed. People said he had a gift for seeing things through, whether it was a wagon axle that needed mending or a barn that wanted raising. Yes, she was proud of him—and herself—for bringing the settlement together. She arranged some thick branches on the blazing flames and, when Beech appeared in the doorway, asked, "Coffee?"

"I'll stay for a cup. Can't let Father tell all the news," said Beech. He had a way of cocking his head that softened the stern line of his nose and reminded Elizabeth of his boyish sweetness.

"Quick and that banker Scadden showed up," said Abraham, hanging his hat and jacket on antler hooks by the door.

Beech hung his jacket beside his father's. "Just like 'em—trying to scare everybody."

Elizabeth put the coffee pot on the stove. "They have much to say?"

"No, didn't stay long," said Abraham. "I suspect they're trying to make the men think before they vote. Thank the Lord we've got the secret ballot."

"Secret or not," said Beech, pulling out a chair at the table and easing into it. "They'll go hard on anybody they think is a Populist."

Elizabeth let Beech take up her role carrying the conversation, though Abraham needed little encouragement. In fact, when he accompanied her on family visits, she sometimes wished he'd leave his preaching and politicking at home. She studied him now, his ice-blue eyes concentrated as he stroked his trim beard. How different life would have been if her first husband, Solomon, had survived the Chattanooga Campaign. She and Solomon shared a soul-deep sympathy, the kind that made them feel they could build a righteous life together—and take joy in the hard work of doing so. She'd married Abraham out of compassion (for he'd lost his first wife) and necessity (mere months after Solomon's death left her a widow). Well, she couldn't complain about

Abraham. He had abundant energy, enough for tending their household and seeing to his causes.

Abraham leaned across the table toward Beech. "Owners depend on the workers. Couldn't make their money without them."

Beech asked, "When it's standing up for politics or feeding their families, which do you think they'll choose?"

"They need to understand the way to provide for their families is to stand up." Abraham slapped a hand on the table, like a preacher who had vanquished all doubt. "And you're the one to help them see that."

There he goes again, Elizabeth thought, badgering Beech. Just can't leave him alone. She spoke up, "Need to get women voting." She shifted the kettle to the hottest spot on the stove. "Hardly a woman alive who doesn't know the harshness of work."

Abraham crinkled a side of his mouth. "I know, Mother. First, we've got to get Weaver elected."

"Well, the sooner women vote, the better off we'll all be." Elizabeth brushed her hands against her skirt. "Women understand fairness better than men."

"I'd like to have an army of women like you voting," said Beech. "Weaver'd be sure to win."

Abraham nodded. "Why, Mother, you and your kind could take the sting out of just about any capitalist."

"Good. I'll keep you fed as long as you work for the woman's vote." Elizabeth raised a finger, for she had a more important point to make. "And bring in enough money so we can afford staples."

Abraham scratched the back of his neck. "I lost my satchel."

"How'd you do that?" Elizabeth, who'd just turned fifty, straightened up beside the stove and rubbed the small of her back. After sitting a spell stiffness always crept over her. She'd watched the arthritis cripple her own mother so bad she couldn't hold a fork to her mouth. Elizabeth found the best way to fight hers was to keep moving.

Abraham shrugged. "Didn't guard it well enough. Someone walked off with it."

"Maybe whoever took it will figure it's yours and give it back."

"Not likely," said Abraham, folding his hands on the table. "Or they wouldn't have taken it in the first place."

"Humph," Elizabeth said, retrieving two cups from the cupboard. "That's a shame."

Beech shifted on his haunches. "Have you seen Florence, Mother?"

"Visited with her at the well yesterday." Elizabeth poured coffee for Beech and Abraham.

"How was she?"

"Seems sad. Everything all right with you two?"

Beech studied his hands. "When I'm around she complains about me being gone. When I'm away I can't wait to get home and see her. Only it just starts up all over again."

Abraham held his coffee cup poised before his lips. "Got to tell her that's just the way it is."

Elizabeth's gaze skimmed over Abraham and landed on Beech. "A woman wants a little comforting now and then. Tell her you understand it's hard on her."

"Can't be coddling her," said Abraham. "That's just the wrong thing."

"Oh, fiddlesticks." Elizabeth plopped the coffee pot back on the stove. "Don't listen to your Father. Knows as much about women as about the bottom of the ocean."

Abraham glowered at Elizabeth. "What kind of thing is that to say about your husband?"

"The truth." Elizabeth turned to Beech. "You talk to her. Tell her you want to make her happy."

Beech met his mother's eyes. "Figure she didn't get the life she bargained for here."

"Show her you know that." Elizabeth came up beside Beech and patted his shoulder. "Don't want an unhappy wife on your hands."

THE CHILLY SEASON

NOVEMBER 1892

Abraham bent into the wind howling down Manistique's morning streets and strode through the drifting snow. He hurried to the door of the *Pioneer Tribune* and tried the handle. Locked. Before Abraham could catch his eye, the worker at the front desk jumped up and hurried back toward the printing press. "Dear Lord," he muttered. "Couldn't they open five minutes early, at least today?"

Abraham turned his back on the entrance and nestled into its alcove, stomping his feet to enliven his tingling toes. At the swish of the door's bolt, he swung around, pushed inside, and came face-to-face with the front desk man, a stiff-limbed fellow who never did a thing without his supervisor's permission.

"Morning, Mr. Heikkila," said Abraham, tugging his wool scarf away from his mouth. "Is the newspaper printed?"

"Certainly, Mr. Byers. Going out for delivery."

"Well, can I buy one?" Irritation crept into Abraham's voice: What did this simpleton think he was here for? All night he'd tossed and turned, wondering about the outcome of the election. Still, he wanted to read it for himself, not hear it from someone who didn't understand how much was at stake.

"I suppose so," said Heikkila, turning on his heel. "I'll bring a stack from the back room."

Abraham surveyed the three desks in the reporters' area—not a single reporter in the office this morning. But he could hear the trundle of the presses, though it was later than usual to still be running the day's paper. Reporters must've worked late, he figured, to put the issue together. Heikkila sauntered back with a stack of newspapers, as casual as if he were on a Sunday stroll. Abraham reached into his pocket for a penny, slapped it on the counter, and, when Heikkila plopped the stack down in front of him, slid the top paper off.

His eyes widened at the stark headline—GROVER CLEVE-
LAND PRESIDENT AGAIN.

"Cleveland?" he gasped, to no one in particular, shaking his
head like a sheriff stunned by the most unthinkable crime. "I can't
believe it."

He folded the paper in half and rushed out and down the snow-
blasted street. Flinging open the door of Chertrand's General
Store, he called out, "Have you seen the news?"

Elmer, the storekeeper, leaned away from his shelves, and two
men and a woman standing at the far end of the counter stopped
their conversation and swiveled around, goggle-eyed, toward
Abraham.

Abraham didn't know any of the threesome, but he quickly
sized them up. It looked like they were from town, since Elmer
had fetched regular supplies for them, a sack of flour and box of
candles. But their attire—the men's crisp bowler hats and the
woman's lacy dress collar—marked them as other than mill workers. Perhaps they're clerks or bookkeepers, or something like that.

"Just got our delivery," said Elmer, glancing at the pile of papers on the floor beside the counter. "You surprised, Abe?"

Abraham brandished the newspaper and leaned against the
ten-foot-long counter. Frowning, he said, "Can't believe Weaver
lost. What did Cleveland ever do for this country?"

"Whatever it was, I guess folks want more of it," Elmer said,
his tone pancake-flat.

The younger man in the group murmured something under his
breath.

Abraham neither discerned what he said nor paused to indulge
him. "The farmers, miners, and mill workers are struggling to feed
their families, and what's Cleveland done about it?"

"What could Weaver have done?" asked the younger man, gripping his lapel like he was posing for a painting. The woman by his
side fixed gleaming eyes on him.

"Plenty," said Abraham. "A whole platform's worth of change."

The older man nudged his glasses up his nose and eyed Abraham. "Weaver never had a chance. You can't tell me you thought
he'd win."

"Oh, yes, brother, if all the common men, like you and me, and the rest of us, if every one of us had heeded the call, then Weaver would have won by a landslide. It's the working man that holds up this country."

"Then why'd most of them vote for Cleveland?" the young man asked.

"This two-party system locks out any but its own. And those corporation bullies are a den of lying snakes, claiming jobs'd be lost if the Populists got in."

"You may be right, Abe," said Elmer, ambling to a shelf at the end of the counter. "Let me finish with these folks and I can see to you."

Abraham nodded to the threesome and unfolded his paper onto the counter, studying its lamentable story. Cleveland didn't even break fifty percent of the vote; he won with only forty-six. And Weaver had received over a million votes, a full eight percent. Abraham figured that was something—a third-party candidate doing that well—but he had prayed for Weaver to stage a win as hard as he'd ever prayed for anything. And now he knew that the two-party candidates had buckled to the moneyed interests and turned their backs on the common worker. Yes, as Jesus is my savior, he thought, this country is in trouble.

Elmer bid the party of three good day and walked down to Abraham's end of the counter. "Now, Abe, what'll it be today?"

Abraham decided against commiserating with Elmer any further about politics; the man was nothing but a lily-livered fool. Reaching into his inside vest pocket, he pulled out a slip of paper and handed it to Elmer. "Here's Elizabeth's list."

Elmer gripped the paper with both hands and studied it, his blue eyes the only sign of brightness in his whey-complexioned face. "How's that hard-working wife of yours?"

"A little lonely with all the boys gone. David and Lenniel rarely write. But that's what happens. They grow up. Get lives of their own."

Elmer squatted down, opened the sugar bin, and eased his scoop into the sugar. "She's still got Beech around, doesn't she?"

"Oh, sure." Abraham watched the tawny-colored grains sliding from scoop to bag. "But he's mighty busy at the mill."

"How're things for him there?" Elmer reached up to a high shelf and grabbed a bottle of vinegar.

"About the same," said Abraham. "Say, you hear many complaints from the workers when they come around?"

"The usual. Griping about stuck wages. Wondering if they'll ever get a raise."

Abraham scanned the back shelves of the store, the ones with household supplies. "I see you've got some nice slabs of cow leather back there. Can I take a look?"

"Sure."

"I'll be spending some time at home mending and such. I'm so disgusted with this election—going to forget about politics for a while."

"If I know you, Abe," said Elmer, the hint of a smile tugging at the corner of his mouth, "you won't forget for long."

⌒∾᷍◠

Abraham trudged in the back door, toting the crate of supplies from town. "Had to put back the vinegar."

Elizabeth lifted a log from the wood stack and spun around from beside the stove. "You don't have my vinegar?"

"No, supplies ran over by the cost of the vinegar," said Abraham, plopping his load on the table.

Elizabeth tucked her chin like a disbelieving parent. "And Elmer wouldn't give you enough credit for a bottle of vinegar?"

"I asked, but he said everybody wants credit these days. Just can't give it out anymore."

"You didn't have enough money for the few supplies I asked for?"

Abraham stiffened. "Well, I wanted to get some cowhide to start on my new satchel."

Elizabeth flung the log back on the woodpile. "You're buying cowhide when I need vinegar for my medicine?"

"I want to work on my satchel and stay away from town." Abraham grimaced. "Got a new president, and it's not Weaver."

"Don't you go blaming the election for what you did. My own sister's husband has the consumption and you're buying cowhide?"

"Who says you have to take care of Eli? What's wrong with Sarah?"

"Don't you tell me who I should and shouldn't see to," said Elizabeth, tightening her fists at her sides. "At least I watch over my family."

Abraham's chest tightened around his heart. "You saying I don't?"

"Saying you think more about your politics than the kin under your nose. One of these days you'll regret your selfish ways."

"You ungrateful woman. Who built this house for you?"

"There's more to family than a house."

"I don't have to listen to this. I'll get you your vinegar."

Abraham stormed out to the barn. He saddled up his trusty steed, Smokey, and rode him hard through foot-and-a-half-deep snow to his nephew Harvey's cabin. He found Harvey at the table, studying his Bible, and Harvey's son, Joseph, tending a pot on the stove.

Harvey leaned back in his chair, his broad shoulders open with welcome. "Well, hello, Abraham, come in and share our dinner with us."

"Why, that's kind of you. I believe I will." Abraham stomped the snow off his boots and shed his coat. The earthy scents of venison and parsnips filled the cramped cabin, drowning out the ever-present smolder of kerosene fumes and ash. "Came over to see if you have a bottle of vinegar you can spare."

"Vinegar?" asked Joseph, tilting his head to a quizzical slant.

Harvey glanced at Joseph and turned to Abraham. "I'm sure we do. Elizabeth cooking up some of her medicine?"

Abraham smiled at Joseph. "Yes, Eli's ailing bad."

"We'll give you what we have," said Harvey. "We're both healthy here, thank the Lord."

"And I thank you, Harvey. You're like another family to me, and I'm grateful for it." Abraham, still stung by Elizabeth's harsh words, truly appreciated Harvey's welcome. He and Elizabeth rarely exchanged angry words, and Harvey's company set his mind at ease: surely Elizabeth would look kindly on him again once this evening passed. He'd found some vinegar for her, and she'd understand Weaver's loss had upset him.

Abraham eased down onto a seat at the table and asked, "Have you heard about the election?"

Abraham recounted the news of Weaver's defeat, Cleveland's return to the presidency, and predictions of doom if the populist message didn't lead to serious reform. Harvey, whose thoughts followed Abraham's like stones tumbling down the same hill, nodded and commiserated with Abraham, matching his scowls and frowns.

Joseph served their dinner up and, as he ate, leaned over his plate and eyed Abraham and his father. Abraham noted his brooding manner and remembered Elizabeth's complaints about his pridefulness. He turned to Joseph. "How's your logging work, young man?"

Joseph glanced up at Abraham and dropped his head. "Don't much care for it."

"Hoping he'll stay on and work this land with me." Harvey bounced his spoon in Joseph's direction. "Plenty of trees to log and land to cultivate right here."

"Your father's right, Joseph."

"There'll always be trees and land," Joseph said, hunching over his bowl. "I'd like to see something of the world."

"All your family is here," said Harvey.

"Family's the most important thing of all," Abraham said. "God setteth the solitary in families, he bringeth out those which are bound with chains; but the rebellious dwell in the dry land."

Harvey nodded to Abraham. "Psalms 68."

"Verse 6," said Abraham.

As Abraham and Harvey smiled assurances at each other, Joseph scooped the last mouthful of stew into his mouth and pushed back from the table.

Abraham rode home late that night with an almost full bottle of vinegar. He put it on the kitchen table where Elizabeth would be sure to see it, went up to bed, and found Elizabeth had left the warming pan just where he liked it—in the middle, where their feet spooned together.

As Abraham had pledged, he did not return to town for several weeks, and then only to sell venison and beaver pelt and buy vinegar, flour, matches, and some leather cord for his satchel. He spent his days splitting kindling to Elizabeth's liking, tending the livestock, and hunting deer and trapping beaver with Harvey. Evenings he worked on his satchel, cutting a pattern to match his old one and stitching it together. With the leftover leather scraps, he sewed a quill-like holster for Elizabeth's cooking spoons and mounted it on the side of her cupboard. While he cut and sewed his leather, Elizabeth sat at the table with him, winding up the kerosene wick and reading aloud from the Bible. Never once did they speak of their argument over the vinegar, though neither forgot the words spoken that day.

THE PANIC OF 1893

APRIL 1893

After Saturday breakfast, Elizabeth spent a good hour reviewing the household ledger with Abraham. The financial panic sweeping the country hadn't passed them over. In fact, the whole settlement buzzed with worry about dwindling cellars and high-priced goods— dependent as they were, with garden harvests so far off, on bought supplies.

Elizabeth shook her head as they completed their inventory. "We have to be careful with our pennies. Be sure we can buy enough flour. And cut back on sugar. It's up to seven cents a pound."

Abraham sighed, "Don't know how much more we can scrimp, with everybody looking to us when their supplies run low."

"We have to help each other," Elizabeth said. "That's what family's for."

"Well, Mother, I'll leave the list-making to you. Now, I promised Harvey I'd help him mend some harnesses, so I'll be getting along."

Elizabeth planned an afternoon visit with her older half-brother, John, and his wife, Elvila, who was also Abraham's niece, making the couples doubly related. John and Elvila mostly kept to themselves, so Elizabeth enjoyed a companionable relationship with them—like that among relations who don't have enough dealings to store up resentment. Still, an unspoken debt of gratitude connected John and Elvila to their kin. When they moved to the settlement in 1883, John was indisposed with carbuncles and unfit for heavy labor, whereupon all the Kepler and Byers men pitched in and built a fine hewn-log cabin for him and his family. Over the next several years John, being a proud man, took pains to leave his mark on his home and the homes of his relations. He coated his interior walls with varnish, sealed the gaps around windows and doors with beeswax, and visited the others' cabins to share his craftsmanship by sealing their walls and leaks, too. He also stocked his three-room home with simple furniture wrought with his own hands: a sturdy kitchen table and chairs of maple; a rocker strong enough for his six-foot frame; a poster bed for Elvila and him; and compact bed frames for their five then-young children. Elizabeth found the tidy cabin's atmosphere comforting, for she apprehended the hard work that went into keeping it so and the reward of relishing its clean coziness when visitors called.

Elvila opened the door wide for Elizabeth, and her plump face lit up. "Lizzy, what a nice surprise. Come on in."

"Well, blessings from Heaven," Elizabeth said, spotting Florence and Beech's children, Goldie and Artie, playing with wood-carved figures on the deerskin rug. "Came to visit you and get to see my grandchildren, too."

Elvila swung the door shut and minced toward the kitchen table, her stout, ample-bosomed body pitching from side to side. "How's the good Lord keeping you, Lizzy?"

"Well enough. Here, brought you some biscuits." Elizabeth had mixed up a batch of biscuits and folded in some of her canned huckleberries. Yes, her pantry had thinned over winter, but she intended to share what she had, for she believed that giving multiplied itself.

"Oh my, and with times like they are. You're a better woman than I am." Elvila put the bundle of biscuits on the table. "Got time for coffee?"

"Don't mind if I do," said Elizabeth. "John out skidding logs?"

"Uh-huh, with the crew across the perimeter road."

"Florence busy at something today?"

"She got it in her head to scrub down the cabin. I'm keeping the little ones for the afternoon."

Elizabeth clucked, "That old stove of theirs sure turns a cabin grimy after a winter."

Elvila plopped her tin coffee pot on the stove. "Good day for cleaning, with this false spring upon us."

Elizabeth and Elvila had a lively visit: How many ways can you cook venison? Other than roasts, stews, and steaks? Have you tried it in hash or shepherd's pie? Potato supply holding up then? Getting low. Venison's good with rutabagas, too. Most of my apples are going bad after all this cellaring. Glad I canned up a good store of huckleberries. Lot you can do with winter squash. I like it baked and mashed for a soup. Goldie—you stay in this room! See much of Beech and Florence, Elvila? Every now and then for Sunday visiting. Eli's doing better. Poor Sarah sure's got a hard row to hoe. Think we've seen the last of the big snows? Never can tell. Could get surprised a time or two before spring.

"Well, I'll be passing by Beech and Florence's on my way home," said Elizabeth, rising from the table. "Want me to bring Goldie and Artie back?"

"No, Florence said she'd come fetch them when she's ready. Maybe you'll meet her on the path."

Elizabeth slipped into her bulky wool coat, but it being a mild April day, left it unbuttoned. Stepping out along the narrow, quarter-mile path to Beech and Florence's cabin, she meditated on the breezes meandering over pockets of snow and around the thick and thin of trees: Where had the wind been? What had it seen? Did it send her scent ahead and warn off bear fresh from their dens?

She knocked and pushed open the door to Beech and Florence's cabin. "Hello," she called, but stillness hung like stale air over the room. Wrinkling her nose at the cabin's acrid odor, she stepped outside and circled the cabin. Florence was nowhere in sight. And the cabin as sooty as usual.

Hmm, she said to herself, I couldn't have missed her on the path. Maybe she's off visiting. Or took a roundabout way to John and Elvila's. Hope nothing's wrong.

Elizabeth headed down the more traveled path to her own home, high stepping to avoid splattering muck onto her skirt bottom. Sixty paces down the path she heard lively voices and turned back toward Beech and Florence's cabin.

She froze in her tracks. It was Florence, running to her cabin, laughing. And Joseph, catching her from behind and yanking her to him. He kissed her—hard and long. Florence shoved the door open. She stumbled inside, slamming the door behind her.

Joseph dashed back into the woods and headed for the perimeter road.

Elizabeth's legs turned wobbly. She braced her hand against a birch tree.

Neither Florence nor Joseph had seen her. She scurried away, her mind a tangle of disbelief and vexation. Beech's wife carrying on with another man. How could it be? The expression on Florence's face fixed itself in her mind—its blend of joy, desire, and playfulness as disturbing and alien as carnival commotion. She'd never seen anything like it: Something about the surrendering tilt of Florence's head unsettled her, as if what passed between a man and woman had nothing to do with wifely duty or bringing children into the world. Does Beech know that side of his wife? And Joseph—how brazen and insolent of him to touch another's wife. And him Beech's cousin!

All afternoon Elizabeth puttered and paced, nervous as a caged cat. What should she do? She'd talk it over with Abraham. They'd have to figure out some way to save Beech and Florence's marriage. She took up the Bible but couldn't concentrate enough to read even the Gospel of John. Finally, she spotted Abraham and Smokey approaching. He hopped off his horse, opened the barn door, and guided Smokey in.

Elizabeth stared at the barn door through the back-porch window, her lips pursed and her mind awhirl, anxious for Abraham to finish unsaddling the horse. When he trudged to the house, she opened the back door and greeted him with, "See Beech on the road?"

"Yes, he rode on ahead of me," said Abraham, stepping inside and pulling off his hat. "Wanted to get home."

"You get those harnesses fixed?" she asked, following close behind him.

"Well enough," he said, pulling an arm out of his coat. "Harvey said he'll be helping me with ours next."

Elizabeth grabbed his coat by the collar and yanked it off from behind, forcing Abraham to spin around to extricate his other arm.

He frowned. "Everything all right, Mother?"

Elizabeth thrust Abraham's coat onto a hook. "No, everything is not all right."

"What? What is it?"

"I saw something."

"What'd you see?"

Elizabeth kneaded her lips.

"Come, now. Let's sit together." Abraham walked her to the table, pulled out a chair for her, and settled into another close in front of her. "Now tell me what's riled you."

Her eyes misted over. "Florence and Joseph—together."

Abraham jerked upright in his chair. "Dear Lord. What are you saying?"

Elizabeth told him everything. How she stopped to visit at John and Elvila's and found Goldie and Artie there. Her walk to Beech and Florence's home. The dank emptiness of the cabin. The excited voices she'd heard as she headed down the path. Florence running and giggling. Joseph kissing her.

Abraham's eyes widened. "He kissed her?"

"He did."

"And she allowed it?"

The look on Florence's face flitted before her. A knot of revulsion twisted her belly. She nodded.

Abraham sprang from his chair. "My Lord in Heaven. That woman, that Jezebel."

Elizabeth snapped her head up at him. "I told you Joseph was trouble."

Abraham's eyes flashed icy outrage. "He sins against God. She's a married woman. She sins against God *and* her husband."

"We have to help Beech," said Elizabeth.

"He cherishes that woman. Against all reason he cherishes her."

"Joseph's got to leave," Elizabeth said, holding his gaze. "Or there'll be no saving that marriage."

Abraham clapped a palm over his forehead. "What'll I do?"

"Go to Harvey. Tell him what's happened. Ask him to send Joseph away."

Abraham paced from the table to the front door and back. "Yes, Mother. I believe you're right. And Florence?"

"Oh, I don't know," said Elizabeth, wringing her hands. "I don't want to hurt Beech. We have to spare him."

Abraham nudged his chair close to Elizabeth's, sat down, and took her hands in his. "We'll pray, Mother. We'll pray for guidance."

Abraham and Elizabeth sat together at the table, and Abraham read aloud from chapters one to four of the Epistle of James. He said there was much to commend in this epistle, and he would preach from James at the morning service.

But Elizabeth could think only of her son's devotion to his wife and the wild joy on Florence's face when Joseph embraced her. "I'm afraid for Beech," she said. "We have to help our son."

THE DEVIL'S ROAD

APRIL 1893

Abraham, more somber than usual, nodded to the settlement congregants as they filed into his barn for Sunday service. They seated themselves on the makeshift hay-bale pews. When those filled up, the younger of the men surrendered their seats to the ladies and moved to the standing space at the rear. Abraham caught a few men glancing at the even plane of shovels, pitchfork, adze, and hoes hanging on antler hooks. Yes, his commodious barn was even neater than usual. Nervous and fretful from a poor night's sleep, he'd risen early to clean out the three livestock stalls, feed the cow and horses, put up his implements, and even sweep down the walls. But the clean barn failed to dispel the gloom hanging over him this morning.

The hour for the service arrived, and Abraham kept the doors propped open to let in the mild April day's light and expel the lingering fumes of horse and cow excretions.

Standing before the four rows filled with settlement families, Abraham opened his Bible. "I will preach today from the Epistle of James."

Taking in and expelling a deep breath to seize the force of conviction, he read, "My brethren, count it all joy when ye fall into divers temptations; knowing this, that the trying of your faith worketh patience." He looked up at his flock. He could not keep himself from seeking Joseph's eyes. "But you must turn from temptation. You must never let temptation pull you from God's path to the devil's road."

Joseph jerked his gaze away from Abraham, and Abraham turned back to his Bible.

"'But every man is tempted when he is drawn away of his lust and enticed. Then when lust hath conceived, it bringeth forth sin: and sin, when it is finished, bringeth forth death.'"

Abraham closed his eyes as the gravity of sin's wages reverberated to his core. His heart overflowed with sorrow, knowing two of his flock had strayed. Please Lord, he prayed, bring them back to the fold. Make me your instrument.

Abraham scanned his congregation of some forty men, women, and children. They knew not what sinfulness was afoot among them. He must speak now to Florence. And Joseph. Like tinder put to the match, fervor blazed up in him.

He leaned toward his attentive flock and unleashed his words. "Sin bringeth death. And this death is the death of the soul, the death of life everlasting with our Lord in Heaven."

He swung his head this way and that, taking in the upraised faces, stopping his eyes on Florence, then Joseph, long enough to assure himself they attended to his words. He took in Harvey's questioning gaze, too. Poor Harvey. Soon he would share the shameful news with him. Oh, Harvey, then you will know this same sadness and wrath. How I wish you could be spared.

"The toll of lust's way is a seared soul. Do not let lustfulness lead you away from God's path. Do not cast the Lord's commandments out of your heart lest you be cast out of God's keeping."

As he approached the pinnacle of his sermon he settled back on his heels and collected himself. Taking up his Bible again, he read, "'Ye adulterers and adulteresses, know ye not that the friendship of the world is enmity with God? Whosoever, therefore, will be a friend of the world is the enemy of God.'"

He clapped his Bible shut, set his jaw, and looked out on the silent faces before him. Gripping his Bible to his chest, he said, "Harvey, will you please lead us in hymn?"

After a restrained round of "Bringing in the Sheaves" the congregants milled about, partaking of each other's fellowship. But their voices were low, and their manner subdued. Abraham could tell the sermon had affected them, and then he remembered how last summer he'd preached on thievery and the week after that news had spread that a new snaffle bit had gone missing from Harvey's barn. Eli and Sarah's youngest son, Clifton, confessed to taking it, though he said he only wanted to show it to his father and ask him to make one like it, and then he planned to return it. Yes, Abraham had known about the thievery before the sermon. Still, he'd intended today's preaching for the two who most needed to hear it, and he hoped the others would take the references to lust and adultery in stride and not give themselves over to wild imaginings.

Abraham bided his time during the fellowship, circulating among the gathered until most had dispersed, waiting for a chance to talk with Harvey. Finally, he found occasion. "May I have a word with you, Harvey?"

Harvey nodded, his deep-set eyes more shadowed than usual as he looked down on Abraham. "Why were you preaching about adultery? You told me Elizabeth gave you the idea for a sermon on the loaves and fishes."

"Yes, that is what I must talk to you about."

"I'm listening then," Harvey said, leaning in. Although he towered over Abraham, both knew his height afforded no advantage with Abraham.

"Come, let us walk," said Abraham, and he and Harvey passed out of the barn and put distance between themselves and the ones remaining there.

"Harvey, there are sinners among us."

"Well, that's what I was wondering. Just tell me what you mean."

Abraham widened his nostrils with aggrieved resignation. "It's Joseph. And Florence."

Harvey swung around to face Abraham. "What about them?"

Abraham stopped in his tracks and gazed up at Harvey, his expression at once hard and pleading. "Elizabeth passed by Beech and Florence's yesterday. She saw them together outside the cabin. She saw Joseph embrace Florence."

Harvey cocked his head to the side. "Embrace? You calling that adultery?"

Abraham stared beyond Harvey at the desiccated snow in the woods, its dank, dispiriting scent filling his nostrils. "She saw Joseph kiss Florence."

"I don't believe it," said Harvey, shaking his head. "It can't be."

Abraham peered into Harvey's pained face. "Something must be done. You're his father. You must see to him."

"No, no, this makes no sense. Sure he fancies her, but it's just a boyish liking. He'd never do what you're saying."

"He did do it. They have sinned. Against God and against Beech. And now something must be done."

Harvey stretched out his neck. "What, Abraham, what must be done about my son?"

Abraham dropped his gaze and then lifted his face to Harvey. "He must leave. He must get away from temptation."

"You're asking me to send my son away?"

"Yes, he must turn from the devil's road."

"And Florence. What about her?"

"Florence must atone for her sin. I'll see to her. You see to Joseph."

"You're talking about my only son."

"I know, Harvey. It's a great sadness to me."

Harvey turned from Abraham's gaze. "I can't believe what you're accusing."

"Then talk to him. Ask him to tell you the truth before God. And warn him that the Lord hates a lying tongue."

"I know my Proverbs—chapter 6, verse 17."

Abraham pulled in his lower lip and swallowed hard. He took no pleasure in Harvey's knowledge.

Harvey shook a finger at Abraham. "I will talk to him. And then I'll be speaking to *you* again." Turning his back on Abraham, he hurried down the road.

When Abraham stepped onto the back porch and stomped his boots off, Elizabeth rushed up to him. "Sarah and Eli were asking me what you meant by your sermon."

"Nothing for them to bother about," said Abraham, hanging his coat and trudging to the stove in the main room.

"I told them you decide your own sermons." Elizabeth followed and took up the opposite side of the stove. "What if Beech figures who it's about?"

"He'll find out sooner or later, Mother," said Abraham, spreading his hands over the stove and feeling its warmth rise against his thighs and chest. "And then Florence will have to make amends."

Elizabeth bit at her lower lip and heaved out a sigh. "How'd Harvey take it?"

"Hard. I told him Joseph should go away."

Elizabeth flattened a hand over her heart. "Will he send him away?"

"I hope so. He doesn't want to believe what passed between them, but he said he'd talk to him."

Shaking her head, Elizabeth said, "Just don't know any other way to save that marriage."

The stove's blazing heat reached through Abraham's trousers, overheating his thighs. He inched back from it. "Something must be done about Florence."

"I don't know," said Elizabeth, her brow arching up. "Isn't that for Beech to decide?"

"She has wronged him, and she has wronged God."

Elizabeth cupped her hands together. "She's been unhappy. Maybe Joseph said things that tempted her."

"Doesn't matter who did the tempting. Neither one turned away from it."

"What do you mean to do then?"

"I told Harvey I'd see to Florence."

"How? How you going to see to her?"

"Oh, Mother, I don't know yet." Abraham wagged his head. "I don't know. I can only pray the Lord'll show me the next step."

Elizabeth squared off her shoulders. "Well, I'm praying for Florence's forgiveness and our son's happiness. And you should, too."

"Yes, Mother. I think I'll go to the woods now to walk and pray."

Late that afternoon, as the weak sun stretched its rays over the snow- and mud-pocked fields and woods, Abraham spotted him, riding up to the house, his saddlebags packed for his work week. He announced, "It's Beech."

Elizabeth pulled the last of the dinner plates from the steamy water reservoir. "Oh, my."

Beech stepped inside. "Mother, Father," he said, standing erect before them. "I've not had much peace this day."

Abraham looked up at him but said nothing.

Elizabeth dried her hands on her apron. "What is it, Beech?"

"Harvey came by earlier." Beech turned to his father. "Said you was saying untrue things about Joseph and Florence."

"Sit down, Son," said Abraham.

Beech didn't budge. "I'll not sit at your table. You tell me what you said."

"Told him what was seen between Joseph and Florence."

"And what was that?" Beech poked his chin out in challenge.

Abraham turned to Elizabeth, his eyes beseeching her.

Coming to Beech's side, Elizabeth said, "I just saw playfulness between them. Nothing that can't be fixed between you two."

"What do you mean, Mother? What kind of playfulness?"

Elizabeth shot a glance down at the floor, then looked up at Beech. "I saw them laughing and running outside your cabin yesterday."

Beech shuffled his feet. "Probably just humoring the children."

"The children were at John and Elvila's," said Abraham.

Beech glared at his father. "Not a sin to laugh and run, is it?"

Abraham rose from the table and leaned in, bracing his hands flat against it. "Beech, your mother saw them kissing. And I have asked Harvey to send Joseph away because of it."

Beech searched his mother's face.

Elizabeth met his gaze, her eyes filling with tears and her pursed lips trembling.

Beech's face reddened, and he turned on his father. "Why you telling Harvey this before speaking to me?"

Abraham tempered his voice. "I wanted to tell him to send Joseph away. He should get away from Florence."

Beech stomped a foot. "You keep your righteousness out of my marriage."

Elizabeth reached her opened hands toward Beech. "We were trying to help."

Beech waved his mother off and mumbled, "Lord help me." He swung around and hurried out of the house, springing into the saddle and urging his horse back toward his home.

⌒~⌒

In the days that followed Abraham lamented that he did not know what to do next. Elizabeth said they'd done enough, that Beech had been right, they should have talked to him first, not Harvey, and now they should just leave the matter to Beech. A doleful Abraham accepted Elizabeth's advice and stayed close to the cabin to avoid Joseph or Florence and to pray and wrestle alone with his agony. Abraham restrained himself from going to visit Harvey. Although it pained him to be alienated from him, he knew that Harvey did not see the matter as he did.

On the afternoon of the third day, when Abraham caught sight of Harvey approaching the house, his heart quickened. Harvey strode toward the house, his face stiff and determined, his hat pulled down tight.

Harvey stepped inside and nodded, "Abraham, Elizabeth."

Abraham lifted his brow in somber hopefulness and leaned forward in this reading chair. "Hello, Harvey."

Elizabeth pushed her shirt-mending aside and rose from the table. "Coffee, Harvey?"

"No, won't be staying long," said Harvey, pulling off his hat and clutching it two-handed over his chest. "Came to tell you Joseph is leaving in a day or two."

"I'm sorry, Harvey," Abraham said. "I know it pains you."

"Yes, it pains me." Harvey stared at Abraham. "You ought to know that Florence is leaving, too."

Abraham shot Elizabeth a wide-eyed glance.

Elizabeth gripped the back of a chair and said to Harvey, "She's got two children. She's got a husband. She can't just up and leave."

Abraham leaned over his knees. "She leaving with Joseph?"

Harvey stood stock still, his eyes shifting from Elizabeth to Abraham and back.

"Does Beech know about this?" asked Elizabeth.

"Best you talk to him about those matters." Harvey swung his hat onto his head, nodded at them, and strode out, closing the door with a solid thud.

"Oh, dear Lord in Heaven," gasped Elizabeth.

"I expect Harvey got some satisfaction from delivering his message," said Abraham. He set his jaw and crossed his arms.

Elizabeth spun toward him, hands on hips. "Doesn't matter what Harvey thinks or feels. What about your own son? Your own grandchildren? Or don't you care about them?"

"Course I care. Don't you be putting this on me. Sinning is sinning."

"You stop your talk of sin. We got to think. What about Florence? What about Goldie and Artie?"

Abraham brushed a hand over his brow and dropped his arm onto his lap.

Elizabeth gripped the chair back, her knuckles whitening. "We must speak with Florence."

Abraham studied her. "You go speak with her. You're good with her. I don't believe I could face that woman just now."

"Yes, I will. And you? You going to talk to Beech?"

Abraham leaned back in his chair. "I'll ride into town first thing in the morning."

"Well, I'll go see Florence right now."

THE RECKONING

APRIL 1893

Elizabeth knocked on the cabin door, eased it open, and stepped inside. "Florence, dear child, can I speak with you?"

Florence looked up from the table and nodded. Redness circled her eyes, and wisps of her bound hair fell unevenly around her face. She held her arms tight around Artie, who squirmed on her lap. Goldie sat pouting in the chair beside her. The remnants of a meal—plates, cups, and an emptied canning jar—lay scattered on the table.

It broke Elizabeth's heart to imagine her grandchildren without their mother. No, she couldn't let it happen. She strode up to the table. "Goldie, dear, let's go rock Artie."

"Don't want to," said Goldie, slipping down from her chair and running into the bedroom.

Elizabeth took hold of Artie, wiry now without his baby fat, and carried him to the bedroom. After some rocking and cajoling, she settled Goldie and Artie for naps. What, she wondered, had passed between Beech and Florence? *I must convince Florence to stay with her husband. How much power does Joseph have over her? The children—what mother could contemplate leaving these dear ones? If nothing else, a mother's love should keep her here.*

Returning to the main room, she pulled a chair up close to Florence and spoke to her in a low voice. "Harvey says you're leaving. Is that so?"

Florence sat crumpled over, deflated as a busted bellows. "How can I stay here? I can't live like this."

"How can you leave? You've got two beautiful children and a husband that loves you."

Florence grimaced. "You know what people are saying, don't you? Harvey says it was Abraham told him."

"I don't care what people are saying," said Elizabeth, leaning toward Florence and softening her voice. "Can you make it right with your husband?"

"How? How'm I supposed to make it right after bringing shame on him and me?"

Elizabeth sighed and said, "By letting Joseph go away. And by staying and making amends to your husband."

Florence flopped her head down and folded her hands on her lap.

"Think of your children. That darling Goldie. Every little girl needs a mother to brush her hair and wash her skinned knees. And what would Artie do without you to rock him to sleep?"

Tears dropped onto the front of Florence's blouse, streaking its whiteness.

Elizabeth reached out and cupped a hand over Florence's. "Tell me you'll stay. Tell me you'll give your heart back to your husband and your family."

"I'll try," Florence sniffled.

"That's my brave girl."

Florence burst into shoulder-rocking tears.

Elizabeth stood and stroked Florence's head. "There, there, dear. Just give it some time. I'll help you find your way through."

The next morning Abraham rode into town to give Beech the news that Florence had decided to stay. Elizabeth took advantage of the mild weather and kept close to home. She spent the day hoeing the winter-hardened garden soil, planting beet, kohlrabi, and spinach seeds, and scrubbing windows, floors, and chamber pots. Come Friday afternoon she paid Florence another visit. Two days was too long to leave the poor girl alone, distraught and plagued with guilt as she was. No sooner had Elizabeth set off down the path than she spotted Beech and Abraham riding up to the house, earlier than usual for Beech's return. Just as well, she thought, though leaving the mill on Friday meant Beech'd lose two full days of pay on the week. But he was probably anxious to see his wife. Elizabeth turned back to the house, relieved to know Beech and his wife would soon reunite.

"We told the supervisor it was a family emergency," Abraham said to Elizabeth as he and Beech trudged in from the barn.

Beech followed his father through the back door and walked over to his mother. "I appreciate you talking to Florence, Mother."

Elizabeth looked up at her son. "Everything'll be fine, Beech. Now, you sit down while I warm up some soup. Florence won't be expecting you anytime soon."

Abraham hung up their coats and joined Beech at the table. "Your mother and I'll do what we can to help, Son."

Beech knit his hands together on the table. "Living with these poor conditions has been hard on Florence."

"Times are hard everywhere," said Abraham. "I don't imagine things are any better for her family down in Indiana."

Elizabeth gave the soup a stir and covered the pot with a lid. "She's just confused and unhappy. You two can work this out if you try."

Beech asked his mother, "Joseph gone yet?"

"Don't think so," said Elizabeth. "Probably soon though."

Goldie's voice pierced the cabin walls. "Mama, I don't want to go."

Beech, Elizabeth, and Abraham turned toward the door as it flung open.

Florence stood holding Artie against her hip and a whimpering, off-balance Goldie by the upper arm. At the sight of Beech, Florence's eyes widened.

Through the open door, at the end of their drive, Elizabeth spotted a wagon with two chairs, a table, and bed frame tied down in it. Joseph sat perched on the driver's seat, peering into the house.

Beech stared out at the wagon, his jaw dropping in unspoken question.

Florence pushed Goldie through the door. "Daddy," she cried, running to her father and wrapping her arms around his knees.

Florence strode into the cabin and thrust Artie into Elizabeth's arms. "Here," she said, turning and darting for the door.

Elizabeth grabbed Artie under the arms and pulled him to her chest. Artie twisted around and reached out his arms, calling "Mommy, mommy."

Hoisting her skirt to mid-calf, Florence bounded off the porch and down the drive.

Beech unwrapped Goldie's clinging arms and shoved her toward Abraham.

Goldie landed against Abraham's leg, and he reached out and caught her by the shoulders.

Beech raced out the door after Florence. Catching her, he grabbed her elbow and jerked her around.

"Let me go," she wailed, flailing her whole body, trying to twist out of Beech's tight hold.

Joseph bolted to standing in the wagon seat and glowered at Beech.

"What are you doing?" Beech demanded, tugging at Florence.

Florence stiffened her arm and pushed him away. "I'm no good for you. I can't stay here."

"No, stay." Beech held his free hand out to Florence, his open palm pleading for her hand. "Stay with me."

Florence locked eyes with Beech, freezing in place.

"Mommy," Goldie cried, slipping out of Abraham's grip and running out the door. Goldie's blond tresses swung wildly as her four-year-old legs propelled her forward, faster and faster. A few steps from her father, her feet tangled up. She pitched onto the backs of his legs and shrieked in pain.

Beech twirled around at the impact, releasing his grip on Florence.

"Florence," Joseph called out.

Florence turned and dashed for the wagon, springing up into the seat. Joseph caught her in one arm, shook the reins with his other hand, and hollered "Git."

The horses broke into a trot. The wagon jerked forward, jolting Joseph and Florence against the wagon seat. Joseph righted himself, concentrating on the horses and shaking the reins with the urgency of a fleeing bandit.

The wagon bumped down the road with Florence and Joseph jostling about on the wagon seat, looking straight ahead.

"Mommy," Goldie hollered, scrambling to her feet. Dirt streaked her knees. She turned around and ran toward the house. "Nana, I want my mommy."

Beech thrust his fist into the air and hollered, "To hell with you."

Florence hunched forward on the wagon seat and braced her hands over her ears.

Beech watched the wagon carrying his wife away. As his shoulders bowed inward and his head sunk, Elizabeth discerned the desperate sorrow welling up in him.

Inside the cabin, carrot soup gurgled down the pot sides and onto the stove top.

Beech not speaking to Abraham stung him to the core. He had to ask himself: Did Beech blame him for Florence's desertion? Had he been wrong to preach about adultery and implore Harvey to send Joseph away?

No, Abraham could reach no other conclusion: He was the pastor of his flock and he'd done what needed doing—confronted the evilness of sin and cleansed his congregation of it. Shouldn't a preacher keep the souls he's responsible for on the path of righteousness? After all, Florence and Joseph had left, and in the weeks that followed his flock greeted him in the same respectful manner and spoke naught of the adultery that had sullied the settlement. Surely this was a sign, not only of vindication, but of affirmation of his role as their spiritual leader.

But Florence's departure meant Elizabeth had to care for Goldie and Artie six days of the week. Abraham could tell that seeing to the children tired Elizabeth something awful. She never complained about it, but when he grumbled about Beech not even saying a hello to him, she cut him off: "That's between you two. Don't be bothering me about it."

And now Abraham couldn't bear the sight of Beech, so wounded was he by the rejection. When Beech dropped Goldie and Artie off on the Sabbath and picked them up the next Saturday, Abraham steered clear of the house. In fact, being unaccustomed to young children underfoot and recognizing Elizabeth had little patience for him, Abraham spent more time in his shop, garden, and the woods than usual.

To make matters worse, Harvey no longer came visiting, and Abraham knew he wasn't welcome at Harvey's cabin either. So whenever Abraham hunted or checked his traps, he took one of his older sons—Elonzo or Link—instead of Harvey, though he would have preferred Harvey's company.

Five weeks after Florence and Joseph's departure Abraham was in his shop fixing up a beaver trap when the door swung open. He looked up from the latch he'd been pounding into shape.

Harvey stepped inside and eased the door closed behind him. "Morning, Abraham."

"Harvey," said Abraham, laying down his mallet. "How've you been keeping?"

"Well enough." Harvey shuffled his feet. "Been doing a lot of thinking. With the jobbing pay so bad and Joseph gone now, I'll be putting my land up for sale."

"Why, look here, Harvey, you're not the only one torn up by this," said Abraham, feeling the blood drain from his face.

"Not saying I am."

"Beech lost a wife. And he's still not speaking to me."

Harvey gripped one of his suspender straps. "Maybe you got what you deserved—stirring things up like you did."

Abraham shook a finger at Harvey. "It was your son who started all this."

"It was you spread suspicion all around," Harvey shot back, pitching forward. "How was Florence to go on here with everybody treating her like an adulteress? You pushed her right into Joseph's arms."

"I did no such thing. Tried to remove temptation from both is what I did."

A smirk fluttered over Harvey's face. "Well, it didn't work, did it?"

Abraham scowled at him. "If you'd have sent Joseph away like I asked things would've turned out different."

"Spare me your feeble excuses. I've no interest in them," said Harvey, stepping back toward the door. "Thought I ought to tell you about my land, in case you know somebody who might want to buy it."

"No, I don't," said Abraham, his heart clutching. "And I don't figure it'll be easy to sell. Who's got money to buy land these days?"

"It's good land. It'll sell." With a quick nod, Harvey turned and left.

Abraham paced the confines of his shop. Lord in heaven, what am I to do? Harvey—my friend in faith, the son of my departed sister, my dearest companion—turned from me. Beech miserable. Elizabeth standoffish and running herself ragged. This isn't working, he thought. Strife is cleaving the bonds meant to sustain us. We've started this settlement at just the wrong time, with the financial depression eating away at the country. We can't go on pretending like everything will work out if we just keep at our orchards, hunting, and logging.

No, deep in his bones Abraham knew something needed changing.

"Mother," he announced that night as he folded back the bed sheets and eased under the covers. "Times are hard. Maybe we should see how the old farm is faring."

Elizabeth sat at her dresser brushing her hair out, her back to Abraham. "It'd be a welcome relief to stop a spell with Josephine and Ira."

Abraham had sold their Van Buren County farm, at a special family price, to his daughter, Josephine, and her husband, Ira. Abraham folded his hands behind his head and studied the ceiling. "Will you write Josephine? Tell her we'll be coming for a visit?"

"What about Goldie and Artie?"

"Could someone else keep them for us?"

"I suppose Elvila and John might. I'll talk it over with Beech."

Abraham decided the time was ripe to try his plan out on Elizabeth, though he didn't imagine she'd take to it right away. "Wonder if we should try to sell this land here. Could use the money to get us going again down in Van Buren."

Elizabeth swung around and frowned at him. "You honestly thinking about selling?"

"You see how hard it is for everybody here," Abraham said, propping himself up on his elbows to meet Elizabeth's gaze. "This depression is grinding us down. We can hardly get enough for our crops or venison to afford flour and kerosene. I just wonder if we'd be better off on the old farm. We could throw in with Josephine and Ira."

"Well, I don't want to sell. Look how hard we worked to build up this settlement. Got most of our kin here now. Can't turn our backs on them."

"Some of them are having doubts, too. Like Harvey. And we're getting old. Maybe the younger ones can manage here, but I can't do much more heavy work myself. And conditions are bad. We've got to think about ourselves."

"Never thought I'd hear you talking like this."

"Well, I have to consider our future. I think I ought to run an ad and see if anybody's willing to pay us well."

Elizabeth shook her head. "We have most of our family right here, all around us, and you're talking about turning away from all we've built?"

Abraham relaxed onto his side, and his voice turned plaintive. "All this privation weighs heavy on my heart, Mother, with Beech's troubles and Harvey putting his land up for sale. Our produce won't bring in much money this season and then next winter'll be even harder to get through. I say let's get the garden planted, ask the others to tend it for us, and then go see if we can do better down there."

"I don't like what I'm hearing. You can run your ad, but I'll be wanting a say if someone proposes to buy. I'm only agreeing to this so we can see how things are down in Lower Michigan."

Two weeks before Abraham and Elizabeth boarded a train for Van Buren County, Abraham placed an ad in the late May issue of the Manistique *Saturday Morning Star,* instructing the paper to run it every week until they heard otherwise:

> Farm for Sale: 160 acres, 12 miles north of Manistique in Hiawatha Township. 40 acres improved, good house, new frame barn. 2 acres set to fruits, the balance first class hardwood land, all but 5 acres of good cedar and the best of springs. The cheapest farm in Schoolcraft County for $1500. Call and see the owner, A.S. Byers.

Abraham and Elizabeth spent the height of summer with Josephine and Ira in southwest Michigan. Many an afternoon Abraham rode out on the country roads and spoke to farmers he'd once neighbored with. Come August, upon their return to Hiawatha, Abraham stopped at the *Saturday Morning Star* and asked them to run a notice:

> Abraham Byers and wife, who have been visiting relations in Van Buren County for two months, returned Wednesday. Mr. Byers says the outlook for the farmer in the Lower Peninsula is very discouraging. The wheat was a light crop, the cornfields and pasture lands are burned, and the fruit crop is next to nothing. He said that he had been advertising his farm for sale at $1500, but now $3000 would not buy it because the outlook is so much better here than in the Lower Peninsula. He has taken his farm off the sale list.

Yes, Abraham thought, I just needed time for reflection and rest to renew my homesteading spirit. Shortly after their return, Harvey stopped along the road to tell Abraham he was moving to Wisconsin even though his land hadn't sold.

"Joseph is in Eagle River with Florence, and I'm wanting to join my son," Harvey said, looking down on Abraham from his horse.

Abraham shook his head. "I fear you'll regret your decision, Harvey, but I wish you well."

He hated to see Harvey leave. Abraham and Elizabeth had taken Harvey in after he lost his mother and raised him like a son of their own. So Harvey leaving on such bad terms on top of Beech not speaking to him pained him doubly bad.

There was nothing to do but set aside his fretting about Harvey and Beech and prepare well for the coming winter.
By God, he thought, maybe Harvey has lost faith in me and this settlement, but I've got dozens of kinfolk here that need someone to buck them up.

TIME FOR RENEWAL

MARCH 1894

"Can't say it's gotten easier," Beech said. On his way home from town, he'd stopped to pick up Goldie and Artie, but Elizabeth sent them to their bedroom and insisted Beech sit with her a little. It'd been four seasons since he'd lost Florence, and still he moped around, insisting he couldn't bear to think of taking a new wife.

"It's time to set your sorrow aside and consider your children." Elizabeth figured a year was long enough for mourning. She'd lost her first mate—to the Civil War after only three months of marriage—and over time her sorrow had abated. Sure, she indulged in some reminiscence of her beloved Solomon from time to time. On their wedding day, he'd given her a rose-colored shawl of spun wool. Every time she wrapped it over her shoulders, she remembered the proud look on his face when he presented it to her. But rememberings didn't keep her from living each day as best she could. In Abraham she'd found the steadiness, loyalty, and comfort of a well-made marriage, even if he sometimes peeved her.

"I know it's hard on you taking care of them, but I just can't seem to leave off hoping Florence will come back."

"I'd never say this to your father but marrying him helped me heal after Solomon died." To her way of thinking remarriage was like a spring rain rushing into a dry creek bed. "It was terrible hard losing a new husband, but after your father's Henrietta died, he needed someone, just like I did."

Beech shook his head and studied the tabletop, like he couldn't imagine what that had to do with him.

"You're a good man, some woman out there would be fortunate to have you."

"And be saddled with two young'uns from another woman?"

"Happens all the time."

"It was different for you. Your Solomon was killed. My Florence is still alive."

Elizabeth had to think on that. Maybe the pain of a wife deserting was worse than being widowed. Death isn't a willful abandonment, but a passing ordained by the Maker himself. A final passing at that. She nodded, "Yes, I can see that."

"You had no choice. But I'm left wondering if Florence might come to her senses."

"Will you at least consider how much longer you should wait on her?"

"You make it sound like it should be easy to do, Mother."

"Well, I hope you can set your mind to it." She loved her son, but this self-indulgence was trying her toleration.

It was only two weeks later, a month shy of the one-year anniversary of Florence's departure, that Beech invited Elizabeth onto the front porch for a private word. "I've had a letter from Florence. Says she's wanting to marry Joseph."

"Oh, Lord," said Elizabeth, hoping the news would break up this logjam. Beech needed to find a new wife, and not only for himself and the children. Elizabeth just couldn't spend the next decade and a half caring for Goldie and Artie. Not with all her other obligations. "How you taking it, Son?"

"I'm done with her. What kind of woman leaves her children like that? She doesn't deserve them."

"I liked your Florence, I did. Thought she might be some kind of daughter to me. But she disappointed all of us." Elizabeth stood beside Beech, taking in the scent of fresh-sprouting grasses around her house.

"I'll be filing divorce papers soon as I can. Might as well be free myself."

"You're making the right decision," she said, thanking the Lord for Beech's turn of mind. "Spring's upon us. It's time for new beginnings."

Elizabeth could leave off worrying about Beech for now. She had plenty of other troubles hanging over her. The winter had been harsh, and the settlement had suffered a shortage of staples. One settler, James Rose, had died from the lung fever, and Elizabeth knew they all ought to be grateful only one had succumbed to winter's cold and scarcity. More winters like the last would sorely test the settlement. She hated to think it, but maybe Abraham had the right idea about starting over in Van Buren County.

DELIVERANCE

MARCH 1894

Abraham feared Beech'd never speak to him again. But over fellowship the first Sunday of April, as the congregation dispersed, Beech sidled up to him and announced, "Gus says the Company is lowering wages again next week."

Abraham glossed over the fact that these were Beech's first words to him in a year. "Dear Lord," he said, "could it get any worse?"

Beech stared out the open barn doors. "I figure once the mill closes for the season, they'll cut pay in the camps, too."

Abraham had stood by while the Chicago Lumbering Company reduced wages for mill workers, lumberjacks, and even independent jobbers by twenty-five percent in under a year's time. They'd started out trimming pay by five percent and then, a few months later, by another ten. Wages had dipped to three-quarters of what they'd been ten months earlier, and it was then Abraham had observed the workers and their wives stopping along country roads, on street corners, and in shops to commiserate.

"I wouldn't doubt it," said Abraham, glancing at Beech's impassive profile. "Those company men know just how much they can get away with. It's harder for the men in the camps to organize, with them all spread out like they are."

Beech poked his chin toward the few remaining congregants, the small circle made up of his older brothers, Elonzo and Link, and their wives and children. "I feel sorry for them that's got even more mouths to feed than the likes of us."

Abraham pursed his lips with determination. Although the renewal of the father-son bond gratified him, he sensed distance in Beech's manner and determined that patience was the best course. He bowed his head. "With the Lord's guidance, we'll help each other."

Beech nodded. "Gus is organizing a workers' committee. To consider a strike. Wanted me to ask if you'd be there."

"Course I will," said Abraham, relieved that the estrangement between him and Beech had ended—and thankful about being asked to join the workers. He'd do whatever he could to help the five hundred men at the Manistique mill and the few hundred more at lumberjack camps in the area. It wouldn't be easy fighting the Lumbering Company. No other business in the three-county area came close to employing so many people. And the company's tentacles reached into other parts of town as well. It operated a commissary and box and broom factory and controlled the Soo rail-shipping line. Manistique was what they called "a company town." Sure, the townspeople appreciated the steady work and the community of workers and families it supported, but Abraham knew they also resented the control the Company exerted over them.

Abraham leaned against the side wall of Manistique's Township Hall. He'd declined young Gus Highland's invitation to open the meeting: "No, you've got the fire—and grounds—to call for a strike, Gus. You're the one the workers ought to hear from." Gus was a natural-born speaker, with gangly arms that he used to pound the air for emphasis and a rusty head of hair that stood out in a crowd.

Abraham figured some four hundred mill workers had gathered in the hall. By God, he thought, these men are finally ready to teach that Company a thing or two. And since the managers at the mill watched over the men as they labored hard and long, Abraham hoped they'd understand these men didn't grumble over trifles. The managers lived in their midst and ought to show at least a stitch of sympathy for the children's shabby clothes and wives' complaints about skimpy meals.

Gus stood at the podium gazing out on the well-packed hall. Dusky light shone through the wide hall's side windows, and electric light bulbs glittered along its back wall, lighting more of the men's backs than anything else. After one beat of his gavel, Gus announced, "Thank you for coming, men. I'm pleased to see so many of you here tonight."

The size of the crowd and the dimming light of day seemed to infect the men with the bravado of anonymity, and several of them hollered greetings back at Gus: "Speak up, Gus" . . . "About time we did this" . . . "Got good call to be here."

Gus, his cheeks mottled up with the headiness of rabble-rousing, continued, "A committee of us, these men seated here"—Gus pointed to Beech and three other workers seated at the table next to him— "have drawn up a resolution for you to consider. We'll read it to you, and then we'll have an up or down vote whether we sign and deliver this statement to the company management tomorrow. First I'll ask the other men to speak."

Gus relinquished the stage, and the committee members took turns at the podium lit by a dangling electric bulb. The first speaker, a young widower with no children, read from an article in *The Coming Nation* that urged workers to fight against profiteering companies. Next Beech recounted the early history of the Lumbering Company—how it had encouraged families to move to the Upper Peninsula and promised steady work and good wages. Another man told the story of the American Railway Union workers who had struck against Great Northern Railroad one year earlier and, after only eighteen days, forced the railroad to rescind most of its wage cuts. The last speaker reminded the group that the mill was processing more lumber now than ten months ago, which was not surprising since they'd increased hours. And, to boot, they had the gall to pour salt in the workers' wounds and cut their wages.

The crowd, quieted by the sobering words spoken to them, held themselves still, their faces lifted to their leaders. Gus approached the podium and glanced at Abraham. Abraham nodded once, urging him on. Gus had made him an honorary member of the planning committee, but Abraham resolved: It was Gus's time to shine and the workers' place to call for a strike.

"Here's the resolution for you, men." Gus clenched the sheet of paper, two-fisted, and raised it to chest level. "We, the workers of the Manistique Mill, resolve that all employees of the Chicago Lumbering Company have a right to a living wage and work hours that are respectable. We demand wages be raised fifteen percent, starting with five percent now, another five percent on May 1, and the last five percent on June 1, and that weekly hours be no more than fifty-four, starting now. We request a response to our demands within forty-eight hours of delivery of this resolution. If our demands are not met, we resolve to strike until they are."

Gus put down the resolution and called out, "Now, men, we'll hear your questions."

An arm shot up in the front row and a hollow-cheeked older man spoke. "Is it foolish to ask for both the wages and reduced hours at the same time?"

All eyes turned to Gus. He leaned over the podium. "We considered that. You know the Company has whipsawed us— lowering wages *and* increasing hours. If we don't ask for both wages and reasonable hours, they could give us the wages, then turn around and make up for it in more hours. That's what our thinking was."

"I say ask for the whole fifteen percent now," yelled a man from the middle of the crowd. A buzz scudded over the group.

Gus pounded the gavel twice and waited for the crowd to still. "I'm glad one of you asks for less and another for more." Chuckles rose from the committee and many in the hall. "It means maybe we got it right. Did we, men?"

The committee members clapped. Mutters and clapping coursed through the crowd of bobbing heads.

Gus raised his voice over the din. "Are you ready to vote then?"

From the back of the hall, a clear tenor voice sounded out. "You asking all of us to sign?"

"If we vote in favor of this resolution," said Gus, weaving his head to spot the man who'd voiced the question, "we back it up with our signatures and deliver it with all the force of our numbers."

"What about them's not here?" called out the same one. Abraham raised himself up on his toes to catch sight of the man—an oily-haired fellow of perhaps twenty-five years.

"Well, some are on their shifts now," said Gus. "The others I can't account for. But we have many more than half of us here. If all of us carry through on the strike, we'll shut that mill down."

The same one hollered, "Then how'd we feed our families?"

"Can hardly feed them now," said Gus, but his response was lost in the commotion stirred by the question.

The crowd of men shifted about, forming clots of debaters, and the din of rising voices fed on itself as they spoke louder to get in their say. The heat of the men's leathery bodies and long-worn woolens rose in the hall.

Gus brushed his sweat-beaded brow and pushed up the sleeves of his flannel shirt. He hammered his gavel on the podium three times, and the men quieted.

"Conditions are bad for all of us—those that are here and those that aren't. The only way to get on the road to righting the wrongs done us is to demand fair treatment." Gus stiffened an arm against the podium and spoke up loud and sure. "I urge you to vote in favor of the resolution. A strike will bring the Company to its knees. Then we'll have the wages we need to feed our families. I ask all of you to stand together—for your families and your fellow men."

"Stand together," hollered a lone man, and the crowd took up the chant, "Stand together, stand together," till the whole hall shook from the stomping of their feet.

At the first hint of a downturn in the chant, Gus held his arms up high to bring it to a close and called out, "Talk to those who aren't here. Tell them of this resolution—of the hundreds of us gathered here. Tell them we must stand together."

Stepping out from behind the podium and coming to the edge of the stage, Gus bellowed, "We will win if we stand together. Do you hear, men?"

A cluster of men in the first row yelled, "Hear, hear." Those behind them clapped, and the crowd erupted into cheers. Gus seized the opportunity and called for the vote, which was as near to unanimous as the committee had hoped it would be.

During the cheering and voting, Abraham scrutinized the workers, trying to gauge their mood. Was it confidence or angry desperation he discerned in their bouncing heads and flashing eyes? A few men in the back looked down during the vote and then shuffled out the door before the signing got underway. No matter, he thought, all these signatures will deliver a strong message, and afterward he congratulated Gus on running such a spirited meeting.

⌒───○

The next morning Gus and Beech delivered the resolution, with 371 signatures, to Manager Artin Quick, explaining they expected an answer at the same hour two days hence.

Their answer arrived sooner than that. The next day Abraham and Elizabeth's son Lenniel rode up to the house bearing the news. He handed the *Manistique Weekly Tribune,* folded to an article on the front page, to his father. "Thought you should see this."

Abraham and Elizabeth's third son strode to the table and plunked down in a chair. Lenniel, who was taller than his father by a half-foot, had inherited his height from an earlier generation. Elizabeth said he was the handsomest of their sons, but Abraham thought his deep, close-set eyes and long, fleshy ears gave him a hang-dog look.

"What were you doing in town, Son?" Elizabeth asked.

"Poking around at the newspaper offices, asking about work," he said, flattening his palms on the table.

Abraham, who had settled down in his chair to read the article, sprang up. "Mother, listen to this." He read aloud, "'About three hundred lumber mill workers came together for a general meeting on the evening of April 10 by a small group of agitators headed up by Abraham S. Byers.'"

Abraham looked up from the newspaper. "Those lying skunks."

"What else does it say?" Elizabeth asked, worrying her hands.

"'The workers were riled up about conditions and told they could beat the Company if they went on strike with their demands. But the Chicago Lumbering Company will not answer to outside agitators and will not buckle to unreasonable demands. Loyal employees know the Company is under dire financial threat because of the general depression sweeping the whole country. The management is doing the best it can by its workers and does not have the financial resources to meet the agitators' foolish petition. The Company sympathizes with the hardships of the workers and pledges to raise wages again when finances improve. Meantime workers should report for work on April 13. Supervisors will report any workers who do not show up for their shift and release them from work.'"

Abraham slapped the paper against his palm.

"They're using you, setting the workers against you," said Elizabeth.

Abraham flushed. "Those scoundrels, those low-down good-for-nothings."

Lenniel swung around in his chair and hitched his arm over it. "Well, did you, Father? Did you organize that meeting?"

Abraham huffed, "No, I did not. I was invited to show my support."

"Not the first time the Company used dirty tricks," said Elizabeth.

Lenniel shook his head and pushed back in his chair. "Guess I won't be getting an accounting job at the mill."

Elizabeth sat down next to Lenniel, who had recently returned from his studies at the Valparaiso Business School in Indiana. "You'll get something. Not many around here with your education."

Abraham threw the paper onto the table. "And that newspaper with its mealy-mouthed reporters lets them get away with it."

"Not much you can do about it," said Elizabeth. "Good thing you don't work at the mill."

"They'd have fired you long ago," Lenniel said, staring at his father.

"That's just it." Abraham bounced his arm. "This is a red herring. They're trying to say that an outsider caused the strike. See? It takes away from the real story—how they've done wrong by their workers. They're not only ruthless—they're lying evildoers."

"Think this'll hurt the strike?" asked Elizabeth.

"Sure is intended to," said Abraham with a wide sweep of his head. "How can they stoop so low?"

Elizabeth sighed. "Must figure it's their privilege to decide the rightful order of things."

Abraham raised his eyes skyward, "As God is my witness, their way is not the right way."

"Those men are desperate," said Lenniel.

Abraham said, "Hope they can see through the Company's conniving ways."

Lenniel clunked his heels on the floor, as if to signal certitude. "I imagine most of them are more worried about feeding their families than prognosticating about the Company."

Abraham grabbed his satchel and stuffed the paper inside. "Well, I can't stand by and let them get away with this lying. Pack me a dinner, Mother. I'll be getting into town right away."

Abraham saddled up Smokey and hurried into Manistique, heading straight for the newspaper office. He demanded to talk to a reporter, who sat at his desk, arms folded, listening to Abraham's vociferous complaints about the newspaper's failure to check the accuracy of its story.

The next day the paper ran two articles. One reported on Abraham Byers' emphatic denial that he had instigated the strike, and the other explained that the lumber mill strike had not materialized as nearly all workers had reported for work that morning.

Abraham was sorely disappointed the strike had failed—and disgusted at how the Company had used him to defuse it. Corporations were corrupt, he declared, and capitalists without conscience. Was there no end to the insults this government and the corporations would heap on the farmer and working man? First Weaver lost, and now depression and inflation gripped the country. Right here in Schoolcraft County the Chicago Lumbering Company is taking advantage of every worker by shaving wages and increasing hours. There was only so much a man could take before resorting to drastic action.

And now the possibility of such action crystallized in Abraham's mind. In the February issue of *The Coming Nation* Abraham had learned of a new book, *The Product-Sharing Village*, by Walter Thomas Mills. He'd ordered a copy and read it cover to cover—twice. Thrilled by its vision, he resolved: The time is ripe for deliverance.

A NEW VISION

Chill breezes swept over the snow-patched landscape as the men, women, and children of the Byers' Settlement streamed into Abraham's barn for Sunday service. In accordance with their custom to come to God humble, they greeted each other with silent nods and filed to their places on the hay bales and in the standing space. Some of the children slumped into the tied bales, and their parents elbowed them to attention.

Abraham stood at the door, clenching his hands behind his back as he smiled at the gathering congregants. Anticipation hummed in his brain, and he recalled his sermon of one year earlier about adultery. Well, he told himself, I doubt any will think of that today. When his pocket watch showed ten o'clock, he rose before the gathering.

This Sabbath he preached his "Love and neighbors" sermon, taking from Leviticus, "Love thy neighbor as thyself," from Proverbs, "I love them that love me," and from John, "Know that ye are my disciples if ye have love one to another."

"Brothers and sisters," he announced at the close of his shortened sermon, "before fellowship time I have some important business to take up with you." He reached down to his table, gripped the book that he now considered second only to the Bible in importance, and raised it up for all to see. "Walter Thomas Mills, a fine Christian leader who speaks for the common man, has offered a vision for a new way of life. He calls it the product-sharing village."

Abraham sauntered before the rows, holding the book up so all could read its cover. He stopped and clutched the book to his chest. "We, my dear brethren, can bring this vision to life."

Two of Abraham's sons from his first marriage, Elonzo and Link, glanced at each other across the standing space in the rear.

John Kepler, Elizabeth's older half-brother, cocked his head in question. Husbands and wives turned and muttered to each other.

Abraham held Mills' book close and relaxed onto his heels. "I know this is sudden and that none of you, except my Elizabeth here, have heard of this idea, but I wanted all of you to come to it at once and consider it together."

John, the eldest of the Kepler clan, spoke from his seat in the second row, his baritone voice rich with resonance. "I know you have read about such things as this, Abraham, but I have not, and I expect most of the others haven't either."

"Why, yes, John," said Abraham. "Let me read how he explains this general notion."

Abraham opened the book to his first marker. "'By product-sharing I mean the voluntary organization of workers to provide for their own wants with the products of their labor—and the distribution of these products among themselves based on their share of the production. The special form of organization discussed is one which provides that the workers shall have the total product of their labors without paying to others than themselves either wages, profits, interest, or rents.'"

Abraham, inspired all over again by these words, lifted his eyes from the book and beamed at his flock.

John cast a look to each side, including as many of the gathered as he could in his glance. "I must ask you to tell us more, in words we can all understand. I know nothing about this product-sharing notion."

"Of course," said Abraham. "The idea is for the village to plan its labor and products, being mindful of how it can best meet the needs of all. Think of it this way, John: You plant your garden with one row each of potatoes, carrots, and turnips for winter storage. But still you're dependent on your jobber's earnings to purchase kerosene and sugar and flour—even as the Lumber Company keeps cutting your earnings. But if we as a village grew whole gardens of potatoes, carrots, and turnips, then we would have enough for our own cellars *and* enough to sell. With the profits from our agriculture, we could buy our kerosene and staples."

John tugged at the scraggly bottom of his beard. Unlike Abraham, he eschewed trimming and let his beard grow freely. "It sounds like it'd take quite a lot of figuring and fussing."

Abraham pitched forward, as if he were bucking a strong wind, and spoke, eyeing his sons, Elonzo, Link, Beech, and Lenniel. After all, his own offspring ought to back him up. "Don't our households already produce much of our own food? And furniture? And clothing as well? Do we not harvest the berries that grow on our land? And take deer and beaver from our woods? And fish from the streams and lakes?" He smiled in response to their bobbing heads. Turning to John, he said, "We are halfway to this vision already."

Abraham sliced a finger into the second place marked in Mills' book. "'In starting such a village, four things are necessary: members, organization, location, and capital. Members should be working people accustomed to hard labor who care for educational and social advantages for themselves and children and who seek an opportunity to serve society, not simply to make money.'"

Sweeping his arm to take in the gathering, Abraham said, "You are all accustomed to hard labor, and you know the value of it for yourselves and your children."

Returning to his marked passage, Abraham read on. "'The location would not need to be extensive. It should be healthful, fertile, able to produce a great variety of products, and, if possible, afford a beautiful location for the village itself. The purpose is not to do again on the frontier what has already been done there; but to make it possible for the workman to obtain the full returns of his own labor by imitating the frontiersman in adopting, as he has always done, the plan of product-sharing, but now in permanent form reinforced with the best machinery.'"

Abraham looked up at the gathering. "Do you see? This is the very path we have already set ourselves on. We have tried to live as much by our own means as possible. Mr. Mills only puts into words and gives method to the very things we prize and practice."

Abraham again brought the book up before him. "'The most difficult question will be that of capital, but a large amount of capital is not necessary. The usual cost of a favorably located and well-stocked farm large enough to engage a capable farmer is not less than five thousand dollars. For an ordinary farm hand to start such a farm with only his hands is an undertaking which means the labor and the savings of a lifetime. But there are large numbers of young farmers who can raise five hundred dollars. Now if one hundred of these would combine it would make a total capital of fifty-thousand dollars which, invested in lands, machinery, and stock, would be enough to make an ample beginning for such an association.'"

Abraham looked up, his eyes sparkling with enthusiasm. "Dear brothers and sisters, we already own this land. We have logging and farming equipment, woodworking and blacksmithing shops. And we could have others join us, requiring that they contribute funds for the purchase of whatever else we need to make our community sufficient unto itself."

John Kepler, who was much taller and sturdier than Abraham, stood. He wore the German socks and knickers of the lumberjack, and his gray-with-age cotton long johns showed at the opening of his heavy flannel shirt. "Is there much risk to us, Abraham, in undertaking such a village? I wouldn't want to lose what I have worked so hard to build."

Abraham turned toward his brother-in-law and squared his shoulders. "You are a prudent man, John, and you deserve a thoughtful answer to your question. Let me read one last passage in reply."

John nodded at Abraham and sat.

"'But if it is difficult for men working together to make a start, it should be borne in mind that the only other alternative is for each to start alone on his own account; and that working alone he will never be able to buy with his own earnings the best machines, and, if he could, he could not run them without the help of others—it is either working with his fellows for himself, his children, and the common good, or working for others under the bondage of the wage system.'"

Abraham clapped the book closed with one hand and bounced his other hand before his chest, like a general exhorting his troops to courage. "You have witnessed the damage done by bondage to the Chicago Lumbering Company. The mill workers, lumberjacks, and jobbers among us have seen their pay cut and lies told by the company about why they do this."

Abraham allowed a twinkling smile to creep onto his expression. "Now we have an answer to their greediness. By turning our settlement over to a product-sharing village we can bring in enough capital to start our own milling operation. We would cut our own building lumber, and we could sell milled wood to our neighbors with no middleman or profiteer to shrink the value of our hard work. We can increase our farming with better plows and more hands. How can we not gain when we grow our own food, sew our own clothes, and sell goods direct to the people? We can free ourselves from the bondage of the wage system."

Abraham dropped his arms and sighed with satisfaction. He would let his words rest on the ears of the waiting.

John looked to Abraham and then turned his glance to the men sitting beside him. "You mention the amount fifty-thousand dollars to begin. But we have no such money among us."

"Mr. Mills is referring to the total assets available. I've had our settlement lands appraised, and with our personal properties, they are valued at fourteen thousand. But, what's more important, we already own much of the equipment for logging, blacksmithing, and furniture-building."

"Still," said John, "we'd be needing more equipment, thousands of dollar's worth."

Abraham tilted his head in thoughtfulness. It was right and good for John to push for particulars. "We would require those joining us to bring in assets for the purchase of additional machinery and supplies. And remember: We're not starting from scratch. Look what we've already done for ourselves here—taken this wilderness land and built homes, gardens, and orchards, made income by our own logging and work on it. With that and the funds and labor of the newcomers, we cannot fail."

Abraham placed Mills' book down on the table beside him. "I would not want to lead you wrong. You are my brothers and sisters, my children and brethren. We will not go forward unless you understand this plan and can give yourselves over to its ideals."

John's brother, Alva, tapped John's shoulder and whispered a few words to him, which Abraham could not discern. John nodded his assent.

Alva turned to Abraham and asked, "What about all the work? How can we be sure we have enough hard laborers among us?"

Ah, thought Abraham, Alva always had been quick to complain about others not contributing their share at the house raisings. "That's an important question, to be sure. And Mr. Mills in his wisdom has considered this matter. All able members of the village should make a contribution, and their work is recognized in the form of time credits. These credits are then used by the workers to purchase their goods. There's no need of outside wages, for the village would honor and credit the very work we already do in our settlement."

"I would like to hear from others what they think about us taking this path," said John, glancing about from his seat.

"Thank you, John," said Abraham. "I'll not go forward without being satisfied you all understand and agree to this plan. Let us hear your questions."

Edgar Huey, the twenty-three-year-old son of Elizabeth's sister, Sarah, rose. "You say time credits would be used to purchase goods. But what about those who are elderly or unable to work?"

Abraham had always been fond of Elizabeth's good-willed nephew, and even now, as Edgar questioned him, Abraham admired his mettle, for he knew Edgar was only speaking out of concern for his ailing father. "You are right to raise this question, Edgar. The Christian spirit requires us to care for those among us who cannot care for themselves. Time credits can be awarded to those who care for these persons, and, in the true sense of Christian community, we should provide for the needy among us. Mr. Mills even explains how to do this in his plan."

Alva blurted out, "What about our land? What does this mean about the land we own?"

Abraham had suspected that Alva, who had an ornery streak as long as a skunk's stripe, would be a naysayer. Rubbing his palms together to bide his irritation, Abraham replied, "The village would own the land according to an agreement signed by all landowners and village members. We would use it in ways that would be of the greatest benefit to the whole village. And as the village enlarges its financial coffers it could acquire even more land—land that would then be available for all of us—for fishing, farming, and logging. By being the stewards of our own land and labor, we all benefit directly."

There were more questions, not about Mills' book, but about how to translate his ideas into practice and who would undertake the organization of it. Abraham, well versed in Mills' vision, answered according to the strictures of the book, only once venturing beyond its pages by proposing a name for their village, Hiawatha Colony, to honor its citing in Hiawatha Township and to exemplify the spirit of living in harmony with the land.

Once the group's questions were exhausted, Abraham asked, "Shall we go forth then? Shall we study whether to embark on a product-sharing village?"

Abraham stood with folded hands and looked upon the gathered, his gaze settling on John Kepler.

John spoke. "I would want to see exactly how this plan would work out for all of us."

John's wife, Elvila, smiled in assent, and, like the ripples in a pond, nods of agreement spread from this center.

"Very well, we can begin by drawing up a proposal for the management of our village," said Abraham, spreading his arms out as if to embrace the gathered, wanting with all his heart to bring his flock together under this vision. "I'll need a committee to work on the partnership agreement. Who would like to join this committee?"

Abraham's eldest son, Elonzo, raised his hand, and his younger half-brother, Lenniel, did the same. Gus Highland, who had started traveling from Manistique for the Sunday service, said he'd be willing to join in if the settlement members thought it proper, and after Elonzo and Lenniel signaled approval, others nodded and muttered their agreement, too.

Abraham looked to John. "Would you like to join us, John?"

"Will you come back to the whole group with this partnership plan?" asked John.

"Why, yes," said Abraham. "We'll want the consent of all to go forward."

"Then no, I'm not a committee man. I'll leave it to you and these other men," John said. "But I'll not turn away from the Lumbering Company's pay until we've got supplies enough for a good many months."

"I take your point, John."

"Wouldn't want a repeat of what happened at the Furnace Company."

Abraham passed over John's reference to events that took place over a decade ago in Van Buren County. With a nod to John, he straightened and addressed the whole group. "I'm gratified by the spirit of willingness and trust among us. I'll request that the committee meet this very day and begin planning and designing an agreement. And I'll write to Mr. Mills and ask if he would like to join our community. I doubt he will, but maybe he'd consent to help in fashioning a village after his own vision."

Straightaway after the committee's first meeting Abraham composed his letter to Walter Mills.

Dear Mr. Mills:

Having studied your admirable book The Product-Sharing Village, I write with a proposal which I hope you will consider as seriously as it is ventured. There is here in Hiawatha Township a large homestead of 1080 acres appraised at $11,095 and personal property at $2,576, for total assets of $13,671. We are considering turning all this over to a product-sharing village. We would be honored to have you join us, but we will go forward with a study of your fine idea with or without your assistance. I invite you to come and visit our community, see our homesteaded lands, and consider whether you would like to aid us in bringing your vision to life in the beautiful woodlands of Upper Michigan.

Respectfully yours,

Abraham S. Byers

Abraham sent his letter and resolved not to wait for a reply, but to organize and do everything necessary to launch a village in accordance with Walter Mills' ideas. He set his committee to work reading Mills' book and drafting the partnership agreement. Traveling all around Schoolcraft County, he spread word of the proposed cooperative community and found many receptive ears among the populace. The same could not be said for the newspapers, one of which wrote: "Mr. Byers is now bedecked with badges on hat and coat, announcing to the world that he's a grubstaker for product sharing."

IN EDEN WE SHALL MEET

APRIL 1894

Much to Abraham's surprise, a reply came from Mr. Mills a mere twelve days after he'd posted his letter. Mr. Mills would like very much to visit. In fact, if Mr. Byers would make the arrangements, he'd happily address Michigan audiences on the Christian community and his product-sharing ideas. Abraham had no difficulties securing the finest and most capacious hall in three counties—downtown Manistique's Star Opera House—for a series of lectures by renowned author and speaker Walter Thomas Mills.

Once news spread that the famous Mr. Mills had accepted his invitation, Abraham discerned a shift among the editors at both the Manistique *Weekly Tribune* and *Pioneer*. They took a more respectful tone toward him and welcomed his visits. No, he'd not tarry when such opportunity presented itself. He straightaway capitalized on the moment, scheduling appointments with reporters and sharing news of his plans for a product-sharing village.

Once satisfied that his cause had garnered broad exposure in the newspapers, he ran an announcement in the *Weekly Tribune*: "The citizens of Schoolcraft County and the public at large are cordially invited to meet at Manistique's Township Hall for the purpose of discussing the formation of a cooperative colony in the Byers' Settlement. A.S. Byers will preside."

In the days leading up to the meeting, Abraham fretted over how to manage the meeting. He reasoned no other address or sermon he'd ever delivered—or might yet deliver—exceeded this one in importance. Everything he'd ever done in life—to serve the Lord and the working man—seemed to converge on this opportunity. Every mistake he'd ever made could be righted if he succeeded with Hiawatha Colony. He devoted every waking hour of his day to mulling the possibilities and anticipating the challenges.

If the colony was to be a success, it would need new members, members who could bring not only a true spirit of cooperation and enthusiasm, but also capital for the purchase of machinery and building materials. And although John and Alva Kepler and the others in the settlement seemed to be coming around to the plan, Abraham expected that the eagerness of outsiders might just nudge his community of kin toward complete acceptance. And without the cooperation of everybody in the settlement, it wouldn't work.

The evening before the Manistique meeting, he paced about his cabin, sketching out his thoughts for the talk. Come ten o'clock Elizabeth hollered down, "It's late, come to bed."

Although Abraham wasn't satisfied with his speech, he trudged upstairs and gave himself over to fitful sleep. In the middle of the night, he awoke with a refrain ringing in his ears. He leaped from bed, scurried down to the kitchen, and lit a candle. Hunkering over the table, he wrote out the whole of his talk, and then, for the first time in days, slept soundly until morning.

Abraham arrived at Township Hall an hour before the meeting. Because he wanted to be on the floor with his guests, he carried the podium down from the stage and placed it before the rows of benches. Satisfied with this new arrangement, he brought a chair down from the stage and sat beside the podium to review his notes.

The door at the back of the hall creaked open. Abraham looked up. A man of perhaps sixty with a shock of wavy gray hair entered. "Mr. Byers?" he asked, a slight smile gracing his clean-shaven face.

"Yes, welcome," said Abraham, standing and approaching the man.

The gentleman marched in, black bowler hat in hand. He was tall, about six feet, and carried himself with thrown-back shoulders. His double-breasted suit fell in straight lines down his trim frame, and a black bowtie set off his crisp white shirt. "I'm Gideon Noel. I live just outside Manistique."

Abraham reached out a hand, and he and Mr. Noel exchanged a hearty handshake. "I'm pleased to make your acquaintance, Mr. Noel."

"I've long admired your causes, Mr. Byers. And I've read Mr. Mills' book, too."

"Have you? It's a visionary work, isn't it?"

"Yes, visionary—that's the very word for it."

Abraham slipped his notes into his pocket. "Mr. Mills will be here next week. Will you attend his lectures?"

"I wouldn't miss them for anything. I'm most interested in his ideas—and your cooperative village."

Warmed by the prospect of a new backer, Abraham smiled at his compatriot. "What is your line of work, Mr. Noel?"

"I run the Apothecary and Spice Store in Manistique."

"Why, yes, I recall your name now."

"Been there sixteen years. But it gets harder and harder to make a business of it with the commissary for competition."

"Ah, I can see how that would be, with the company pushing its coupons. They do everything they can to keep the money in-house."

"Yes, they do. I've done well in my business though, and my brother, who lives in Detroit, made a small fortune in patent medicine. Anyway, I hope to throw my support behind your village."

"I'm happy to hear that," said Abraham, trying to contain the excitement rising in him. Hearing the rattle of the door, he peered over Mr. Noel's shoulder. A party of four, two men and two women, shuffled in. Looking back to Mr. Noel, he said, "Would it be possible to meet afterward?"

Arrangements with Mr. Noel made, Abraham hurried to the back of the hall to welcome the foursome and all the other newcomers, taking pains to commit their names to memory. As the hour to commence approached, he encouraged them to take their seats.

Striding to the podium, Abraham looked out on the crowd of some thirty townspeople. It was a convivial group, made up of couples and also some men on their own, all who had greeted each other with knowing smiles and eager handshakes.

He raised his head high and braced his hands atop the podium. "Fellow citizens, you show courage and a forward-thinking temperament by venturing out to hear of the plan for a product-sharing village. You know these are hard times in our country, difficult times for the hard-working men and women of the Upper Peninsula, times that call for idealism and vision. For too long we have been at the mercy of poor economic conditions and the whims of the Chicago Lumbering Company. It is now we must take the teachings of our Lord to heart in our every action.

"We must follow the way Christ showed us: at the holy temple when he forced out the money-changers; in the kindness and forgiveness he showed sinners; in his Sermon on the Mount. We must build a community devoted to these Christian ideals. And that is what we will do, together, in Hiawatha Colony.

"We'll model this community after Walter Thomas Mills' vision for the product-sharing village." Abraham held up Mills' book and thumped the air with it. "An agreement of the very kind Mr. Mills suggests will govern our colony. In this way, all members will contribute their work and abilities. No family will go hungry, no child unclothed, no elderly man or woman uncared for. We'll watch over each other, and we'll work for the good of all. We'll produce nearly everything we need among us and sell what is surplus. In this way, we'll have funds to purchase the things we cannot produce ourselves. This is the general plan, brothers and sisters."

Abraham put down Mills' book and stepped out from behind the podium. Fervor gripped his heart and his eyes gleamed with purpose. "When, my fellow citizens, we banish greed and selfishness by sharing the fruits of our labor—from our gardens, our workshops, our woods, and homes—then, in Eden we shall meet.

"When we have rendered every man and woman equal in contribution by prizing the labors and abilities of all who join in this new place; when we have forged ties of loving kindness each unto another and practiced the giving ways of our Lord by organizing ourselves for the good of all then—I say to you—in Eden we shall meet.

"Fellow citizens of Christ, when we turn our backs on the ways of sin, the evils of mammon, the profiteering of corporations; when we show by our actions, we value the welfare of each other more than the almighty dollar, then, in Eden we shall meet.

"Dear children of God, when we have vanquished the differences among men that are of this world—differences in station or birth, in wealth and inheritance—when we show that it is our likeness with God that should be treasured and that each soul is equal before God, it will be so: In Eden we shall meet.

"Dear brothers and sisters, I beseech you, turn your backs on worldly riches, come join me and my brethren in the Hiawatha Colony, and with us build the riches of another kingdom. For those who do this, I promise: In Eden we shall meet."

THE MILLS COME CALLING

MAY 1894

As Elizabeth spooned up the stew, she noticed Abraham bouncing his folded hands on the table. Ever since Mr. Mills had agreed to visit Abraham had turned restless as a puppy.

Elizabeth twisted around and eyed Goldie and Artie. "That's enough fiddling at the wash basin, you two."

Goldie bounded to her seat at the table, and Elizabeth lifted Artie onto his chair. She plopped four plates of stew at their places and sat.

Abraham bowed his head. "Thank you, Lord, for this food from our own land, for the good health of our families, and for the promise you have wrought for Hiawatha Colony. Amen."

Elizabeth reached for Artie's plate, sliced his venison and potato chunks into bite-size pieces, and flapped her hand to cool them. Abraham watched and waited, kneading his lower lip. He must have something he wants to talk about, she thought, slipping Artie's plate in front of him.

"Mother," Abraham said, planting his forearms beside his plate, "I would have you join me at the lecture next week."

"Don't think I can. Not with Goldie and Artie to watch over."

"Papa," said Goldie. "I want to stay with Papa."

"Yeee, Papa," chimed Artie.

"Hush," Elizabeth said. "Your papa'll be working then."

"You don't get much chance to go to town, Mother." Abraham held his fork over his steaming stew. "I'd hate for you to miss Mr. Mills' lecture. Everybody in town is talking about it."

"Don't much care for going to town," said Elizabeth, and she slid a healthy spoonful of stew into her mouth.

"Mrs. Mills'll be coming along. I'd like to have you with me to welcome them. I'm only asking you to come to the first lecture."

Elizabeth applied her napkin to Artie's smudged mouth.

Abraham waited to catch her eye. "Won't you please find some-one to take the children?"

Elizabeth sighed. Maybe she ought to hear out this Mr. Mills, what with the colony idea being the only thing Abraham and her kin talked about these days. "Well, I'll ask around."

The next afternoon, before Goldie returned from school, Eliza-beth told Abraham, "I'm going visiting. To see if John and Elvila can watch the children. Will you take care of Artie?"

"Why, yes, I'll be glad to watch the little fellow," said Abraham, and he took Artie by the hand and led him out the back door. "Come along, little man, let's give Tilda some fresh hay."

Elizabeth shook her head. She'd never seen Abraham so en-thusiastic about watching a young'un. She donned her shawl and hiked through woods thick with hardwood lily blooms. As she neared her half-brother's home, she heard chopping sounds, steady and solid as a church bell's peal. She spotted John in front of the cabin, lost in the rhythm of his work, reaching for a chunk of wood, centering it on his chopping block, swinging his axe in a half-circled arc, splitting the chunk clean, then starting on an-other.

"Hello, John," she called.

John swung around, the surprised wideness of his eyes giving way to a crinkly smile. "Well, Sister. How you be?"

John left off his work to join Elizabeth. Opening the cabin door, he said, "Elvila, Lizzy's here."

The stout Elvila sat settled in her rocker, mending a sock. "Taking a break from your chores, Lizzie?"

"Here on another one," said Elizabeth, joining John at the ta-ble. "I was wondering, will you be going to the lectures?"

"I'm not much for lecturing," said John. "Abraham expect me to go?"

"Don't know if he expects you to. He's so excited, thinks every-body else is, too."

John smoothed a hand over his cheek, as if contemplating a broken wheel. "I know I should, but it's not the sort of thing I hanker after. Don't take to it like Abraham does."

"Well, he asked me to go and I said I would if I could find some-body to watch Goldie and Artie."

"We'll watch them, Lizzy," said Elvila, tying off the thread of her needle.

"That's kind of you," said Elizabeth.

Elvila eased up out of the rocker. "I'll put the kettle on."

John folded his hands together on the tabletop. "I'd like to hear what's said about this cooperative idea. I expect Abraham will tell us?"

"I'm sure he'll be glad to oblige." Elizabeth cocked her head. "Ever know a time he passed on a chance to declaim?"

John allowed himself a constrained smile. "I wonder about this village notion. You think it'd change things much?"

"I suppose. Some things more'n others."

Elvila plunked coffee cups down on the table. "What things you think'll change?"

"We'll have more people among us," said Elizabeth, shrugging a shoulder. "Suppose that's good and bad. More to share in the work and fellowship. More to cause trouble, too."

John brushed at the frizzy bottom of his beard as if trying to tame its tangle. "Don't mind saying, Sister, it troubles me."

"How's that?" asked Elizabeth.

"Not sure. Just like my life the way it is."

Elizabeth fingered the handle of her coffee cup. She wasn't so sure about the whole notion herself. But it was like a train rolling down the tracks now. "Abraham gets these ideas. They take hold of him, and not much stops him once he gets the fire in him."

"Uncle Abe is a fine man. Upstanding and Christian," said Elvila, for though most called him Abraham, she used the more familiar address, being his niece. "But I don't like to think of mixing with newcomers."

Elizabeth knit her hands around her cup. "Seems to me it'll be the new people who'll change their ways of living—over to ours—not the other way around."

"I hope you're right, Sister," John said.

Elizabeth and Abraham arrived at the Star Opera House a full hour before the lecture. The largest hall in town and the pride of

Manistique, it offered the liveliest entertainment a body could find in the three-county area. And it housed the celebrated Gorsche piano: When the Gorsche thumped, people said, Manistique jumped. But tonight's bill featured more serious fare.

Elizabeth followed Abraham up to the stage. The podium stood close to the stage edge, with a table beside it. On the table sat a milk bottle filled with water and a tall clear glass.

"Yes," said Abraham, "it's arranged just according to Mr. Mills' instructions."

Elizabeth hung back while Abraham summoned the ushers and instructed them to rope off eight seats in the middle of the front row for their party. Then she accompanied him to the Ossawinamakee Hotel.

"Why don't you make yourself comfortable," he said, pointing to the plush burgundy sofa in the lobby. "I'll let the reception desk know we're here."

Elizabeth sat and studied the oil paintings hung on the peony-patterned wallpaper walls: one of a black bear standing tall on its hind legs, another of an alert ten-point buck in a meadow dotted with red and orange wildflowers.

Abraham joined her on the sofa, leaned over his knees, and said, "Can't keep myself still."

"He's just a man," Elizabeth said. "Don't get yourself in a stew."

At the sound of bright steps on the stairway, Abraham snapped his head up, stood, and bolted for the stairs.

When the man reached the bottom of the stairs, Abraham greeted him with a smile and hearty handshake. "Why, Mr. Mills, welcome, welcome. I'm Abraham Byers."

So this was the famous Walter Thomas Mills. He was surprisingly short, about five feet. Only rarely had Elizabeth encountered a man shorter than Abraham. Nevertheless, Mills was a commanding presence—sturdy, with an overly large head, even for his stocky frame, and great fuzzy muttonchops. He looked about forty years old, and his broad, clear forehead and the delicate perch of his spectacles gave him a bookish appearance.

"Mr. Byers," he said, his eyes dancing with enchantment. "So pleased to make your acquaintance. This is my wife, Mary," he said, turning to her.

Mrs. Mills wore a fox-collared wool coat. She tilted her head back a touch and nodded, "Mr. Byers."

"Pleased to meet you, ma'am," said Abraham.

Elizabeth joined the circle, and Abraham took her arm. "And this is my Elizabeth."

"Mrs. Byers." Mr. Mills bowed his head. "A pleasure, to be sure."

"Why, thank you, Mr. Mills," said Elizabeth, feeling the hint of a blush rise to her cheeks.

Mrs. Mills held a limp hand out to Elizabeth. "Pleased to meet a north woods woman, Mrs. Byers."

Elizabeth accepted the fingertips of Mrs. Mills' gloved hand and noticed her eyes drop and linger on the round-toed boots below her black homespun skirt. "Pleased to meet you," said Elizabeth, the color in her cheeks deepening. No, she didn't own any fancy shoes, and she disliked being made to feel ashamed of it.

"Mr. Mills," said Abraham, "the town is alive with excitement this evening. Your visit has been greatly anticipated."

"I must say, Mr. Byers, I'm full of eagerness to know more about your settlement and what plans you've made."

"Well, we're mighty pleased with your interest. Now, would you like to see the hall?"

"Yes, lead us on," said Mr. Mills, though Elizabeth figured he wasn't the type to require much leading.

The foursome walked out of the hotel and strolled down the street, gentlemen in front, ladies behind.

Abraham turned around to the ladies and said, "Watch your step, Mrs. Mills."

Mrs. Mills dropped her gaze to the slat-board sidewalk and, stepping over a shiny brown cow pie, exclaimed, "Oh, my!"

"It's one of our local peculiarities," said Abraham. "Free-roaming cows."

Mr. Mills chuckled and said, "How very quaint."

"They do sometimes abuse their privilege," said Abraham.

Elizabeth added, "The paper is filled with complaints about ruined flower boxes and cowbells ringing all hours of the night."

Mrs. Mills wrinkled her nose and cast her gaze downward as she minced along in her shapely, fawn-colored shoes. Elizabeth imagined Mrs. Mills, with her powdered cheeks, doll-size mouth, and fancy gloves, had little affection for cows—or livestock of any sort. But Abraham said he had high hopes for Mr. and Mrs. Mills moving to the settlement, so she thought she owed her friendliness, at the least.

"Have you lived in Chicago all your life, Mrs. Mills?" asked Elizabeth, for she knew they had traveled all the way from there.

"Only since '88," said Mrs. Mills, glancing at Elizabeth. "I hope you'll visit Chicago someday, Mrs. Byers. It's such a modern city, with all the arts and the very best architecture."

Elizabeth couldn't think how to respond. Chicago? Why in the world would she go to Chicago? Finally, though too late to sustain the easy back and forth of polite conversation, she settled on, "Thank you kindly for the invite, Mrs. Mills."

MR. MILLS' ADDRESS

MAY 1894

The Manistique newspapers had extolled the event with keen anticipation, and now the crowd in the Star Opera House tingled with animation. After Abraham settled Mr. Mills backstage and escorted Mrs. Mills and Elizabeth to their front row seats, he scurried out to the foyer to survey the house. A stream of townspeople filed through the front doors, some milling in the foyer, most passing through to the auditorium. At the far end of the foyer, Abraham spotted the mayor fawning over two mill managers and their wives. Humph, he thought, why ever would Lumbering Company managers, all decked out in plug hats and tailored suits, attend? They're likely to hear ideas that go against *their* way of doing business.

Scanning the crowd, Abraham noted the many mill workers with wives in attendance, all of them dressed in their Sunday finest, walking proudly about, like they belonged here as much, if not more than, all the town dignitaries. Abraham smiled with satisfaction: Now they'll learn there's another way for the common man, one that doesn't require bowing down to the Lumbering Company.

From the foyer doorway Abraham spied a threesome of reporters seeking seats halfway down the hall and toward the side. They probably want to scrutinize the crowd's reaction, he thought. Hope they get it right this time. Well, no matter, we'll have a full house and the people can decide for themselves what they think of Mr. Mills. They won't have to rely on those high and mighty newspaper men.

Abraham ambled down the aisle and stood between Elizabeth and his sons Elonzo and Lenniel. Gus Highland, the other member of the Hiawatha Colony Planning Committee, scurried down the aisle and joined them in the front.

"Quite a turnout," Abraham said to Elizabeth and Mrs. Mills, rocking back on his heels and gazing out on the crowd.

Mrs. Mills glanced back at the crowd out of the corner of her eye. "The big cities have even larger halls, and he fills them, too."

Abraham spotted Gideon Noel and his wife, Alberta, standing in the doorway and searching the hall. Signaling to them, he hurried up the aisle and escorted them to the front row.

"What an auspicious occasion, Mr. Byers," said Mr. Noel, smiling on the crowd.

"I couldn't be more pleased with the attendance," said Abraham. "You must stay afterward so I can introduce you to Mr. Mills."

Mr. Noel glanced at this wife and nodded to Abraham. "We'd be honored."

Abraham introduced the Noels to Mrs. Mills, Elizabeth, Elonzo, Lenniel, and Gus before turning to Elizabeth. "Guess I better get up there."

Abraham exited the side door of the hall and hastened up a narrow corridor to the backstage, where Mr. Mills sat calmly reviewing a scribed sheet.

"Are you ready for your introduction, Mr. Mills?" asked Abraham.

"Yes, Mr. Byers. Let's begin."

Abraham strode onto the stage. The crowd hushed. He clutched the podium sides and spoke, "Ladies and gentlemen, I have the great honor tonight of introducing one of our country's foremost citizens, Walter Thomas Mills. You may be acquainted with his visionary book, *The Product-Sharing Village*, but that is not all he is famous for. He has carried out a homebuilding program for the needy in Chicago. He has built an industrial school to provide employment to workers. He has lectured in every corner of this country, from San Francisco to New York, on such diverse topics as 'Shall government of the people fail?', 'Forgotten factors in the labor problem,' and 'The wisdom of temperance.' None other than Clarence Darrow has proclaimed him one of the greatest orators of our time. Mr. Mills is truly a leader of men and a forward thinker who understands today's troubles. Tonight, he will address us on an important and timely topic—Christian citizenship. Ladies and gentlemen, I give you Walter Thomas Mills."

The crowd welcomed Mr. Mills with sustained clapping, and Abraham hurried down the stage steps, stooping to avoid obstructing anyone's view as he made his way to his seat.

Mr. Mills bowed from the waist and took up his place behind the podium, nodding at the sea of faces, at once acknowledging and quieting their applause.

"Thank you, Mr. Byers," said Mr. Mills, extending a hand toward Abraham. His gaze swiveled out across the expansive, jam-packed hall. "It is a pleasure to be here with you, in this bountiful, beautiful land of lake and forest."

Mr. Mills, attired in a dark gray jacket, matching vest, and white shirt, tucked a hand inside his vest and struck a thoughtful pose. "Christian citizenship? What is meant by this? Are we not all citizens of God? Do we not all heed the teachings of Christ?"

Mills removed his hand from his vest and swept it before the audience. "But we all struggle in this world to transform our Christian beliefs into action. This leads us to the question: How do we unite the teachings of Christ with our citizenship in an imperfect world? This is the challenge for all Christians. This, my fellow citizens, is the matter I wish to discuss this evening."

From his first words, Abraham found Mr. Mills' pronouncements profound and inspiring. In all his days he'd never heard such a fine speaker. Mr. Mills' thoughts bubbled forth, pure and full of sparkle, his magnetic eyes commanded attention, and his voice rose and fell, from soft and deep to fiery and fast, in perfect pitch with his ideas. The man's logic was impeccable; each idea led to a reasoned conclusion and each conclusion to a tangible notion of how to enact it. The hall was so quiet and Abraham so rapt that he hardly detected the occasional cough, stifled as it was, or here and there the unconscious shifting of posture. Only once during the hour and a half address did his mind drift from the speaker—when the slight bouncing of Mrs. Mills' foot gave cause for distraction.

Much to Abraham's delight, the newspapers got it right. Manistique's *Semi-Weekly Pioneer* reported: "The lecture of Walter Thomas Mills of Chicago at the Opera House Sunday night called out an immense crowd of people . . . One of the finest lectures that a Manistique crowd ever listened to . . . He is an earnest and eloquent speaker, voice clear and persuasive, and makes good every point . . . Such men will do a good deal of good in the world."

Schoolcraft County citizens were enthralled by Mr. Mills: a famous speaker spending a whole month in their midst, delivering two to three lectures each week. They hadn't known such excitement since the $75,000 train heist of '93. And most agreed that this topped that by far, since every single person who wanted to could attend one of Mr. Mills' lectures at some point, and only about twenty had squeezed into the courtroom each day of the four-day train robbery trial.

Truth be told, Abraham heard that many of Manistique's citizens wondered why Mr. Mills lingered so long in their town of mill workers and lumberjacks, especially since his wife had left after only three days. But Abraham knew, for he and Mr. Mills had become fast comrades. Why, thought Abraham, Mr. Mills is as enthusiastic about bringing a product-sharing village to the Byers' Settlement as I am.

God had brought them together: Abraham was convinced of it. Mr. Mills' vision and knowledge would put them on the right path. His lectures had stirred so much enthusiasm that Abraham could barely keep up with inquiries from townspeople and reporters about the village undertaking. And, Mr. Mills told Abraham, the Byers' Settlement had made a good beginning already: They had fertile land and abundant wood, hard-working Christian people, and buildings, plows, and tools.

Such a propitious start for the Hiawatha Colony. How, Abraham mused, could it fail to succeed?

The Sunday after Mr. Mills' lecture series Abraham and Elizabeth tramped through the moist, humus-scented woods to John and Elvila's cabin.

"Every time I see your furniture, John," said Abraham upon stepping into their home, "I think of what fine examples of wood-working they are."

"Thank you, Abraham, I pride myself on them," said John, motioning them in. John's leather-trussed boots were the only neat part of his attire, for the sleeves of his bulky cotton shirt bunched about his elbows and his suspenders crossed over his chest at an odd angle.

"I brought some biscuits for dinner," said Elizabeth, handing them to Elvila.

"That stove of yours is never idle, is it, Lizzy?" said Elvila, accepting the biscuits. "Well, come in and sit. Dinner's almost ready."

John, Abraham, and Elizabeth settled around the sturdy maple table while Elvila stirred the kettle on the stove, releasing scents of pepper, salt pork, and earthy rutabaga.

"I say, John, you missed a most stimulating lecture series," said Abraham.

"I've been hearing from Elonzo and Lenniel that Mr. Mills knows how to deliver a message," said John who, even seated, towered over Abraham.

"He's a man of many ideas. Is there a particular topic you want to hear about?" asked Abraham.

"Well," said John, his hand stroking the bottom of his beard. "His notions about our settlement and how we'd run this new village."

Abraham scratched his cheek. "He didn't speak in particular about us in his lectures, though I and the committee have discussed this with him."

"I don't mind telling you," John said, "I'm worried about how we'll be living with this change."

Elizabeth sat with her hands on her lap, leaving all the explaining to Abraham. He'd appealed to her to help persuade John, who continued to evince doubt about the village, but she'd demurred, "No, this is your idea. It's for you and Mr. Mills to peddle."

Abraham told John of as many of the particulars of the agreement as they'd discussed—the time credit system, the requirements for new members, and the various departments of industry they'd institute—and John folded his arms over his chest and pushed out his bottom lip as he listened. Lord in heaven, Abraham thought, what would it take to convince him?

"It's all being put in writing and will soon be brought before us, so then you can see the very document for yourself," concluded Abraham.

"I would like to study it before the meeting if I may," said John. "I'm not as fast at reading and understanding as you are."

"Then I'll have a draft brought to you." Abraham smoothed his fingers over the tabletop. "So you can read it before the meeting and study it as you like."

Elvila carried plates, forks, knives, and napkins to the table for them. "Will Mr. Mills be joining the village then?"

Abraham smiled up at Elvila. "Yes, he has spoken of his intention to join us, with his wife and children."

"I don't know about that wife of his," said Elizabeth, standing and taking the pile of plates and utensils from Elvila. "Doesn't seem like the country type to me."

"She's his wife," said Abraham, wishing Elizabeth wouldn't challenge him before others. "A good wife follows her husband's dreams and wishes."

"You see that fancy coat she wears?" Elizabeth set the plates and napkins in their places. "The softest wool I ever saw, with a red fox collar. And those shoes of hers won't stand up more than a few weeks in the woods."

Abraham pulled his napkin off the table and slid it onto his lap. "What'd you expect? Even the town folk dressed up for the lectures, and she and Mr. Mills were staying at the hotel."

Elizabeth straightened a knife and fork at Elvila's place. "Just can't picture her living among us. She might like to wear red fox, but I doubt she'd take to them roving around her chicken coop."

Abraham shook his head. Dear Lord, he didn't need his own wife throwing obstacles in the way. "I expect she'll contribute like everybody else. I understand she enjoys planning a good meal, so I imagine she knows a few things about kitchen work."

THE COLONY COMMENCES

MAY 1894

With Manistique buzzing about Walter Thomas Mills' rousing lectures, Abraham wasted no time placing a notice in *The Weekly Tribune*:

> The Hiawatha Colony commences. We have 1080 acres of land, personal property in the amount of $16,000, and the promise of more investment to sustain us. Come and help us get our product-sharing rules down to rock bottom. And be sure to do as the whippoorwill when it crosses the desert—bring along a little lunch. Come to the farm of A.S. Byers at noon for a May 19 meeting.

Thanks to newspaper interviews with both Mr. Mills and Abraham, the whole of Schoolcraft County was acquainted with the Hiawatha Colony plan. In fact, many of its citizens displayed curiosity, even admiration, for the undertaking. And, to Abraham's delight, members of the settlement also seemed to be catching the fever of excitement.

In the weeks leading up to the organizing meeting, Abraham and his charges rushed about with the industry of bumblebees, meeting to discuss the rules, consulting Mr. Mills' book and a local attorney, and enthusing to their families and neighbors. Championing this cause left sixty-five-year-old Abraham vigorous as a young man gone courting. Why, he could see it in his mind's eye: the settlement given over to cooperative principles; its members serving each other and the Lord; and everyone freed from the chains of the Lumbering Company and its greed. They'd be a model for all the Upper Peninsula, nay, the whole country. And he'd started it—his drive and idealism had ignited the whole undertaking.

Throughout the planning period, Abraham and Mr. Mills commiserated and calculated, and both agreed on the import of choosing just the right association officers, a matter they discussed one day while strolling on a section of the perimeter road. Abraham, brimming with pride to have Mr. Mills joining their endeavor, couldn't stop himself from showing off the settlement's abundant supply of white pine and, as they passed Dodge lake, slipping in a few words about the first-rate bass fishing there.

"Now, Abraham," said Mr. Mills, for they'd been on a first-name basis for some time, "you must select your officers with great care. My speaking engagements mean I will be absent on and off. You can do the most good by working with your president and officers. In short, I advise you to play the role of a conductor keeping the train on the right track."

"I believe I can do that, Walter," Abraham said. "I've got seven sons and a whole settlement of relations behind me, to say nothing of townspeople who are willing to take up the cause."

"Splendid. Now, you must choose men devoted to the village-sharing principles who won't get mired in minutiae or distracted by naysayers. And they should show you respect and loyalty."

Abraham chuckled. "Why, with all the assistance you've lent, Mr. Mills (for this is what he called him when he wished to feign formality), I believe I can find just the right men for the job and keep the cow catcher clear, too."

Mr. Mills' discous countenance broadened with a smile. "Yes, you have copious energy, Mr. Byers, and I'm sure you'll keep the engine well stoked. Now, tell me who you have in mind for the offices."

On the sun-filled Saturday of May 19, a wagonload of seven townspeople trundled down the road from Manistique and turned onto Abraham and Elizabeth's property. The wagon driver tethered the horses on long ropes in the grassy meadow beside the barn, and the party ambled to Abraham's barn. Many settlement members—Byers and Keplers—made their way on foot to the site, over paths and along the perimeter road. Twenty-four men and women gathered at Abraham's barn for the first official meeting of Hiawatha Colony.

Abraham, standing beside Mr. Mills inside the barn door, gazed at the convivial crowd with the pleasure of a grandfather contemplating his begats. Seven women, Sunday-bonneted and flush-cheeked, broke from their husbands' sides and joined in a cheery circle. Four of Abraham's own sons, Elonzo and Link by his first wife and Beech and Lenniel by Elizabeth, stopped to chat with each other, overlooking the brotherly rivalry that Abraham had long ago determined to neither fan nor discourage. Gus Highland and the four other mill workers in attendance conducted themselves in the most gentlemanly manner, tipping their hats to the ladies and moderating their voices. Even the dapper couple from town, Gideon and Alberta Noel, set aside any misgivings about the rugged settlers and greeted the sturdy Keplers—Elizabeth's brothers, sister, and in-laws—with grace and forbearance.

"Walter," Abraham said in a soft voice, "look how our cooperative venture puts all on high and common ground."

"Ah, yes," said Mr. Mills, his chest expanding with contentment, "that is the very thing it should do."

Abraham surveyed the gathered. "I believe everyone is here,"

"Fine, fine, I'll begin," said Mr. Mills, and he strode before the group and swiveled his great head from side-to-side, signaling to all that the time had come for him to address them.

Abraham sauntered out among the visiting clumps, motioning for them to take up the bale seats, and his relations and comrades trickled into the rows. All eyes turned to Mr. Mills.

"My dear brothers and sisters," began Mr. Mills, "my heart overflows with joy at having found a community of Christian people such as yourselves. I'm filled with unbounded hope as I contemplate the great good we are about to undertake."

Reaching his arms wide, he smiled on his audience. "Never in my life have I been blessed with so many propitious events, rendered more meaningful by our country's troubled times: publishing my product-sharing book; being invited to visit and lecture by your own Mr. Byers; meeting you brave Christian people; and discovering this bounteous land you have homesteaded.

I'm amazed at the convergence of these events and how they or-
dain the new way of life we are about to undertake."

Mr. Mills pressed his palms together, bowed his head, and
bounced his hands in prayerful cheer. "I thank the Lord for such
blessings."

Mr. Mills looked up, his countenance still solemn. "Now, I give
the meeting over to you, Mr. Byers."

"Thank you, Mr. Mills," said Abraham, taking up his place before the gathering. "We have much work before us and many
details to attend to. The committee has begun working out these
matters and committing them to paper so we can go forth knowing we are of one mind on this new path.

"One of the first matters," continued Abraham, drawing a paper from his vest pocket, "concerns the notice for new members.
Here is the draft we propose: 'The Hiawatha Cooperative Colony
invites applications from able-bodied, industrious, and frugal
Christian people to join its product-sharing village. New members
must be able to contribute their labor and skills and pay $100 for
membership. They will be provided housing in the product-sharing village.'"

Abraham looked up from his paper. "Do you favor this notice?"

John Kepler rose from the middle row to speak; his tall frame
towered over the seated guests. His wife, Elvila, twisted around to
look up at him. On her other side sat Sarah Huey, Elizabeth's
sister, whose husband was bedridden with the consumption. In
his stead was their eldest son, Edgar. On John's other side sat
Alva Kepler, another of Elizabeth's brothers, who leaned forward
and eyed Abraham.

Those Keplers sure stick together, thought Abraham, praying
they wouldn't choose this occasion to impugn the plans, for he
knew John was skeptical and Alva prone to fretting.

John asked, "Who will hold the membership fees and how will
new purchases be decided?"

Ah, Abraham thought with relief, this request reflects a reasonable desire to understand the workings of the village.
Although he had, as promised, shown John a draft of the
roughed-out plan a week earlier, he had since added more details,
so he explained, "We'll elect a treasurer to keep the books and a

set of officers to decide on purchases. With permission, this we can do today, in advance of accepting new members."

"And where will these newcomers be housed?" asked John.

"An excellent question, John," said Abraham. "We'll build new houses. Later in the meeting, we'll present the plan for the village buildings—for both homes and workplaces."

"Thank you," said John, sitting, and the Keplers around him nodded at each other.

"With your permission," said Mr. Mills, glancing at Abraham and angling around in his seat to address the gathering, "I would like to invite those who have written me and asked if they might join a product-sharing village. I've had inquiries from people I know in the Chicago area, a gifted mechanic among them, and even a family from Texas. An elderly widow, Mrs. Lucinda Clark, has written and said she would contribute whatever funds are needed to start up a village if she could only join such a noble undertaking. I understand she has a sizable fortune."

The women turned to their husbands and raised eyebrows in delighted surprise, and several of the men failed to stifle pleased humphs.

Abraham, with the know-how of a preacher discerning when words have struck their mark, spoke up, "Mr. Mills, we all agree that new members can bring the very resources—strong arms, special knowledge, and hard-earned dollars—that will speed our village on to its zenith."

As the crowd's murmurs subsided Abraham searched out his eldest son, the one who had taken Harvey's place as his companion in scripture-reading. "Elonzo, will you speak to us on association rules?"

Elonzo, wearing his usual brown vest, which was always so rumpled that his brothers teased him about sleeping in it, came forward, pitching over his bad leg. Settling his weight on his good leg, he said, alternately looking at the ground in front of him and glancing up at his wife, "First I want to say it is my land being considered for the village housing. And I'm honored that the land I have cleared myself will be for new homes."

Elonzo scuffed a foot into the dirt barn floor and drew a folded-up paper from his vest pocket. He read, "The Hiawatha Colony is a Christian village, made for the glory of our Lord. All in it will live by Christian ways. We will allow no tobacco in the village. We forbid intoxicating beverages, gambling, racing, and lewd or disorderly conduct. Sunday services will be held at 10:30, and we will honor the whole of the Sabbath with prayer and fellowship."

Several heads bowed during Elonzo's recitation, either in reverence for the Christian ways of living he espoused or out of sympathy for his shy manner.

Elonzo sucked in his lower lip and folded up his paper. As he shuffled back to his seat soft amens sounded from the rows.

Contented with the spirit of reverence that lingered after Elonzo's speech, Abraham said, "Lenniel, will you come before us and talk about book-keeping and matters of the treasury?"

Ever since Lenniel had returned from his schooling at the Business Institute at Valparaiso, Abraham had noted Lenniel's desire to put his business skills to work, and he delighted at the wonderful concordance between wherewithal and opportunity that the village venture presented.

Abraham remained standing but took a few steps to the side to give Lenniel center stage.

Lenniel, clutching his hands over his belly, strode before the meeting. Abraham twitched in nervous sympathy, for he'd observed that the usually confident Lenniel turned timid in Mr. Mills' presence. As Lenniel reached into his vest pocket and pulled out his notes, his long, fleshy ears brightened like embers. With the exaggerated loudness of an unpracticed speaker, he read, "I've studied Mr. Mills' book and worked out how to keep track of contributions. We'll count hours of labor as time credits; each person's work will be honored and credited in this system. We'll pool our funds, including application money, pensions, and wages of any who work outside the village so that all will have access to the money and can use their time credits to purchase whatever they need from our store of products. And they may use their credits to buy supplies from town. In this way, all men and women will contribute according to their skill and ability and provide for their family's needs, too."

Abraham looked out on the group. "Do you find this system agreeable?"

"Is there to be a general accounting then of each person's money?" asked John, again standing.

Lenniel said, with a dip of his head, "Yes, the idea is to pool our income for the benefit of all."

Mr. Mills rose from his seat and faced John, tipping his head to the side like a tolerant teacher. "In this way, Mr. Kepler, the needs of all can be met. No one who has been destitute will want for food, clothing, or other necessities, and no one who has been wealthy will be given unfair advantage over his fellows."

"Thank you, Mr. Mills," said John, taking his seat.

"Now, with respect to the incorporation of our village," said Abraham, "I would ask Mr. Gideon Noel to address us."

The distinguished Mr. Noel, his thick gray hair parted and combed to swooping neatness, pushed up from his seat and came before the group. "As you know I have run the Apothecary and Spice Store in Manistique for many years. It is incorporated with my brother, who lives close to his own work in Chicago. By incorporating the business, we have defended ourselves from any untoward financial risk. Now, I don't wish to suggest that the village would be exposed to financial problems, but I believe in the prudence of incorporation. Since many of us would come together in this venture, a corporation would allow us to form a singular business to represent us in dealings with other entities or individuals."

Mr. Noel signaled the end of his speech with a bob of his head, and Mr. Mills stood and turned to the gathered. "I'd like to second Mr. Noel's statement. I myself have drawn up several incorporation agreements, and the arrangement, as Mr. Noel has expressed so well, has many protective benefits."

"Thank you, Mr. Mills and Mr. Noel," said Abraham. "Are there any questions on the matter of incorporation?"

Mr. Mills and Mr. Noel scanned the group.

John Kepler stood. "If we ended the corporation, would those who have joined and signed over their land be able to reclaim it?"

Abraham looked to Mr. Noel.

Gideon Noel straightened his spine. "Yes, Mr. Kepler, upon dissolution shares would be returned to the members of the corporation according to the proportion of their contribution."

"Why," said Abraham, interposing himself between Mr. Noel and the gathered, "I hate to hear us talking of dissolution before we've even gotten underway. If we make a good start and take the welfare of all into account, as is our intention, then dissolution will be of no consequence."

Without a word John sat down and took up the study of his knuckles. As Gideon Noel returned to his seat, the Keplers seated around John flashed squinty-eyed glances at each other.

Mr. Mills rocked back on his heels like a lawyer intent on clinching his case. "We are not the first cooperative community, although we'd be the first to follow the particular outline of my product-sharing village. Many cooperative communities are now in place across the land—Harmony Society, the Shakers, and Amana Colony—and all are thriving. I have much hope and great confidence for us, too."

The Kepler's squirming wariness had neither escaped Abraham's eyes nor surprised. He'd known all along of John's reluctance and had long ago resolved to invite a Kepler to join the planning committee. In this way, he hoped to soften the Keplers' qualms, especially in view of what promised to be the most sensitive of all colony matters—land ownership. He turned to Edgar Huey, Elizabeth's nephew and son of her sister Sarah. "Edgar, will you speak on the matter of lands and deeds?"

Edgar, a fresh-faced twenty-three-year-old with a neat brush mustache and the confidence of untested youth, came before the meeting. "I have gathered all the deeds," he said, "and it will only take our signatures to make the transfers. We'll manage this in two steps. First, we will transfer deeds to a trustee—some person we name and bind to hold them. Then, we'll file the legal document incorporating the association and naming its stockholders."

Abraham took up the next part. "In this way, when deeds are transferred to the corporation, those who have signed over their land will be credited with stock in the corporation. That's how they'll prove their contribution."

Edgar scanned the faces of the gathered. "Do you have any questions?"

A few shoulders hunched but no one spoke.

Abraham inhaled in relief, and the barn's ammonia tang tingled his nostrils. "Very well. The details are endless, but we have many hard workers among us who I'm certain will manage them well."

Clapping his hands together, Abraham continued, "We have much building to do for housing and industry. Gus has worked out a general plan for this."

Gus Highland grabbed a rolled-up paper and strode to Abraham's side. Unfurling the paper and holding the two-foot-square sheet by the top corners, he turned from side to side, allowing all in the room to view of his drawing. "Abe," he said, "will you help me hold this?"

Abraham gripped one side of the paper.

Gus pointed to a series of large structures on one side of the drawing, "Here we'll put up the industry buildings—a good-sized barn for wintering the livestock, a dairy building for processing milk and cheese, a sawmill, and a blacksmith shop."

Beech, who worked beside Gus at the Lumbering Company, called out, "When will our mill start up? I'd like to know when I can quit the Lumbering Company."

Chuckles broke from the gathered, and the corners of Gus's bushy auburn mustache lifted in delight.

Abraham, thankful to Beech for interrupting the tension that he and likely others discerned, turned to him. "Son, you don't have to wait until our sawmill is open to quit that job. As soon as we get the building underway you can join in. Your work will be credited—just like Lenniel explained."

"Once we get our own operation going," said Gus, satisfaction spreading over his face, "we won't need the Lumbering Company for wages *or* lumber."

"Can't happen soon enough," Beech said, glancing about, and those whose eyes he met winked or grinned at him.

"Count me in, too," hollered Claude Faust, another lumber mill employee, twisting the end of his handlebar mustache to underscore his point.

The mill worker seated next to Claude called, "I'll be joining up."

"Me too—right now," said the fourth man, rolling up his sleeves with exaggerated flourish.

Titters of amusement infected the crowd.

"Looks like the mill will lose some of its best men," said Abraham, thrilled to join in the fun. When the chuckles subsided, he turned to Gus. "Go on ahead. I know you've more to show."

"We've chosen a cleared area, on Elonzo Byers' lands, to put up buildings for housing in this horseshoe-shaped form," said Gus, pointing to the middle of the drawing. He looked up from his paper. "As we build individual dwellings, families will move into the village. Eventually, we'll all live together in these village buildings."

John's head snapped up. "Must we move out of the cabins we've built?"

Gus hesitated and shot an uncertain glance at Abraham.

Abraham softened his voice. "Yes, John, if we're to be a true product-sharing village, we must live together as villagers."

John stood, crinkling up a cheek. "We have fine cabins on our own plots, and we're accustomed to them. I don't see why we should give them up."

Confound it, thought Abraham as he glanced at Mr. Mills, we've only started and John's already being contrary. Mr. Mills, taking Abraham's cue, rose from his seat and turned to John. "Mr. Kepler, changes such as those we are on the verge of do not come easy. But we must keep our eye on the vision we strive for— a village of all of us finding our way in this imperfect world, living together in brotherly love and harmony."

John clutched a suspender strap and threw back his head. "I don't see that it's necessary, sir. Sometimes living close only breeds trouble. I like my cabin. And my privacy."

Mr. Mills nodded. "Well, Mr. Kepler, I think any moves are off in the future, and perhaps this is something we can discuss as we go along."

Abraham, fearful of allowing John to undermine plans when they were so close to voting time, took up this tack. "Surely, John, you can see we all want to consider what's best for everyone. And as Mr. Mills says, we can continue to talk about this detail."

"Then I'll be holding you to that," said John, plopping down in his seat.

"Now, before we get down to the business of voting," said Abraham, "Mr. Mills has asked to make an announcement."

With deliberate ceremony, Mr. Mills rose from his seat and turned to address the gathering. "To show my dedication to our cause, I am this day contributing two thousand dollars, and I pledge to raise thirty-eight thousand more through lectures, sponsors, and new members."

Mr. Mills paused while his spectators absorbed his message. Abraham had told no one—not even Elizabeth—of Mr. Mills' generous pledge, for he and Mr. Mills had determined the announcement would do the most good at just this moment. Abraham glanced at John, trying to discern his reaction, and noticed him looking to Elizabeth, perhaps wondering if she'd known of this or maybe attempting to gauge her reaction to it. The others sat studying Mr. Mills through the tops of their eyes, as if made meek by the promise of such a grand sum.

Mr. Mills rushed into the admiring lull. "Our village has many needs, but perhaps the most pressing is crops, for we're sure to have more villagers among us by the end of this farming season. I understand that potatoes grow well in the Upper Peninsula, so I've urged the planning committee to commit some of my funds to land clearing and planting, and to not let the month get away without a large crop of potatoes and other promising crops in the ground.

"Next week I must leave to deliver some lectures long ago promised. But my family is now preparing for our remove from Chicago, and in June I shall return to stand shoulder to shoulder with you and endeavor to build this wondrous village of our future.

"I look forward to that time with great hope and eager anticipation." Mr. Mills drew in a deep breath and, nodding to Abraham, said, "Mr. Byers."

Abraham rose, came up beside Mr. Mills, and turned to him. "Thank you, Mr. Mills, for your inspiration and solid backing."

"Here, here," called Gus, putting his hands together in applause, and all the others joined with the polite clapping of an audience unsure of whether it had chosen the right time to show approval. Mr. Mills bowed in acknowledgment and strode to his front-row seat.

Abraham summoned the full, strong voice he used for sermons. "Brothers and sisters, we are getting our rules and ways of operating spelled out. We have only now to see if you consent to these plans and, if you do, we must put them into action. Much must be accomplished before the winter. I ask, have you any more questions? Have you any concerns?"

All eyes turned toward the Keplers in the middle row. John shifted in his seat; his wife Elvila gazed at him.

Twisting around and stiffening an arm against the hay bale, Mr. Mills fixed his eyes on John.

Abraham, too, studied John, lifting his brow in an unspoken question.

John looked Abraham in the eye and nodded.

Abraham blinked in acknowledgment and searched the faces of every other man and woman in the room.

No one spoke.

With a preacher's solemnity, Abraham said, "Very well then. Let us vote on the general provisions set forth today, understanding we'll require signatures for deed transfers and incorporation."

The vote was unanimous. When the calls for officer nominations went out, every office found a man willing to run and, once such a volunteer came forth, that man ran unopposed. By the end of the meeting each office had been filled: for trustee of deeds, Edgar Huey; secretary, Claude Faust; treasurer, Lenniel Byers; vice president, Gus Highland; and for president, Gideon Noel. Abraham was pleased with the vote and officers: He'd not abandon his role as general advisor and promoter; Mr. Mills would continue to provide inspiration; and in the men elected to office he and Mr. Mills would find the able workers necessary to carry the torch, just as the two of them had planned.

JUNE 1894

Elizabeth wriggled into her nightgown and turned around, contemplating the shadowy, candle-lit bedroom. She'd been brooding all day, ever since Abraham showed her Mr. Mills' letter. And Abraham, too, was preoccupied, which only increased her disquiet.

Abraham stood beside their bed unbuttoning his shirt. "Well, Mother, I was surprised to hear Mr. Mills will bring his sons, daughter, and aunt back with him."

Elizabeth let down her hair and sat at her dresser. "And *not* his wife?"

"Why, yes, I'm surprised she won't be coming along." Elizabeth could tell Abraham was considering his words as he tugged off his pants and hung them over a chair. "But so many of his other kin—that I didn't expect."

"The man has a way of persuading, doesn't he?" Elizabeth eyed Abraham's face in the mirror as she brushed out her hair. "Excepting his own wife."

"Oh, Mother, you want me to say you were right about his wife?" Abraham, stripped down to his undergarments, sat on his side of the bed. "Then I'll say it—you figured her right."

Elizabeth took little satisfaction in this minor victory. Mrs. Mills hardly warranted her attention, although knowing at least one person could stand up to Mr. Mills provided recompense. She put down her brush and walked to the other side of the bed. Abraham stood, and they folded down the summer quilt and slid under it.

"Wait a minute before you douse the candle," said Abraham, turning on his side and facing Elizabeth. "Mr. Mills and his family will need a good-sized home. We have nothing in the village that would accommodate them, let alone the other new members we're expecting."

Elizabeth swiveled her head toward Abraham. She could tell he was working up to something. "Might as well tell me what you're thinking."

"I was wondering if we should move out and let them have our home."

Elizabeth's breath caught. "That's what I was afraid of."

Abraham softened his voice. "It'd set an example for everyone about quitting their own homes."

"I don't like the idea one bit."

"I know, Mother. My sweat and blood's in this place—built on this site twice. But if we aim to have a village, then we must be a part of it ourselves."

"Don't tell me *you* want to leave this house. It's set up just how we like it. Got a real nice stove. I know just how to work it."

"We'll have a brand-new stove when we move into village housing. How would you like that?"

Elizabeth turned away from Abraham and stared up at the ceiling. "What I'd like is to keep on in my home."

"Mother, you know there's no way we can do that."

"Why not?"

"The plan is for everybody to live in the village."

"That time's not here yet." Elizabeth hoped this part of the plan would falter, and she knew others did, too. "And seems to me Walter ought to be the one to find a place for his family."

"He's been busy in Chicago raising money for the village. Hasn't had time to make arrangements."

"Gideon's the president. Let him see to it."

"That'd put Gideon in an awkward spot—him being so new here. It'd be a gesture of kindness and sacrifice to let all the Mills stay together, instead of being farmed out to different households. And we've got more bedrooms than we need here."

"Abraham, this is our home. I don't want to move."

"Ever?"

"If I had my way, it'd be never."

"I've signed the association papers, just like every other landowner. We're bound to the rules now."

Elizabeth's breathing turned shallow, and despair overtook her. She hated everything about this village notion.

Abraham reached out and stroked her shoulder.

Tears stung Elizabeth's eyes, and her words turned tremulous. "Abraham, I don't want to leave our home."

"Oh, my dear, dear wife," said Abraham, nestling up against her and wrapping an arm over her. "I love our home too: this bedroom, our sitting area, those cupboards I labored over. Don't like the thought of leaving myself."

Elizabeth pursed her lips and forced back the lump pressing at her throat, for she was not given to the frivolity of tears. "Why, then?"

"So we can live together as a community of brethren."

"I know that's the plan, but I can't stand the thought of leaving this house."

Abraham tightened his clutch and nestled his head against Elizabeth's. "We'll have a sturdy new home just the right size for us. It'll be easier for you to take care of."

Elizabeth squirmed against his grip. "Don't. I don't want to talk about it anymore."

Abraham pulled back his arm.

Leaning over to her bedside table, Elizabeth blew out the candle and settled on her side, with her back to Abraham. She lay still, going through her house and taking inventory of its memories: the porch where family and friends stopped for visits on their way into or out of the settlement; Lenniel, when he was only fourteen, bursting into the kitchen to show off a ring-neck pheasant he'd shot; their bedroom, all cozy with the pipe stove running up along its wall.

She couldn't bear to talk to Abraham any more just now, even if bedtime was their only chance for these discussions, what with children underfoot all waking hours. Now she was grateful for a full day's reprieve. It'd give her time to turn her troubles over, for she found that when she did so some solution usually tumbled forth, often at the least expected moment—while she weeded the garden, kneaded her bread, or indulged in a soaking bath.

She loved this house, and now she'd have to leave it. She must find something good about this village notion. That's all there was to it. And she didn't want Abraham to tell her what that might be. No, she'd work that out on her own.

Come morning, the strain between them persisted as Elizabeth went about the business of coffee- and oatmeal-making. Abraham, sensing her reserve, studied his newspaper and excused himself after breakfast: "I have some business to discuss with Lenniel."

Elizabeth sent Goldie off to school and spent the morning churning and turning her troubles. By afternoon an idea began to emerge. "Come along now," she told Artie, "we're going visiting." She deposited little Artie at John and Elvila's and then spent an hour visiting her sister Sarah.

When bedtime rolled around again, Elizabeth sat down on the bench at her dresser and faced Abraham. "This is how it'll be: We're taking this bedroom set with us, and I want to keep my kitchen furniture and porch rocker, too."

Abraham finished splashing his face at the basin and pulled on a fresh undershirt. "Well, I'd like to keep my reading chair, too. I suppose the Mills could bring their own furniture."

"You and I'll stay with Sara and Eli. We'll use the parlor for a bedroom and store our other furniture in the barn."

Abraham sat on the bed and knit his hands together. "Do you think it wise for us to stay there, with the consumption upon the family?"

"My father always told me—just keep their personal items separate. It's the fluids, the blood and sputum and such, that spread it. That's what I've told Sarah, and that's how she's managed to care for Eli and stay clear of it herself."

"And Goldie and Artie?"

"Can't expect young'uns to be so careful. They'll stay with John and Elvila until we can take them back." Elizabeth braced her hands on the seat. "And when we're all moved to the village, I want us next door to Sarah and Eli. So I can help them with the children."

"Well, I expect I can ask Gideon about that."

"You're not asking. Tell him that's how it'll be. You're taking it on yourself to give up our home for the Mills. I expect some consideration for that."

"Well, all right, Mother. I'll explain that to him."

Elizabeth got up from her seat and signaled Abraham to help with the quilt. They folded it down and crawled into bed.

Abraham turned onto his back and looked up at the ceiling. "It'll be hard for me to get much work done there with such a full house."

Elizabeth glanced at Abraham. "I don't imagine you'll be around much anyway."

"I suppose I'll be spending some time with Mr. Mills. It'll be strange going visiting at my own house."

"Humph," said Elizabeth with a snort, "that's not what I'm worried about. Got a whole house to pack up."

"Well, Mother, I know this isn't easy for you." Abraham cupped his hand over her shoulder. "A man couldn't have a better wife than you."

"I just hope this plan of yours works, seeing as us and everybody else is giving up good homes for it."

When Abraham nestled up beside her, Elizabeth allowed him to knit his fingers into hers. No sense holding onto this anger, she thought. What she needed now was the grit and foresight to see herself and her kin through these big changes.

◦──◦

A week later Elizabeth and Abraham settled around a pockmarked pine table with Elizabeth's sister, Sarah, Sarah's ailing husband, Eli, and their twenty-three-year-old son, Edgar.

"Go on outside, now," Sarah fluttered her hand to shoo along the younger children: their one boy, Clifton; and two girls, Pearl and Evvie.

The three youngsters exchanged put-upon eye-rolls and trotted out the door.

"We appreciate your hospitality," said Abraham.

"You did the same for us. Kept us a good two months when we were just getting settled here." Eli coughed from the exertion of the long sentence, and his thin shoulders quivered.

Sarah patted her husband's back and frowned, severe as an impatient nurse. "Hush now, don't put yourself out."

"I'll expect to do my share around here," said Elizabeth.

"Oh, I know you will, Sister," said Sarah, the deep creases on her pallid brow slackening. Although she was only forty-four, she looked closer in age to fifty-two-year-old Elizabeth.

Elizabeth studied Sarah's droopy expression—she always looked vexed to her—and said, "I intend to watch over Evvie."

"Oh, I don't know when our hardships will end." Sarah clapped her bony hands onto her cheeks and gazed upward in a pose somewhere between prayer and admonishment.

Eli leaned in, as if to speak, and Edgar, who sat on his other side, touched his father's forearm to restrain him. "We're not sure it's the consumption. Have to ask the doctor to look next time he's out."

Elizabeth knew consumption when she saw it. Evvie had it, of that she was sure, and it was getting the better of Eli, too. She turned to Sarah. "Well, best we can do is make sure the whole family gets rest and sunshine and good nutrition."

Sarah pressed her lips together and nodded at Elizabeth.

Eli sucked in a deep breath and spoke through the exhale. "Others going to be moving soon?"

"No, not soon," said Abraham. "The houses we're building in the compound will go to new members arriving this summer. I expect most will stay in their own cabins through the winter season."

Eli worked his mouth at the forming of some thought, and the whiskers under his nose poked out like little porcupine quills. "Hear about Frank Dodge?"

Edgar, perhaps discerning his father's labor, spoke up. "Frank Dodge's been around visiting us. And John and Alva, too."

Abraham's brow fluttered with interest. "Is that so?"

Elizabeth, too, wondered what the old man was up to, since he'd always made it his business to set the Keplers against the Byers. Dodge's property abutted that of John and Alva Kepler, so he had plenty of occasions for visiting the Keplers, and Sara had kept Elizabeth informed about Dodge's rants against the Byers. She'd decided it best not to share the details with Abraham. It'd only upset and inflame him.

Eli pushed his chin at his son to nudge him along.

Edgar tilted his head in studied nonchalance. "Said he didn't see why we should give up our cabins for this cooperative scheme. Thinks Walter Mills is just a showboater."

A vinegary simper took over Abraham's expression. "Why, I'm sorry to hear that. Did Frank attend any of Mr. Mills' lectures?"

Edgar shook his head. "Don't believe he did."

Abraham flapped his hands, like a put-upon parent. "I wish Frank would appreciate it's our Christian ways that are guiding us, not the ambition of any man. Perhaps our success will convince him."

"I wouldn't bother about him, if I was you," said Elizabeth, who'd long ago taken on the job of keeping Abraham from riling up people—and trouble. "Let him and his notions be."

Sundays were visiting time in the Byers' Settlement. All afternoon, Byers, Keplers, and other settlers strolled over paths and along the perimeter road on their way to and from each other's cabins—excepting that of Mr. Mills. No one would have presumed to drop in on the Mills' family, even if they were living in Abraham and Elizabeth's house.

But this Sunday Gideon and Alberta Noel and Abraham and Elizabeth had been invited. Mr. Mills' plump-cheeked aunt, Nettie Mills, had baked a pie with canned peaches, and the party of six now squeezed around the kitchen table over slices of pie and cups of coffee.

"Where are those fine children of yours?" Alberta Noel asked, referring to Mr. Mills' two grown sons and one daughter. Alberta perched her willowy frame on the edge of her chair and, when she wasn't sipping coffee or nibbling pie, kept her hands folded on her lap.

"They packed a picnic and hiked off to Dodge Lake with some of the other young people," said Walter Mills, shuttling his fork under a mouthful of pie. "Lovely day for a picnic, isn't it?"

"Summers can be glorious here." Alberta scratched the red bump welling up above her snug-buttoned collar. "If you can tolerate the mosquitoes and no-see-ums."

"Elizabeth," said Gideon Noel, who sat beside her, "I understand you acquired knowledge of plant remedies from your father."

"Oh, yes," said Elizabeth. "I enjoyed tagging along on his doctor errands."

"You must let me show you the apothecary medicinals I've donated to our store."

Elizabeth smiled at Gideon. "I'd be much obliged."

"Of course," said Gideon, stately in his dark blue jacket and starched white shirt. "They're for all of us to use now. Besides, I'll be busy with my president duties, and I'm sure the villagers will look to you when they need nursing."

"They call on me, it's true," said Elizabeth, keeping pridefulness out of her voice. She liked Gideon Noel. He was a genuine gentleman, respectful and fair to everyone, from what she could tell, and likely the best choice they could have made for president.

Alberta again addressed Mr. Mills from across the table. "Mr. Mills, when will we have the pleasure of your wife's company?"

"I expect her to visit in early July. It's hard for her to quit the Chicago house with all its responsibilities."

Elizabeth shot Abraham a knowing glance. She imagined this was a sore subject with Mr. Mills.

Alberta persisted, "When might she join us?"

Mr. Mills forced a chuckle. "I expect once she sees this lovely land and how quickly the village is being built, she'll give up the burden of the Chicago house."

Nettie, whose fulsome frame rounded her thin cotton dress into soft mounds, flapped a hand at her nephew. "I always said that house was too big, Walter. *I* wouldn't want to keep it up."

Abraham cleared his throat. "Won't you tell us about our applicants, Gideon?"

"Yes." Gideon put his fork down beside his half-eaten pie. "In fact, I should like your opinion on one applicant."

Mr. Mills pushed his clean plate aside and knit his fingers over his belly.

"Mrs. Lucinda Clark, a widow from Peoria, has applied." Gideon turned to Mr. Mills. "Walter, you mentioned her some time ago."

"Yes," said Mr. Mills. "I encouraged her to write directly to you."

"Well, she has made a most singular proposal," continued Gideon. "She appeals, based on her advanced years, to join us not as a laborer but as a financial contributor. In place of the membership fee of one hundred dollars and ongoing labor, she offers to pay three thousand dollars and, if the colony proves a fitting home for an elderly widow such as herself, to consider the colony in her will."

"Oh, I know Lucinda from Peoria," Nettie said. "Everybody knows everyone's business in Peoria. She's positively dripping with money."

Mr. Mills glanced fleetingly at his aunt and turned to Gideon. "Since I recommended her, I feel I should speak. She's frail of body but strong in spirit. She believes in the cause, but she is not herself accustomed to hard labor."

Gideon steepled his fingers. "I don't question the fine woman's spirit or belief. And her offer of funds is generous. But would others among us resent such an arrangement—us bringing in someone who won't contribute work?"

Mr. Mills looked to Abraham.

Abraham cupped his fingers over Elizabeth's folded hands under the table. "If the others understood that Mrs. Clark's financial support benefits us all, then I believe they would accept such an arrangement."

"In my book, I make provision for the aged and infirm," said Mr. Mills. "They must be cared for by the community."

Abraham tossed his head back. "The psalms say, 'What man is he that liveth, and shall not see death?' The physical body is of this world and will someday pass from it. We must show Christian compassion to the aging and sick among us."

All around the table heads bowed, and Gideon and Mr. Mills uttered amens.

Gideon hunched over his clasped hands. "Perhaps we could exempt those who contribute over one thousand dollars in funds or land from work."

"Well, well," Mr. Mills said, cocking his head in contemplation. "We'd have to be certain not to compromise the labor supply by doing so. But your proposal has some merit, I suppose, in recognizing the contributions of the landowners and such bene-factors as Mrs. Clark."

Abraham rushed in, "I believe this proposal would go down well with the landowners—and perhaps increase their dedication to the colony."

Gideon looked up and around the table. "Do the ladies have an opinion? We depend on the ladies to do the caretaking and nurs-ing."

"What sort of person is this Mrs. Clark?" Alberta asked Mr. Mills, her long neck stretched to its utmost. "Is she a companion-able type?"

"Oh, yes," said Mr. Mills with a curt wave of his hand. "I can assure you of that. She's a gracious and learned woman."

"Heavens, yes," Nettie said, picking at the crumbs on her plate. "She has the most delicate way of talking, which is a surprise for someone who keeps her ear horn so handy. And she has more books than you can shake a stick at."

Gideon's eyes darted over Nettie and settled on Elizabeth.

"Well," said Elizabeth. "I could mention Mrs. Clark's applica-tion to my brothers and my sister and see if they have any objections."

"And you, Elizabeth," said Gideon. "Do you see any reason to object?"

Elizabeth kneaded her lips a moment. "If we have plenty of young women joining up, then I wouldn't see any burden among us watching after an elderly lady."

Gideon beamed. "Oh, I can assure you we have that. A newly-wed couple from Texas is keen on joining us. And two farming families from Iowa, with eight grown children, three horses, five cows, and forty-one hogs between them, are ready to load up box-cars and drive their livestock here as soon as we give them the go-ahead."

"Capital, capital," declared Mr. Mills.

Abraham clapped his hands together, Nettie grabbed the coffee pot to pour around, and the party made merry with the good news. But Elizabeth could only wonder if all these newcomers would upset the easy coming and going among everyone in the settlement. And the rules! Every time she turned around a new rule cropped up. How would they keep track of them all?

A NEIGHBORLY VISIT

JUNE 1894

"Oh, I enjoy this fresh air and the abundance of these wild woods," said Walter Mills. He and Abraham strolled along the perimeter road on their way to Frank Dodge's cabin, enjoying the pleasantries of June—the pine-scented breeze, sun-warmed dirt road, and Indian paintbrush blooms speckling the roadside in oranges and reds.

"I remember the day I first walked this land like it was yesterday," said Abraham. "I had a vision then—of angels singing in the breeze. I know now what the Lord had in mind."

"Yes, Abraham, the Lord's blessing is upon us."

As they passed a cut-over pine flat, Abraham remarked, "The Lumbering Company is taking out the pine quicker than it can grow. Where will it end?"

"Not until they've taken all their profits, I expect."

"Those capitalists care nothing for the beauty of the land. They only think of money morning, noon, and night."

Abraham and Walter turned a bend in the road, and in the clearing three hundred feet ahead Frank Dodge's home came into view—a sturdy log cabin with sawed rounds piled into a lumpy hill beside it. This being the Sabbath, Frank ignored the call to split wood and instead sat on the porch in his rocker smoking a pipe. Spotting Abraham and Walter, he stopped his rocking and, like a snapper turtle, stretched his neck out for a good view.

"So, he's a resolute Republican?" asked Walter.

"Yes. I'd advise against speaking on populism. And I should warn you: He's a cantankerous sort."

Frank Dodge eased up out of his rocker. He'd worked hard all his life, that was clear, for the burden of labor had weighed down his aging frame, causing his legs to bow out and his shoulders to hunch in. He served as the local Justice of the Peace, having acceded to the role only after the uncle who raised him had pressed him into service on the occasion of his own infirm retirement.

Abraham waved and hollered, "Hello, Frank."

Frank took his pipe out of his mouth and lifted it a few inches in the air in grudging welcome.

"Cantankerous?" Walter muttered. "I see what you mean."

They strode up the path and onto Frank's porch.

"Frank," said Abraham. "I would have you meet Walter Thomas Mills. Mr. Mills delivered a fine series of lectures in town."

Walter extended a hand to Frank. Frank released his hold on his pipe and clenched it in his teeth, accepting Walter's handshake.

"Pleased to meet you, Mr. Dodge," said Walter. "We're neighbors now."

Frank withdrew his hand and pulled the pipe from his teeth. "I reckon we are."

Abraham said, "There are big changes in the settlement these days, Frank. I thought we should tell you and your wife about it."

"Wife's gone visiting," said Frank, standing stock still.

Abraham scuffed a foot. "Why, do you mind if we sit and talk?"

"I suppose. Was just about to fetch some tobacco." Frank turned to the house.

They trudged to the door of the compact cabin Frank Dodge shared with his wife. Their six children had moved on, the four boys into cabins of their own with their new families, and their two daughters to the homes of their husbands.

As Abraham entered Frank's cabin the reek of pipe smoke assailed his nostrils. I'm surprised his wife allows that dreadful tobacco in her house, thought Abraham. Then, glimpsing the cabin's general disarray—the grime-encrusted stove, the counter strewn with mismatched plates and tin pots, a basket in the corner overflowing with knitting and odd fabric bits, and the penetrating, acrid stink of soot—he comprehended the wife's tolerance for tobacco.

The three men drew chairs out from the table. Frank pulled his out farthest and leaned back in it when he sat down, instead of pulling it up to the table as Abraham and Walter had.

"Mr. Mills here has written a most interesting book," began Abraham.

"May I tell you a little about it, Mr. Dodge?" asked Walter.

"Not much for reading," Frank said, grabbing a tangle of tobacco from a leather pouch on the table and stuffing it into his pipe bowl.

"Oh, that's of no consequence, I assure you." Walter summoned a reassuring smile. "It's understanding the ideas that matters."

Frank clamped down on his pipe and pulled his head back, solidifying his expression into stony regard.

"We are building a product-sharing village at the Byers' Settlement. It's a new enterprise, one in which the villagers are treated as equal in need, but their unique skills and abilities are honored, too. Each man and woman among us has a special job to do for the good of all, and we are bound by Christian charity to care one for another." Walter paused with the speaker's knack for using lull to punch home a point.

Frank pulled his unlit pipe an inch away from his mouth. "Hear you're making everybody move out of their cabins."

Walter planted his forearms on the table and leaned in. "The idea is to come together in a village for the benefit of fellowship. Then we'll use the land around us for its best purpose—logging, hunting, fishing, and agriculture—so it can sustain the whole of the village."

Frank rested his pipe on the table. "Why you telling me?"

Walter opened his hands before him in self-evident certainty. "Here you are, living next to the Byers' Settlement, with your own share of the good Lord's bountiful land."

Frank narrowed his eyes. "You wouldn't be expecting me to join up, would you?"

"I believe when you grasp the benefits, Mr. Dodge, you'll feel compelled to join," said Walter.

With the zeal of a father running off a worthless suitor, Frank sprang up, reached into the corner behind his chair, and grabbed his 45-70. "You get out of my house," he said, poking the rifle at Walter.

Walter, eyes agog, stood.

"Why, Frank," said Abraham, pushing his chair out with the backs of his knees and standing. "There's no call for this."

Frank leveled the rifle at Abraham. "I ain't afraid to use this. Fought in the war, you know."

Abraham flared up his palms to signify surrender. "Fine, fine, whatever you say. Just trying to be neighborly."

Frank bounced the rifle barrel at them. "And if anybody from your fancy village invades my property again, I'll do worse than make him a cripple."

Abraham and Walter scurried out the door and rushed down the road, never once looking back.

A MOMENTOUS FOURTH

JULY 1894

The sun rose over a community of antsy children, industrious women, and mostly contented men on the Fourth of July, the settlement's favorite holiday—excepting Christmas. But this was no ordinary Fourth.

Across the settlement, cabin inhabitants sprang from their beds, ate the simplest of breakfasts, and went about the business of preparing for festivity. Fathers commanded youngsters to gather brush for the evening bonfire, and clumps of cousins and chums disappeared into the woods, boisterous with purpose. Settlement women—the full-fledged and budding—organized themselves into an army of cooks and dispatched their orders. After obtaining permission from the gardening department to harvest some young cabbage heads, Nettie Mills cooked them up with pork sausage that Walter bought in town. And Alberta Noel assembled five pies of fresh-picked huckleberries.

Abraham stood at the window contemplating the compound on this auspicious morning. "Yes, Mother, it's looking like a real village."

After the colony purchased an industrial milling saw, the logging department milled some downed beech, spreading the planks out under the summer sun for drying. But needing well-seasoned lumber for current building projects, the officers had requisitioned all the settlers' lots, explaining that village association rules meant all property was now common property. John Kepler and few others balked on the grounds they might need lumber for mending and such. But they relented after Abraham quoted from Matthew 6:19-20— "Do not store up treasures for yourself on the earth"—and Gideon promised them access to the bounteous supply of new planks.

Then, all of June, on every day but the Sabbath, the building department men had measured and sawed, hammered frames together, and raised walls, completing three homes and framing fourteen more in the U-shaped compound. Abraham and Elizabeth were the first to move into one of the finished village cabins, and today Elizabeth fired up her new stove and undertook preparation of an oversized kettle of venison stew.

Elizabeth looked up from her potato-cubing long enough to scrutinize the walls of their box-square home, as if hoping to see something other than plain milled planks. "It's the finishing, not the beginning, that concerns me."

"Oh, Mother, don't be so distrustful. The building department has its priorities."

"Humph. Wonder if you'll sing a different song when the winter wind's blowing through these walls."

"My bones aren't getting any younger either. I just put my trust in the Lord and the many hard-working hands in our colony."

"Trust?" Elizabeth scooped up the potato cubes and dropped them into the simmering stew base. "You've got enough of that for both of us. Somebody around here's got to do the worrying and prodding."

"All right, Mother, you see to that. I've got to curry Smokey and Bellamy."

Come early afternoon, the settlement's five wagon-keepers, Abraham among them, drove the wagons to the open end of the village compound, arranged them in a semi-circle, and put their horses out to graze. Elizabeth joined the other colony women filing from their kitchens and toting their bounty of food, including enough plates and forks for their own families and the single men, too. With the hour of celebration near, fathers called out for their brush-gathering charges to bring in their last loads, and the compound populated with life. The women arranged all the food on one wagon bed, and the children circled around, sniffing the steaming kettles and ogling the lumpy-crusted pies.

Abraham ambled out among the dispersed group, urging them to come together, and President Gideon Noel climbed onto a wagon bed and called out, "Gather around, everybody."

Mothers collected the children loitering about the food wagon and herded them into the crowd of fifty-some villagers clustered before the makeshift stage. The sun, near its summer zenith, beat down on the browned arms and faces of the men and children, and the women adjusted their bonnets to ward off its rays.

Gideon, towering over the crowd on the wagon bed, gripped his suit lapel and swung an arm before the crowd. "This is a momentous Fourth of July for our village. All around you can see the bounty of our labor and realization of our cause: more buildings rising each day; many newcomers joining us; and the fields shooting up with crops. But that's not all. On this day, we undertake our first legal act as Hiawatha Colony. Abraham and Edgar, will you join me up here?"

Edgar Huey hopped up onto the wagon bed and gave Abraham a hand up. Grabbing a board with some papers tied to it with twine, Edgar stepped to the front of the wagon stage. "I have here," he said, holding up his portable desk, "the deeds for Abraham's two hundred and forty acres—the hundred and sixty with his cabin on it and the eighty up by Stutts Creek. As trustee, I will hold his and all others' deeds until we have signed the incorporation agreement. Then I will transfer all deeds over to the Hiawatha Village Association."

Edgar took a pen from his breast pocket, handed it to Abraham, and held the papers before him.

Abraham raised the pen, swung it down to the paper, and signed his deed over. Returning Edgar's pen, he righted himself before the crowd, beaming. "We are on our way, my dear brethren—the stalwarts who first settled this land and our new members, who bring us their courage. By working together we'll realize our wondrous dream."

The crowd cheered. Abraham shook hands with Edgar and Gideon, and they hopped down from the wagon. As he gazed out on the crowd, Abraham stole a moment to thank the Lord for his good fortune—as founder of the Byers' Settlement turned Hiawatha Colony—to address this remarkable assemblage.

"Now," said Abraham, "it's time to begin our celebration of the birth of this great country. I would ask John Kepler to come up."

John broke from the front of the crowd and sauntered up onto the wagon bed. He had dressed in his finest shirt of blue-checked cotton and exchanged his knickers for a pair of ankle-length pants, which he wore tucked into his boots.

"As all of you know," said Abraham, glancing at John, "John here played a role in the building of our nation. John Kepler, Alva Kepler, and Eli Huey are veterans of the War to Save the Union, a bloody and cruel war that took many lives. These men risked their lives for equality, liberty, and reunification—at Chattanooga and many other battles—and we're grateful to the Lord that they are with us today to celebrate this great country."

Abraham reached up and clapped John on the shoulder. The crowd applauded and whooped. John smiled and studied his boots.

Abraham looked out on the crowd and found the eyes of the restless three-foot-high children and the gangly four- to five-and-a-half-footers. "But you, young ones, should listen up, for nothing comes without hardship and hard work. That has been the story of our nation, and it will be the story of our village. By practicing endurance and brotherly love, we'll create a new way of Christian living."

Sweeping his arm before the gathered, Abraham declared, "Today we make history, and I guarantee that all of us will pass the story of these days down for many generations to come."

Abraham paused to punctuate his pronouncement before continuing, "John will now read the Declaration of Independence and get our festivities underway."

Abraham surrendered the stage to John Kepler, who read, in his deep and resonant voice, the whole of the Declaration of Independence while the villagers lifted their faces up in fitting veneration. Upon concluding, he folded and slipped the document into his shirt pocket.

"It's time for the procession," said John, and he stepped down from the stage, took up Old Glory, and marched in place. Gideon and Abraham motioned the group forward, and men, women, and children formed a loose line behind John, who stepped out and led the group around the U-shaped village compound and back to the half circle of wagons. He stopped at the food wagon, signaled the ladies to take up their serving stations, and everybody clustered around the food wagon to fetch a plateful. The served ones pushed back through the hungry bunch and found seats for themselves, the children on the ground, parents with babes on wagon bed benches, and older adults on chairs set up beside the wagons.

Abraham and Elizabeth seated themselves on crates, using a wagon wheel as backrest. Walter Mills and his Aunt Nettie joined them on chairs set up close by, and Gideon and Alberta Noel climbed up on the driver's seat of the wagon where they'd have a view of the whole assembly.

"If I'm not mistaken," Elizabeth whispered to Abraham when the others were distracted, "our Beech is sweet on that Essie."

Abraham followed Elizabeth's gaze. Sure enough, there was Beech, all smiles and courtliness, escorting Essie from the food wagon. Essie Wright's family had come all the way from Iowa to join, contributing fourteen head of cattle, two roosters, and fifteen hens.

"Yes," muttered Abraham, "they'd make a fine match."

"I say," said Walter Mills, turning to Abraham and Elizabeth, "the building is coming along swimmingly, don't you think?"

"Why, yes, the building department has been all vigor," said Abraham.

"Plenty of strapping young men," tittered Nellie, and the gathering of six continued their companionable meal, admiring the fourteen frames that would soon be homes and appraising the industry building sites.

"Alberta, this is no ordinary huckleberry pie," said Elizabeth, twisting around to catch her eye.

"It's delicious," Walter said.

Alberta leaned around to answer. "You noticed, did you?"

"Now, don't tease us," Nettie said. "Just what did you put in this pie?"

Alberta fluttered her eyelids. "It's my secret ingredient."

Gideon bounced his fork over his plate with business-like seriousness. "I'd say it's preserved ginger from the apothecary."

Alberta flapped a hand at her husband. "Why, Gideon, you've spoiled all my fun."

Abraham leaned against the wagon wheel and stretched his legs out before him. "Lenniel says he's secured sales for huckleberries in St. Paul and Minneapolis."

"Yes," said Gideon. "We'll get as many hands picking as we can to fill all the orders."

Walter poked his hat brim up a notch and wiped his brow. "You can count on all my family."

"I'll instruct the small hands among us," said Abraham, "in hopes more berries find the baskets than their bellies."

Gus sauntered over to the group, scraping his fork over his empty plate. "Mmm, mmm, good cooking."

Gideon hopped down from the driver's seat and leaned against the wagon, joining the circle the men had formed. "Oh, yes, the ladies have outdone themselves."

"Fine day for a celebration," said Abraham, standing and inhaling of the air scented with grasses smashed down by hooves, wagons, and feet.

Walter Mills plopped his clean-as-a-whistle plate on the wagon bed. "It's exciting to see the village going up so quickly. Gus, I must commend you on a superior job of managing the building."

"Why, thank you, Mr. Mills." Gus studied the village compound. "Hard to just look at those half-built buildings. Almost want to pick up my hammer and get back to work."

"Come winter we'll need the community building for meetings." Walter brushed the front of his shirt, sweeping away a few crumbs. "When might that be ready?"

"I'm hoping September," Gus said. "Have to finish the houses first."

"We ought to open the post office as soon as possible," said Abraham. "There's enough of us to warrant them bringing the mail to us."

Gus rubbed at the back of his neck, as if puzzling a problem.

Gideon pushed away from the wagon and tightened the circle of men. "We just haven't been able to attend to those needs yet. Not with being pressed for housing and industry buildings."

Abraham chuckled. "Older I get, more impatient I get. I ought to let you men do your work. You don't need me pestering you."

"It's fine with me, Abe," said Walter. "You saying the things I'm thinking keeps me from getting in trouble."

"That's all right, Walter and Abe." Gideon shot them a sly smile. "We have plenty of work to go around if you care to join in."

"I'm cut out more for speeches than hammers and nails," said Walter, who had pledged to donate fifty percent of all his speaking fees. "Guess I better keep up my work bringing in money and members."

Abraham shuffled his feet, for he felt sheepish that the rules exempted him, in view of his land contribution, from work duty. Then again, he kept plenty busy, serving more or less as Mr. Mills' unofficial secretary, fielding correspondence from prospective members and posting the mail for Mill's speaking engagements. But, being unaccustomed to the role of underling, he chose not to advertise these duties, and instead explained, "I've got an appointment at the *Manistique Tribune* Monday. Just want to be sure to keep the newspapers apprised of our progress. But I expect I can find some time the day after to join the crew."

MRS. CLARK WORRIES

JULY 1894

No sooner had the men started up their business talk than Elizabeth spotted Mrs. Clark approaching with one of Sarah Huey's children, eight-year-old Pearl, in tow.

Once admitted to the colony, the widow Lucinda Clark had donated three thousand dollars, setting off a spending and building spree. Treasurer Lenniel Byers stocked the colony store to brimming with flour, sugar, lard, salt pork, and kerosene. Gus Highland's building department commandeered every wagon in the settlement and returned from Manistique with full loads of windows, stoves, stove-piping, nails, saws, and hammers—everything Gus deemed necessary for the speedy erection of houses and industry buildings. From that day on the swoosh of saws and thump of hammers resounded from the village center to all edges of the colony.

In the run-up to her arrival, villagers gave themselves over to many a debate about the wealthy Mrs. Clark: Would she prove genial or haughty? Would she continue her generous ways or lord her contribution over all? Would she require a maid or was she capable of pouring her own tea?

When she took up residence the men found much to admire in her simple but refined dress, even though some of the ladies considered such attire impractical for the country. But she comported herself with the self-assured practicality of a woman long accustomed to ably navigating the world, and the women soon warmed to her ways. Walter Mills and his Aunt Nettie invited her to take up residence in their cabin, and Alberta fawned over her, insisting she stay with them. But Mrs. Clark would hear none of it: "You'll put me where I can be of use. I may be old, but I'm not feeble. I love children, and I do not shrink from treating the sick." So, she'd gone to stay with the Huey family, and Sarah

appreciated her help nursing Eli and Evvie, as well as her generous spirit and easy way with young Pearl and Clifton. She may
look like a good wind will topple her, Elizabeth had told Abraham,
but she's as spirited as a yearling.

"Mrs. Clark," called Elizabeth, "please join us."

"Good day to all of you," said Mrs. Clark, who gripped her cane
in one hand and held Pearl Huey's hand with the other.

"How are you, Mrs. Clark?" asked Alberta, speaking loudly in
deference to the widow's poor hearing.

The petite Mrs. Clark lifted her cane up a few inches and
plunked it down with authority. "Fit as can be expected."

"How's your family, Pearl?" Nettie asked the skinny, sallow-
faced girl.

Pearl looked up at Mrs. Clark, who urged her on with a smile.

"Momma's home with Daddy and Evvie," said Pearl.

Elizabeth asked, "Will they be joining us?"

Pearl hesitated.

Mrs. Clark shook her head. "I don't believe so."

"Well," said Elizabeth, pushing up from her seat, "we'll just
have to bring them some stew and such."

Nettie and Alberta declared they'd stroll around the circle, and
Elizabeth headed for the food wagon with Mrs. Clark and Pearl,
leaving the men to fend for themselves.

"That sure is a pretty dress you have, Pearl. Your momma sew
it?" asked Elizabeth as she, Pearl, and Mrs. Clark made their way
down the path to the Huey's cabin.

Pearl shook her head and looked down at her pale-yellow cotton dress, still crisp with newness. "It's from Mrs. Clark."

"Well, it sure is nice," said Elizabeth.

"Pearl," said Mrs. Clark. "Will you run ahead with the biscuits
and pie and tell your mother we're coming along?"

"Yes, ma'am," said Pearl, and she scampered ahead on the
path, swinging her basket.

"I've been wanting a word with you, Mrs. Byers," said Mrs.
Clark, slowing her pace.

"I hope you're not having any problems getting settled in," Elizabeth said. Truth is, Elizabeth admired Mrs. Clark's spunk and
hoped when she herself turned white-haired and withered, she'd

be as lively and clear-headed. "We're all grateful to have you, you know."

"It's nothing to do with me. It's your sister's family I worry about."

"Well, I worry about them, too," said Elizabeth, trying to keep her voice calm. "I do what I can to help Sarah with Eli and Evvie."

"Of course you do, Mrs. Byers. And your sister's very grateful to you. She looks up to you—almost more like an elder than a sister, I'd say."

"I don't expect her to treat me any different than a sister," said Elizabeth, steeling herself against the consternation welling up in her. "But what is it you wanted to talk about?"

"Sarah would never tell you because she doesn't want to disappoint you, but she's worried sick about Mr. Mills' plan to move everybody into the village. Says she can't live in a drafty place with her husband and daughter ailing with the consumption." Mrs. Clark looked sidelong at Elizabeth. "And I'm inclined to worry for the same reason."

"But Abraham told them they won't have to move right away. They can stay in their cabin this winter."

"What about after that?" asked Mrs. Clark. "How solid is your new home?"

"I have to admit it's not as sturdy as our old cabin." Elizabeth minced along with her pot of the last of the venison stew. "But it's not finished yet. The building department plans to shore up the walls. Shouldn't have any drafts come winter."

"I hope so," said Mrs. Clark, swinging her cane with the ease of a lady on a Sunday stroll. "You know I believe in the cause, or I wouldn't have given myself over to it. But I wouldn't want to see anybody harmed. I've grown fond of the Hueys, and I know you, too, care very much for them."

"I appreciate your concern, Mrs. Clark."

"I felt I should tell you the things your sister is reluctant to say. After all, you're in a position to calm her worries."

Elizabeth gazed ahead at the winding path. "Yes, I'll keep an eye on this matter. We should all have sturdy and warm houses."

"Good," said Mrs. Clark. "I knew I could speak with you like this. And perhaps it's best that we keep this between us—so Sarah won't appear to be stirring up trouble."

"Yes, I'm inclined to think of it just so myself."

Elizabeth brought what cheer she could to her visit with the Hueys: Oh, you should've seen the children gobbling up the pies; yes, Mr. Mills likes to parade around on that white horse of his; and it'll be nice to have a community building for services and gatherings in the cold months.

But gloominess dogged her as she hiked through the shadowy woods back to the village compound. She didn't know whether to welcome Mrs. Clark's confidence or resent her intrusion. And she'd already made inquiries about the plans to chink house walls, so she wasn't sure what else she might do.

Batting away the evening onslaught of mosquitoes, she found Abraham at the bonfire's edge and sat down beside him, wrapping her skirt tight around her ankles. As youngsters paraded around the blazing heap of brush, she sat mesmerized by the bonfire sparks flying high into the indigo sky and then, turned lifeless gray flakes, drifting back to earth. She hoped she and the others, especially the Hueys, wouldn't suffer from poor housing, not just this winter, but all winters to come.

ENEMIES ON THE OUTSIDE

SEPTEMBER - OCTOBER 1894

When Abraham spotted his son Lenniel picking his way toward him over the potato field, his belly tightened. There was something about the haste in Lenniel's lurching gait—the reckless plant of his feet on the uneven earth—that didn't square with his usual deliberate ways. But Abraham wanted to finish the row, so he pushed his hands back into the loose earth and groped among the fibrous roots.

Lenniel stopped and stood over Abraham, facing into the wind and gripping his flapping jacket sides together. "Father, I must speak with you."

Abraham pulled his hands out of the tangle of roots and dropped two fist-sized potatoes into a basket. "I thought you'd be in town all day."

"It's about that." Lenniel glanced at the harvesters in the nearby rows and lowered his voice. "Can you come away to talk?"

"Why, yes." Abraham braced a hand on his knee and stood, dusting the dirt off his hands and wriggling the kink out of his back. As afternoon wore on, the wind had increased and the clouds rumbled into steel swirls, prompting President Noel to summon all hands to assist with the potato harvest.

As Abraham stood, a chilly gust blasted him and tingled the sheen of perspiration on his chest and back. He followed Lenniel past the potato pickers: men and women, young and old, in fact, everyone except the building department men and schoolchildren. Abraham came up beside Lenniel at the edge of the four-acre field and scanned the bent-over pickers working their way down the rows. Filled baskets laid scattered in their wake, with empty ones spaced out before them.

Lenniel planted his feet wide and firm, as if bracing himself on the deck of a pitching ship and worked his thumbs over his closed fists. "Just came from the shipping department at the Soo Line office."

Abraham studied Lenniel's severe profile. "Something's wrong, isn't it?"

Lenniel turned to his father. "They want to charge us twenty dollars per hundred bushels to ship to Chicago."

"Dear Lord," said Abraham. "That's robbery."

"Sure is." Lenniel's stone-stiff jaw insinuated blame, righteousness, or perhaps plain acerbity—Abraham couldn't tell which.

"I don't understand," Abraham said. "Rates were reasonable for the huckleberry shipments."

"Lot less poundage for the berries. And they claim they'd have to bring up empty cars special for our shipment."

Abraham's stomach sank with dread as he scanned the field scattered with bushels and bushels of potatoes. "Did you try to reason with them?"

"Asked to speak to the manager right off. Didn't want to talk to a clerk about such a big shipment."

"Artin Quick?"

"He's the one I talked to." Lenniel cocked his head and observed his father out of the corner of his eye. "Seems he has something against you. Said the colony was another of your hair-brained schemes."

"Why, those capitalist crooks," said Abraham. "Remember when Chicago Lumbering accused me of inciting that strike last spring? Quick was the one behind that lie."

"Guess they've got the upper hand now," said Lenniel.

Abraham usually admired Lenniel's forthright manner but the sarcasm creeping into his voice soured him on it just now.

"It's not easy going up against that company," said Abraham. "They have no compunction about throwing their weight around."

"Maybe you should have told me to watch out for Quick before I tried to deal with their shipping line."

Abraham fastened his gaze on Lenniel. "Never occurred to me they'd charge us such exorbitant rates. My mind doesn't work that way, Son."

"Should've known after what happened down in Van Buren."

"Don't go bringing that up now." It was true, after Abraham had pressed the Furnace Company to put accident insurance in place, they'd fired the eight others who stood with Abraham—and John Kepler, too, just because of his relation to Abraham. But Abraham couldn't stand by after young Andy McPherson had gotten burned, leaving his family destitute. Somebody had to face down these capitalists. He'd followed his conscience, and if more had done the same, they'd have met with success. Had he erred, thinking he could do some good? He supposed the company bosses intended just that—to cow people like him into submission. Lord in Heaven, these companies had too much power, and the government stood by and did nothing.

Lenniel faced his father, his expression taut with restraint. "Now what? You got any ideas?"

"Well, you're the treasurer," said Abraham. "Better tell Gideon about this."

That very evening President Gideon Noel summoned all his officers and Abraham to a secret meeting. Vice President Gus Highland suggested they meet in the community building, and he and Secretary Claude Faust carried a table and chairs from Gus's cabin over to the hollow hall. The men, solemn in their duty, settled around the table. Abraham stole glances at the others, and shadows from the evening's dusk intensified the grave cast of their countenances, as well as his own glumness over the powerlessness pervading him.

Gideon asked Lenniel to report to the group on his encounter with Quick at the Soo shipping office. Abraham explained the Chicago Lumbering Company's animosity toward him, recounting how they'd falsely accused him of trying to incite a strike.

"Damn them," said Gus. "I was the one behind the strike. That's the truth of the matter. The company just lied about Abe. And they said they'd increase wages as soon as they could. But those mill workers haven't seen a penny more since then. That's how good their word is."

Claude, whose wiry body was rarely still, grabbed his pen, flicking it between his fingers. "It's subter, subter..."

"Subterfuge," Abraham offered.

"Right, can't trust them, that's for sure," said Claude, tapping the top of his pen against his paper.

"But they own the rail line," Gus said. "No way around dealing with them."

Gideon drummed his fingers on the table and asked Abraham, "Do you know Mr. Mills' traveling schedule?"

"He's in Iowa right now. He'll be passing through Chicago on his way back, stopping a while to see his wife."

Gideon squinted in thoughtfulness. "Could send him a telegram. See if he'd intercede at the Soo Line office down there."

Abraham nodded. "It's worth a try."

"We've got to," said Gideon, "even though the Manistique operation is bringing big money in for them now. Not likely they'd undermine the bosses up here."

Lenniel spoke up. "It was Mr. Mills that found us the produce dealer down there. Maybe the dealer would have some influence with the rail line."

Gideon planted his forearms on the table and knit his hands together. "I'll mention that, too."

Gus shook his head in disgust, his red hair backlit by the dim evening light. "I can't believe how devious that company is. Got us in a real bad spot here."

Abraham looked around the table. "Time is short. Some of the potatoes are out of the ground now, and we need to either ship or store them."

"It sure doesn't pay to ship at twenty per hundred bushels," said Lenniel. "We can't come out even on the deal."

"Might as well keep the potatoes ourselves," said Gus. "Got a good-sized cellar under this building here."

"We'd need to bring in plenty of sand for storage," said Abraham. "It'd take some effort, but it might be the only thing we can do."

"I sure was counting on the income from those potatoes," said Lenniel. "We'll need more lard and salt pork and other supplies for the winter."

"Well," said Gideon, "one thing at a time. I'll send a telegram to Mr. Mills and go on into town myself and talk to Quick. And I'll ask you, Abe, to see about hauling in some sand. Even if we manage better rates, it may pay for us to keep a good amount of those potatoes instead of sacrificing them for meager gain."

Abraham, Gus, and Claude nodded in agreement.

Lenniel asked, "What about the funds we need for winter supplies?"

Gideon inclined his head in a pensive pose. "Let's think on that a few days. And while we're pursuing the possibilities, I suggest we keep this matter to ourselves. No need to alarm the others."

One week later, Gideon received a telegram from Mr. Mills: "Attempts to secure better shipping rates to no avail. Will return October 8." Neither had Gideon had any success intervening with Quick.

Upon receipt of Mills' news, the officers secured a loan of two hundred dollars from Mrs. Clark, explaining it'd be repaid in the spring, most likely from newcomers' membership dues and sales of other products. Gideon announced the failed potato sale in a general meeting and the plan to allot four bushels of potatoes for each adult and child. They stored the harvested potatoes under the community building for dispersal through the winter months, but many remained in the field for lack of storage space. Then the ladies proceeded to cook potatoes morning, noon, and night: potatoes with eggs from the chickens; potatoes with carrots and rutabagas; potatoes with snippets of salt pork; and, though it was not hunting season, potatoes with venison. Children protested the abundance of potatoes on their plates, but the ladies persisted, for they knew supplies of other food varieties were limited and that even with all their efforts some of the potatoes would rot.

Walter Mills' returned on a snowy October day and, two days later, invited Abraham and the downhearted colony officers to an evening meeting in his cabin. His son Francis joined them at the table, and his aunt, Nettie, served coffee.

Gus wagged his head. "Looks like any long-distance shipping of our produce or goods is out of the question."

"Unless we can negotiate the Soo Line down on their rates," said Lenniel.

Mr. Mills crossed his arms. "I'm willing to approach Mr. Quick and see if I can make any headway."

"He was not receptive to my pleas," said Gideon. "But I urge you to try."

"I will," said Mr. Mills. "There's too much at stake."

Lenniel spoke by turns to Gideon and Mr. Mills. "Production's moving along on the cant hook and peavey stalks. Maybe we could try for more contracts on those."

"I don't believe there's much call for more stalks," said Gideon. "Took some doing to root out the contracts we have."

"Money's tight for finishing the barn," said Gus.

Claude squirmed in his chair. "We'll lose some of the livestock if we don't get that barn finished soon."

"Yes," Gideon said. "We have to finish the barn."

"I'd like to have another set of eyes on the balance sheets from here on out," said Lenniel. "Just to be sure I'm not missing anything."

Mr. Mills' son, Francis, a thirty-year-old with sandy brown hair and his father's stout stature, spoke up. "I'll work with you on that, Lenniel."

Abraham figured Francis might as well give Lenniel a hand since Francis hadn't yet taken on any assignment. And he recalled Elizabeth and a few others muttering about his unruly nature.

Gideon nodded at Francis and looked around the group. "We mustn't be caught off guard like this again."

"Next season we should plant more varied crops," said Abraham. "Think about growing what we can sell locally and use ourselves. No more big potato crops."

Gideon said, "You're right, Abe. But we've got to get through this winter first. The officers and I are considering a mortgage of some of the land."

Mr. Mills frowned at Gideon. "Mortgaging must be a last resort. You have the loan from Mrs. Clark for expenses."

Gideon braced his arms against the table, lengthening his torso, and addressed Mr. Mills. "Mrs. Clark's money is spent, and the store is still low on flour, lard, and kerosene. We can't afford to put our people and livestock at risk. We'll need more building supplies for that barn and more than just potatoes and venison for our kitchens."

Lenniel looked around the table as he spoke. "I see no alternative to mortgaging some of the land until we garner income from our agriculture and other products."

"I'm for it," said Gus.

"Me, too," said Claude.

Gideon flattened his palms on the table. "Sounds like all the officers are in agreement."

Mr. Mills leaned back in his chair. "I go on record as opposing this incursion into debt, but you're the officers."

Turning to Lenniel, Gideon said, "I'll direct you to look into mortgaging some acreage, up to eighty acres, to get us through the winter."

"Yes, sir," said Lenniel. "We should settle on which acreage that would be."

Gideon rubbed his cheek. "It should be land of sufficient value to bring in the needed funds, but nothing central to the village's housing, industry, or agriculture."

All the men fell silent. The creaking of Nettie's rocker overtook the room's quiet. Abraham was the only one among them who'd been a landowner.

Nettie halted her rocking. Silence saturated the air, like humidity on a still day, and Abraham knew there was only one thing to do. Holding his head high, he said, "My eighty up on Stutts Creek seems to fit the bill."

Gideon let out a deep breath and smiled at Abraham. "Yes, Abraham, I believe it fits perfectly. Lenniel, will you see to it?"

Nettie took up her rocking again.

Lenniel swung his head in assent. "And does that mean we can spend what's left in the treasury to finish up the barn?"

Gideon patted his hands on the table. "I'd say you can go full steam ahead on the building."

"All right then," said Gus. "Claude and I'll get the men back on it right away."

Gideon leaned back in his chair and sighed.

Nettie, who hadn't spoken a word during the meeting, stood and brought the coffee kettle to the table. "I don't mind telling you—with the snow setting in, the ladies are nervous about this problem with the potatoes. They know flour and lard are in short supply."

"The village needs a cheering up," said Mr. Mills, clapping his hands down on the table. "Let's inaugurate our community building with a celebration."

Nettie's face brightened. "Perhaps a Halloween party? The children could amuse themselves with costumes."

Abraham shot Nettie a disbelieving squint. A pagan holiday didn't sit well with him, though he agreed with Walter that the people needed cheering. He raised his eyebrows at Walter.

"Hmm," said Walter, stroking his chin. "I suppose that could work."

"Yes, with music and dancing," said Claude.

Francis, the other single man in the group, smiled and appealed to Gideon with wide-open eyes.

Gideon looked into the hopeful faces of Claude, Francis, Walter, and Nettie. His gaze came to rest on Abraham, and, sighing, Abraham acquiesced with a dip of his head.

Gideon thumped a hand on the table. "Very well then, a Halloween celebration it'll be."

Nettie, standing by the table, clutched the coffee pot with both hands. "Maybe I could organize a potato recipe contest for the ladies."

The men laughed, and even Abraham allowed himself a chuckle. Not a half-bad idea, he thought, conceding everyone's amusement at the notion. But he couldn't vanquish the image of the thousand bushels of potatoes in storage and the even greater quantities in the ground that would rot there. Such a wicked behemoth the Lumbering Company was. Did Quick thwart the potato sale for sport or mere greed? And now, eighty of the acres he'd deeded over to the village would be mortgaged. This was not the beginning he'd envisioned for his utopia.

HALLOWEEN FRIGHT

Wind howled through the pines surrounding the village, and fresh-falling snow swirled about in airy vortexes. Bending his head against the snowy needles and stepping over uneven drifts, Abraham clutched Elizabeth by the arm and guided her forward. As they approached the community building, Abraham raised his voice over the blizzard's din: "I bet the newcomers've never seen the likes of this," to which Elizabeth replied, "Maybe now they'll understand all the fuss about preparing for winter."

They hastened into the hall and slammed the double doors behind them. Abraham stomped his feet and brushed the snow off his shoulders.

"Well, look at that," he said, unbuttoning his coat and regarding the banner festooning the sixty-foot wide side wall. Odd bits of stitched-together fabric made up its length, with the colony motto embroidered in navy blue lettering and red stars:

Hiawatha Colony** For GOD**and Humanity**

"Didn't work on it myself," Elizabeth said, shucking her hat and gloves. "You ask me, making winter clothes is more important."

"I suppose so," said Abraham, declining to further discuss the matter, grateful that the villagers had captured the proper spirit of the celebration.

At the front of the hall men in wool flannel shirts and thick trousers, women with sturdy boots and high-buttoned dresses, and costumed children congregated around two blazing stoves: in one corner a full-sized cook stove and in the other a potbellied variety. As the well-stoked stoves warmed the hall, coats and hats landed on hooks and chairs, men clumped up in conversation, and the ladies gathered about the built-in table to discuss their potato recipes and peek at each other's creations. Children outfitted in flour sacks painted up as sundry frightening creatures—skeletons and ghosts, witches and devils—ran about, showing off their costumes to each other and sneaking up behind a preoccupied mother, aunt, or congenial uncle and popping out in front of them with a "BOO."

On the twelve-foot wide stage midway between the stoves, Alberta Noel played strains of Foster's "Beautiful Dreamer" on the new community organ. The organ itself wasn't new, but it was new community property, recently called in from Alva and Ann Kepler's home. Elizabeth had told Abraham how her brother Alva had grumbled about Gideon's request to place the organ in the community building, complaining: If Ann and I have to give up our organ why should Mills have that white stallion all to himself? But Ann, always the pragmatist, had countered, I rarely use it; it might as well go where the children can learn to play it. And she volunteered to earn extra work credits for organ-teaching duty, which, Elizabeth told Abraham, took the edge off Alva's grousing.

President Gideon Noel mounted the stage, came up alongside the organ, and signaled for Alberta to stop playing. He clapped his hands to get everyone's attention. The crowd quieted.

"Welcome to our Halloween celebration," Gideon called out, smoothing the lapel of his trim, black wool jacket. "We have much in store for this evening's festivities. Before we commence with judging the potato recipes, I have some important announcements."

Gideon motioned to his officers, Gus, Claude, and Lenniel, and all three joined him on the two-foot high stage. Facing the crowd, Gideon beamed with satisfaction. "In anticipation of our gathering, the officers and our trustee have been working hard on securing deeds. It gives me great pleasure to announce that all one thousand promised acres have been signed over to trustee Edgar Huey."

Gideon invited Edgar to the stage, and Edgar read his list of owners who had deeded their land to the association, allotting ample time for applause between each: from Abraham Byers, two hundred and forty acres; eighty from Elonzo Byers; one hundred sixty from Lincoln Byers; his own eighty; from his father, Eli

Huey, forty; and Alva and John Kepler, each bringing one hundred and sixty to the colony.

"And last but not least," said Edgar, "Mrs. Emily Rose has signed over her eighty."

A warm round of applause went out to Mrs. Rose. Edgar nodded to Gideon and descended from the stage.

Gideon extended an arm to the now widowed Emily Rose, his expression soft and solemn with sympathy. "I must add that all of us are sorry about the loss of your husband, Mrs. Rose. Please know that our hearts are open to you."

Mrs. Rose, standing near the front of the crowd, clamped her lips together in sad acknowledgment and nodded to Gideon.

Gideon bowed his head to show respect and sympathy, and then looked up with calm eyes and uplifted brow, signaling it was time to move to other matters. "Now I have one more announcement, this one more difficult to convey. All of you are aware of the spoiled contract for our potatoes, and I know this has been a source of worry. But we will persevere in our endeavor to build our product-sharing village. We've secured a mortgage on Abe's Stutts Creek property, and that will see us through the winter— as harsh as it may be—just fine. I must thank all my officers, and Abe, for their steadfastness and good work on our behalf."

Gideon led up the applause.

"Three cheers for President Gideon Noel," yelled Gus, and all joined in the hip-hip-hoorays.

After a modest allowance for the cheer and applause, Gideon dismissed his officers from the stage and held out his hands to subdue the crowd. "It is a tribute to all of you that we have been able to proceed with such dispatch on colony business. We've suffered a hardship, but we're working together, and we have wonderful benefactors among us. I must mention here Mrs. Clark and Mr. Mills, who have lent financial support when it was most needed."

Gideon looked toward Mrs. Clark, who sat in the row of chairs along the side wall, and Mr. Mills, who mingled among the ladies over the potato plates. As Gideon extended an arm toward Mrs. Clark and then Mr. Mills, polite applause broke out.

Abraham followed Gideon's eye across the hall to where Mrs. Clark sat, and by her side he spotted young Clifton Huey, the son of Sarah and Eli. At the sight of Clifton's costume, his breath escaped him. It was a devil, that was clear, for he wore a black sack that sprouted a tail, and he had somehow fashioned a headband with horns. But what caught Abraham's eye was the very large nose he sported, a nose that Abraham had seen before.

"Now," announced Gideon, "I ask Mr. Mills to judge the potato recipes before we partake of our dinner of the prize winner and runner-ups."

As Gideon stepped down from the stage and headed for Mr. Mills, Abraham made his way across the hall.

"Good evening, Mrs. Clark," he said. "I trust you're well."

"Oh, goodness gracious." Mrs. Clark looked up at Abraham from her seat, tightening her shawl over her shoulders. "Now that I'm out of that storm I am!"

Abraham smiled over her head at Clifton. "Why, Clifton, what kind of costume is that?"

Clifton hunched his shoulders in and looked down, as if he were being reprimanded. "A . . . a devil."

"Wherever did you get that nose?"

"I found it."

"Why, yes. And where did you find it?"

Shifting his eyes from side to side as if in search of some escape, he said, "I found it, that's all."

"Well, that's quite a disguise," said Abraham, summoning the tone he used to settle a riled horse. "Do you know who made that noise?"

"I didn't steal it," Clifton said, turning his eyes upward in his bowed head. "Honest."

"I'm not accusing you of that." Abraham remembered how Clifton had stolen a snaffle bit some time back and suffered shaming from the whole settlement. "Just wondering how you came by that unusual nose."

Clifton bit his lip and looked down at the ground.

Mrs. Clark turned about and studied Clifton's downcast face. "You go run along, Clifton, and find your sister."

Confound it, thought Abraham, where could Clifton have gotten that nose? He watched the boy disappear into the crowd of children in the corner.

Mrs. Clark angled a glance at Abraham. "It's wonderful of Mr. Mills to help draw up the incorporation papers, don't you agree, Mr. Byers?"

"It's not him. He's paying for the lawyer to draw them up," said Abraham. But what he was thinking was that Clifton must have come by that nose somewhere around here, either in the settlement or at school.

"Would that be his lawyer in Chicago?"

"Yes, yes." Still, he thought, most of the children in Hiawatha North School are from the settlement.

"Oh, and when will the incorporation papers be ready?"

"Why, most likely in the next few months." The very person who robbed me two years ago could be in this hall, Abraham thought. Or it could be a neighbor. Such traitorous perfidy!

"Will we hold a meeting to review them?" asked Mrs. Clark.

"Most likely," said Abraham, looking about for Beech—the only other person who knew about the robbery at the hands of the man disguised behind a big nose. "Mrs. Clark, will you please excuse me? I must have a word with my son."

Abraham made his way through the milling crowd toward Beech. Beside him stood Elizabeth and Essie, the young woman with whom Beech had been keeping company of late.

"Well," said Abraham, clapping a hand on Beech's shoulder. "Good to see you, Son. And Essie, that's a lovely dress."

"Thank you," Essie said, dropping her eyes. "Don't get a chance to dress up much."

"It's very nice, Essie." Elizabeth nodded her approval at Essie's blue, billow-armed dress.

"Haven't the children outdone themselves?" asked Abraham, and he caught Beech's eye and directed his gaze in Clifton's direction.

Beech studied the boisterous clump of children. "Quite impressive, all those costumes."

Abraham asked, "Did you see Clifton's get-up, with that big nose?"

Beech bobbed his head, trying to get a glimpse.

"I wonder where they got all those parts and pieces." Abraham lifted his eyebrows knowingly at Beech.

"Oh, fiddlesticks," said Elizabeth to Abraham. "They brought flour sacks to the sewing department, and everyone helped them make up costumes. You saw what Goldie brought home."

Abraham shrugged and shuffled his feet.

"We have a winner, all," Gideon called from the stage, motioning Mr. Mills to join him. "If you will direct your attention here, please."

Gideon signaled Alberta, and she played a three-note roll on the organ. The crowd turned to the stage.

"Our judge, Mr. Mills, will announce the winner of the potato recipe contest—the first and only ever conducted in the country." Gideon's voice flattened in understatement at the last phrase, drawing titters from the crowd.

Mr. Mills stepped onto the stage. "The winner of the potato recipe contest is Emolene Odell for her scrumptious creation, savory potatoes with salt pork. It is the most delectable of dishes, and Miss Odell has consented to reveal her secret to any who would like the recipe."

Mr. Mills bowed to Miss Odell, and polite applause ensued. Miss Odell swung her head about like a playful colt. Behind her, a cluster of four young women exchanged sidelong glances.

Mr. Mills smiled at the foursome and continued, "But there are many fine runner-ups. I found not a disagreeable dish on the table. So, I encourage you all to partake now of our Halloween feast."

Mr. Mills stepped down from the stage and strode over to Miss Odell, shaking her hand.

Abraham and Elizabeth queued up to get their dinner, and Beech and Essie fell in behind them.

"Oh, I just knew he'd pick her," said Essie.

Elizabeth turned around. "How did you know that?"

Essie hesitated, and Beech flashed a smile at his mother. "Mr. Mills has had his eye on Emolene for weeks now. He likes the pretty young girls."

Abraham eyed Beech. "Mr. Mills is a married man. I'll not tolerate such disrespect, to say nothing of falsehood, about the man."

Not waiting for a reply, Abraham turned his back to Beech. Elizabeth too turned around, but Abraham caught her sharing a smile with Beech.

After the party of four served themselves, Beech and Essie trailed off to find Essie's parents.

Abraham and Elizabeth joined Alberta and Gideon Noel at their table, and the foursome settled in for the evening, enjoying the variety of potato dishes and, after dinner, the youngsters' costume contest. Confound it, thought Abraham as he studied Clifton's costume, if I could find out where he got that nose, I might recover my robbed satchel.

"A fine celebration," Gideon declared as the gathering broke up.

"Oh, yes," Elizabeth said. "The children enjoyed themselves."

"And the food," said Alberta. "I never knew there were so many ways to prepare potatoes. I'm quite inspired!"

"Yes," agreed Abraham. "It was just what we needed—a little cheer and fellowship."

As they donned their coats, Gideon maneuvered to Abraham's side and steered him away from the ladies. "Abraham, I think you should know that Mr. Mills takes great issue with me announcing the mortgage of the Stutts Creek acreage."

"Oh?" Abraham studied Gideon's worried face. "Well, what's done is done. We've had hardship, and we're dealing with it as best we can. We must all work together now."

Gideon's nostrils widened in exasperation. "I don't want any hard feelings with Mr. Mills. We must avoid strife among us at all costs."

"I agree with you on that, Gideon." Abraham took a step toward the door, for he wished to close the conversation. "Don't worry too much about it. I'm sure it'll blow over."

AS DIFFERENT AS DAY AND NIGHT

NOVEMBER 1894

From the shelter of her cabin Elizabeth watched Goldie and Artie, all roly-poly in their oversized coats, trundle over the snowy terrain with Beech, Essie, and six other children. She had relinquished Goldie and Artie to a Sunday sledding party, but only after warning Beech and Essie to be mindful of reddened noses and ears and to guard against any of the children straying off. "It's cold enough to damage tender skin. And children don't know their limits," she'd lectured.

Winter was in full swing, but Elizabeth's worries about one matter were assuaged. Upon her insistence, Abraham had coaxed the building department to tar paper the home exteriors and seal the double-hung windows with pitch-soaked cloth. Although grateful for the benefit of these measures, she still complained: The plank walls seemed flimsy compared to the old-style log construction and on the windiest days she was forever throwing wood on the fire to keep the stove stoked to a high blaze (though she granted it was a nice modern stove). And the most recent cold snap had set her and Abraham to squabbling over who should alight first to scoop out the cold ashes, start up the day's fire, and empty the thunder mugs. Between giving up their long-time home for this boxy house and tending two children, she wasn't willing to carry these household chores by herself anymore. Yes, at fifty-two she was much younger than Abraham, but it was no great leap for her to justify her demands: He was about the liveliest sixty-five-year-old around, so he might as well pitch in and help, seeing as he was the one who got them into this situation.

"Oh, there go Walter and Nettie," said Elizabeth, bobbing her head toward the path to the Noels' cabin.

Walter Mills, less than his regal self in bulky wool pants and a flap-eared hat, and his aunt Nettie, who clung to his arm like a vine on a tree, high-stepped through the here shallow and there drifted snow on their way to the Noels' cabin.

Responding to the silent signal of long-married folk, Abraham rose from his reading chair. Craning for a view out the window, he said, "Humph, don't know why they don't use the snowshoes."

Elizabeth turned from the window. "Probably not accustomed to them."

"This whole business makes me edgy," said Abraham, helping Elizabeth into her coat. "Gideon's awful anxious to set things right with Mr. Mills."

Elizabeth scooped up her basket of fresh-baked yeast rolls. "I expect that's why he asked us along."

Elizabeth and Abraham stepped out onto their porch and tied on their snowshoes. A gust of wind buffeted them, lashing their scarves about their faces and whisking them along the path to Gideon and Alberta's home.

Alberta flung the door open as they hurried up to it and flicked her arm at them, as if to hasten them in on whiffs of air. "Oh, come in," she commanded, slamming the door shut. "This wind'll be the death of me."

Greetings spread all around amongst Abraham, Elizabeth, Walter, Nettie, Gideon, and Alberta. The four guests shed their wraps, handed them off to the welcoming arms of Alberta and Gideon, and gravitated toward the metal bosom of the new cast iron stove. The Noels' cabin was a simple one-room design, at least for now. During the construction season, the building committee had considered it a priority to erect as many houses as possible. But they'd run out of seasoned lumber for the internal walls; next spring, they promised, they'd take that up.

"You know," began Gideon, sidling up to the stove, "we're grateful for this one-room design. Now that we've got a good drift of snow against the north and east sides, this stove warms the whole place."

"Yes, I'm so glad I insisted that last contribution go toward the best of stoves," said Walter, fanning his hands over the stove's glowing warmth.

Nettie, who'd been assessing the cabin's furnishings and decorations, joined the circle around the stove. "Alberta, those wall hangings are new, aren't they?"

Alberta turned around to glance at her embroidered renderings of dainty flowers. "I'm so glad you noticed. I just love those sweet pansy faces."

"Ah, what a relief everyone got settled before these first snows," Gideon said to no one in particular. He pulled out a seat at the table and motioned the others to join him.

Elizabeth couldn't help but notice how Abraham kept glancing from Gideon to Walter. Only days after Gideon shared his confidence with Abraham, Walter too had approached him and explained his displeasure with Gideon for announcing the mortgage. Abraham reported he'd told Walter the same thing he'd told Gideon: We must all work together as best we can. But Elizabeth knew that the solicitation, subtle as it was, from both men that Abraham take their side in the matter rankled him. "Nope," Abraham had told her, "no good can come of setting one against the other, even by showing the slightest favoritism." And she agreed: "Keeping out of the fray is the only way to stay on good terms with both of them."

"Indeed," intoned Walter. "I'm new to the fierceness of the winters here. The building department did just what was needed for the good of all."

Abraham settled into his seat. "I must add my own sentiments to Walter's, Gideon. You gave just the right instructions to the department."

"Oh, you men," said Nettie, pouring coffee while Alberta served plates of roasted venison and boiled potatoes. "Do you never tire of business talk?"

Elizabeth unveiled her rolls and placed the cloth-lined basket in the middle of the polished dining table. "If my husband ever does, I'll assume he's gone deaf and dumb," she said, evoking chortles from all the others. Abraham even gave up a humble smile.

"This venison is so tender, Alberta," remarked Walter, slicing through a thick slab of the mud-brown meat.

"Oh, thank you, Mr. Mills," said Alberta.

"The snow is so bright and pretty from indoors, isn't it?" asked Nettie.

Gideon smiled to Elizabeth with outreached hand. "Will you please pass your rolls, Elizabeth?"

"Don't let it fool you," Elizabeth said, conveying the rolls to Gideon. "You can never be too careful with these winters."

Abraham caught Walter's eye across the table. "You should use those snowshoes I left hanging in the back porch."

"Oh my," said Walter, with a shake of his great head. "I'll be needing a lesson in strapping them on if I'm to make any use of them."

"Nothing to it," said Gideon, leaning toward Walter. "Just tie the leather straps about your shoes and be sure your feet don't flop on the surface before you take to the snow."

Such a convivial dinner party the gathering of six regulars made. Perhaps, Elizabeth thought, all will be well between Gideon and Walter. They both seemed set on showing goodwill, and Abraham's fretting about the antagonism was turning tiresome. With these thoughts, she gave herself over to enjoying the conversation that ensued—about the prospects for deer hunting in the coming week, the new glove-sewing project the ladies were undertaking, and even some gossip about the pairings of young men and women they'd observed at the Halloween party.

"And now," announced Alberta, rising from the table, "I have a special treat for all of you."

"Why am I not surprised?" asked Nettie, helping Alberta gather up the dinner plates. "You're determined to outdo me in the kitchen, aren't you?"

"Oh, Nettie," Alberta clucked, "your peach pie beats them all, and you know it."

"I'll not even try to outdo you two." Elizabeth fetched the coffee pot and poured all around. "But if you keep up all this good cooking, you're likely to find my husband at your dinner table."

Elizabeth settled again in her seat, her belly full, extremities warm, and the company affable—the best contentment to be had on a chill Sunday afternoon—and watched Alberta prepare dessert. From a tin she extracted thick, round white biscuits, cut each in half, and arranged the halves on plates. Uncovering a bowl, she spooned out a huckleberry concoction, thick and gooey as a hard jam, and shook a dollop onto each biscuit half. With eyes bright and lips pressed in cheery anticipation, she slid a plate of her prize before each guest.

"Now just what *is* this?" Nettie poked the biscuit. It sprung up at the release of her fork.

"It's sponge cake," said Alberta, as if everyone ought to know.

Walter extracted an empty fork from his mouth. "It's so delicate. And the huckleberries are scrumptious."

Gideon smacked his lips. "My dear, you've outdone yourself."

"Why, these are the best huckleberries I've ever tasted," said Abraham.

"So, this is what you've done with all those huckleberries," said Gideon. "How long were you going to keep this from me?"

"Oh, you know you can't keep a secret," said Alberta, sitting up straight as a schoolmarm.

Elizabeth concentrated on the tastes on her tongue. "You've added some spice to the berries, haven't you?"

Alberta nodded coyly.

Nettie slapped a hand on the table. "Must we beg to hear how you've done these huckleberries?"

"No, I'm content with a little flattery," said Alberta. "I cooked them down and added cinnamon and clove."

"Ah, that's what it is," said Elizabeth, for she'd detected cinnamon, though she'd never tasted clove used with fruit before.

"You've made a big batch, then?" Walter asked, stroking his chin.

Gideon's eyes latched onto Walter.

"Yes, and I'll be glad to send you all home with some," said Alberta.

As the party broke up, Alberta insisted that the other two households accept some of her huckleberry topping. She opened her cupboard and asked Gideon to reach to the top and take down four jars from the shelf packed with twenty-some jars of the purple concoction.

"No, no," said Walter. "You needn't give us any."

"Nonsense," Nettie said, accepting two jars. "We'd love some."

As the last rays of day skittered over the snowy knolls, Walter, Nettie, Abraham, and Elizabeth quit the dinner gathering and leaned into the wind on the way to their own cabins, the stoking of their stoves likely foremost in their minds.

Abraham and Elizabeth joined forces against the cold that had overtaken their house, feeding the glowing embers in their stove. As they huddled before its radiating comfort, Abraham said, "Well, I believe Gideon and Alberta's dinner gathering did just what it should have—restore good faith between Gideon and Walter."

"Maybe," said Elizabeth, "but those two are different as night and day."

"It's true," Abraham sighed. "But I hope this spat has blown over."

TOO GOOD TO BE TRUE

NOVEMBER 1894

Two days after the Noel's dinner party, Abraham glanced out the window at the sparkling, scooped-out snowdrifts. He couldn't have asked for better hunting weather: A body could keep warm walking at a steady pace, and the snow was soft enough to muffle steps without being so deep as to curtail progress. He provisioned himself with dried venison sticks, strapped on his knife holster, and bundled up in a knit sweater and thick coat. Taking his Winchester down from the wall rack and pocketing a small box of bullets from the cupboard, he announced, "Hope we won't be long. Elonzo spied some deer yarding up at the cedar swamps last week."

"I'll be needing you to cut some kindling when you get back," said Elizabeth.

"It'll be the first thing I do." Abraham stepped out the door and headed down the path to Elonzo's cabin. Before he'd gone thirty paces, he heard Gideon call out, "Abraham, can you spare a few minutes?"

Abraham spun around. Gideon stood on his porch, coatless, flapping his crossed arms over his chest against the cold. Confound it, thought Abraham, he must have been watching for me. What can it be now?

Without a word, Abraham turned and trudged toward Gideon's cabin. Gideon bounced back and forth on his feet, watching Abraham approach. The closer Abraham got, the clearer it became that Gideon, usually the picture of equanimity, was out of sorts—very much out of sorts, if his agitated movements and refusal to quit the cold were any indication.

Abraham stepped up onto the Noels' porch, and still Gideon made no motion to retreat indoors. "What is it, Gideon?"

"Walter came around this morning. Told us keeping large stores of goods for ourselves is against the rules. Hauled all of it away."

"Stores of what?" asked Abraham.

"Canned huckleberries. The ones Alberta served on Sunday."

"Oh, my," said Abraham.

"Alberta is beside herself," said Gideon, folding his arms over his chest. "And I'm none too pleased myself. We're talking about huckleberries. Can you imagine making such a fuss about some jars of jam?"

"Well, what does he expect you to do about it?" asked Abraham. Yes, it was ridiculous to fuss about it, though he decided not to grant that point. Rules were rules, whether it was jam, lumber, or potatoes.

"Said we ought to apologize to you and Elizabeth and any others who know we broke the rule."

"I don't know what to say, Gideon. Maybe you should do what Walter asks and get on with your business as president." Abraham was losing patience with the animosity between Gideon and Walter. Was Walter set on antagonizing Gideon or was he merely enforcing product-sharing principles for the good of all? He hoped Gideon would do as Walter asked and put this behind him. The colony had more important matters to attend to, like keeping enough flour, sugar, and kerosene in the store to match the needs and work credits of all the men and women.

"Well, that's the problem, Abraham. I'm the president, and I'm trying my best to do right by everybody. I wouldn't call anybody to task over what a wife might put up in her own kitchen. This is downright pettiness. And Walter is overstepping his bounds. He's not an officer."

"I can see your point there," said Abraham, squirming as he watched Gideon shivering on his porch.

"And Alberta is upset. She was just trying to please everybody. Even gave some jars to Elizabeth and Nettie."

"Why, yes." Abraham lowered his eyes and brushed the back of his neck. He lifted his gaze to Gideon and softened his voice. "I promised to meet my son, so I have to be getting along. Can I think on this matter and visit you later this afternoon?"

"Yes, yes, please do," said Gideon, turning and gripping the door handle. "I'll be seeing you then."

It'd been too good to be true—the goodwill between Walter and Gideon that Abraham had observed over dinner. What'll it take to ease the strain that's sprung up between them, he wondered, meditating on the snow whooshing out from under his footsteps as he hiked to Elonzo's cabin.

∽≈⌒

"I don't know, Father," said Elonzo, his crooked leg forcing him to slow his pace over the snow-drifted path. "Perhaps you can appeal to them with Peter, the second epistle, about brotherly love."

"Why yes, that's a good source." Abraham called up the verse: "'And to godliness brotherly kindness; and to brotherly kindness charity.'"

"That's the very one I meant." As Elonzo smiled at his father his snowshoe snagged a bush and he pitched on his weak side.

Abraham looked away from Elonzo as he stumbled, allowing him to right himself on his own. He hated being reminded of Elonzo's lameness. It only dredged up the memory of Henrietta scolding him for letting thirteen-year-old Elonzo help break in a new horse. A boy had to learn how to be a man at some point, he'd argued, but Henrietta had countered that a busted-up leg would make it harder for Elonzo to do a man's work for all time. She'd been right, of course, and he'd never gotten over the recrimination she'd heaped on.

"I believe I'll speak with each of them and try to patch this up," said Abraham, swiping at the drip of moisture gathering on his nose, "though I hate playing go-between. Maybe we need a village sheriff—so Walter doesn't have to take it on, which it looks like he has."

The path narrowed and Elonzo held back and let his father step ahead. "You're the only one Mr. Mills'll listen to. And everyone in the settlement looks up to you."

Abraham nodded, but it wasn't his son's fawning that he wanted now. He needed someone to help him figure this whole thing out. It made him miss Harvey. Harvey would've commiserated and offered solutions. "I suppose you're right there. Just because I'm not an officer doesn't mean I don't have a responsibility for all of us."

"It's more your village than anybody else's. You brought Mr. Mills and Gideon here."

"Yes, I feel the weight of it all," said Abraham, staring into the distance.

As they emerged from the woods onto the perimeter road Elonzo eased alongside his father. "It's not been easy for the colony. With the potato problem and now this trouble between Gideon and Mr. Mills."

Elonzo cleared his throat and studied his father. "You think there's any cause to worry about the colony's future?"

"Oh, no," said Abraham. "You worried about your land?"

"We all took a big risk, signing our property over. And now the land I cleared for grazing is covered with buildings. What would I have if the colony fell apart?"

"Don't bother yourself about that, Son. We've got able people in charge. A little squabbling won't undermine the ideals we've all given ourselves over to."

"Yes," nodded Elonzo. "We've taken God's commandments to heart in our village, haven't we?"

"Why yes, we have. Now, we best stop this talking if we're to take down a deer today. And I wouldn't mind thinking about something other than the wrangling between Gideon and Walter for a while."

THE LADIES DEBATE

NOVEMBER 1894

After Abraham set off on his hunting excursion, Elizabeth finished her morning chores and bundled up for her afternoon outing. The day before Alberta had invited her to join her for sewing duty, and Elizabeth had accepted. Not that she looked forward to Alberta's company. Alberta was nice enough and a hard worker, too, but Elizabeth had little patience for her crowing about this or that recipe or special ingredient. Still, the village was stocked to the gills with deer hide, and Gus had secured enough glove orders from Manistique stores to keep all twelve of the village's sewing machines busy for a good month. So Elizabeth had consented to walk Alberta to the sewing room and instruct her on how to work with leather.

"Oh, Elizabeth, I just don't know if I can go today," said Alberta after she urged Elizabeth to step inside.

"Are you not feeling well?" asked Elizabeth.

Alberta's eyes bulged with surprise. "No, it's this business with Walter. It's got me so upset."

"What business?"

"About the jam. Didn't Abraham tell you?"

Elizabeth cocked her head. "I don't know what you're talking about. Abraham's gone off hunting."

Alberta kneaded her hands together. "Walter came and told us we're breaking the rules. He took away all my huckleberry topping. I can't believe the fuss he's making. It is *so* unnecessary."

"Oh," said Elizabeth. "And what does Gideon say about all this?"

"He's very displeased, very. He *is* the president. What right does Mr. Mills have to call him to task about something that is none of his business? Can you see Gideon making a fuss over such a petty matter?"

"No, it wouldn't be Gideon's way," granted Elizabeth. "But you shouldn't get so upset about it. I'm sure Gideon can take care of this with Walter."

"Well, I am upset. And I don't see any reason I shouldn't be. I try my best to be a good wife and good member of this community and look what insult I suffer for it!"

Elizabeth took in a deep breath and studied the floor, hoping by her mere composure to encourage calmness on Alberta. Looking up at Alberta, she said, "Maybe Mr. Mills shouldn't have done what he did. But best thing for you is not to let him know you're riled about it."

"I don't mind one bit him knowing I'm riled," Alberta huffed. "He's got no right."

"All right then," said Elizabeth, leaning back, as if to avoid an unpleasant odor without giving offense. "But what do you aim to do about the sewing? Are you coming or not, because I have to go."

"No, I'm not. You can go on without me. And I don't mind one bit if you tell everybody there what Walter's done."

"It's not my place, Alberta. It's for you to tell."

"That's fine, Elizabeth. Do just what pleases you. And so will I."

"Good day, then," said Elizabeth, reaching for the door.

"Yes, good day," said Alberta, her manner cooler than it had been at the outset of the call.

Elizabeth trudged the hundred yards to the community building and climbed the stairs to the second-level sewing room. Already, four others had gathered: her sister Sarah, sister-in-law Elvila, and two younger women, Essie and Emolene, who huddled over two sewing machines in the corner, lost in their own conversation.

Most of the women in the village took pleasure in sewing duty—and not just for the conversation and respite from their regular household duties. The colony had purchased twelve new Demorest sewing machines in the summer; at $22 apiece they were the most modern machines money could buy. During the days they were under the command of Mrs. Ida Smith, supervisor of the sewing department, but in the evenings anyone could use them for personal sewing projects. And each woman found that the more hours she put in the more proficient she became at her own sewing. Besides, reporting for sewing duty during the day earned them work credits, and though no one spoke about this, most of the women delighted in the newfound respect they earned by tallying up work credits alongside their husbands. Elizabeth wasn't required to sew, for she and Abraham were exempt by virtue of their contribution of land, but it was easy enough for her to do while Goldie was at school and Artie at the children's room in the community center. Neither she nor Abraham thought it wise for them to shirk colony labor or the extra work credits they could accrue by their contribution, and Abraham didn't mind feeding the cows and pigs and cleaning out the livestock barn, which didn't require too many hours.

Elizabeth, relieved that Alberta had not come along, took up a station at the sewing machine closest to her sister Sarah and sister-in-law Elvila.

"Lizzy, have you heard what Mr. Mills has done?" asked Sarah, leaning close to Elizabeth.

Elizabeth surveyed the stack of cut glove pieces piled beside her sewing table. Could word have spread already, she wondered. "What's that?"

"Well, he told Gideon and Alberta that they violated the rule about not keeping more than a month's supply of goods and hauled off all their jam. Do you believe the man's gall?"

"Where did you hear that?" asked Elizabeth.

"Gideon told Gus," said Elvila. "Alice was at home and heard every word. It was her told us."

"Yes, I heard about it," said Elizabeth. "I wish people wouldn't make such a fuss about it."

"Mr. Mills started this," said Sarah. "I don't like that man. I don't like him one bit. Been living among us only a few months and he's acting like he's king or something."

"Gideon is the most decent man I know," said Elvila. "He's a real gentleman."

Sarah said, "He's been doing right by all of us, and then Mr. Mills has the nerve to order him around like he's his servant."

"Yes, Gideon's a good man. I agree with you on that," said Elizabeth, noticing that the young women had stopped their own talking and were listening in on their conversation. "I hope he can straighten things out with Mr. Mills. He has a way about him when it comes to bringing us together. That's what makes him a good president."

"Wouldn't bother me one bit if he gave Mr. Mills a piece of his mind," said Sarah.

Emolene called out from the corner. "I think Mr. Mills is doing the right thing. Somebody's got to keep order among us."

Sarah swiveled around in her chair to eye Emolene. "You call barging into someone's kitchen cupboards keeping order?"

The door swung open and Ida Smith entered the room. "Well, ladies, did you all work over the lunch hour?"

"Hello, Ida," answered Elizabeth. "I'm just getting started myself. Guess I better sign in." Elizabeth had forgotten about signing the work-credits ledger, distracted as she was. She didn't like all this bickering among the women, nor did she appreciate Alberta's theatrics, which would only add fuel to the fire. She'd have to urge Abraham to direct the men to settle the matter before it got out of hand. Not that it hadn't already.

THE PRESIDENT PROTESTS

NOVEMBER 1894

Abraham and Elonzo hadn't spotted a single deer, which was mighty unusual, but then they'd talked a great deal and not properly given themselves over to their hunting. And this flap between Walter and Gideon flummoxed Abraham. The sooner it got settled, the better. Like Elonzo said, he was the one to set it right. He thought it might be prudent to hear what Walter had to say before speaking to Gideon again, but he'd have to pass by the Noel's house first and Gideon might be watching for him, so he figured he'd stop there on his way home.

Gideon greeted Abraham at the door. "Come in, Abe. It's good to see a friendly face. Give me your coat."

"Hello, Gideon, Alberta," said Abraham, shedding his coat. Alberta stood over the kitchen table wrapping plates in cloth. Oh, no, thought Abraham, this doesn't look good. "What's happened?"

Gideon took Abraham's coat and folded it over a chair. "We're leaving. Soon as we get our belongings packed."

"But you're our president." Abraham couldn't believe what he was hearing. "You've done a good job by us. We need you, Gideon."

"I can't stay without the confidence of the village. And it's been badly undermined."

Alberta slammed a bundled plate onto the table and burst into tears. "That man," she managed between sobs. "How dare he?"

Gideon hurried to Alberta's side and gripped her by the shoulders. "We'll be fine, dear. We've got family to go to. Everything'll be fine."

Abraham lingered by the door, feeling like an interloper.

Gideon stroked Alberta's shoulders, and her sobs quieted. He eased her down into a chair at the kitchen table.

Gideon turned toward Abraham, shaking his head in an ain't-it-awful manner. "I wish it hadn't come to this."

Abraham held his folded hands over his stomach. "Are you sure then? Won't you please consider staying?"

"I've no choice. Everybody's heard about this incident. If I apologize, I lose the faith of the village and compromise my leadership. And If I don't, I risk enmity from Walter and his backers."

Dear Lord in Heaven, Abraham thought, what an awful state of affairs. "You have my respect and confidence, Gideon."

"I appreciate that, Abe, but Mr. Mills has cultivated a following among the young people. I can't make a move without feeding dissension."

"Won't you let me help work things out?"

Gideon sighed and said, "I'm sorry. I am. But neither Alberta nor I can live with Mr. Mills' ways."

A PROPOSAL FOR ABRAHAM

NOVEMBE 1894

Snowshoes clomped outside the door. Abraham froze—right in the middle of drawing a leather strand through the harness he was mending.

Elizabeth twisted around from the stove reservoir, her hands still deep in the warm dishwater. "Who could that be?"

Abraham and Elizabeth didn't expect any visitors this evening. In fact, they'd had enough of togetherness to last awhile. Two days earlier the villagers had celebrated Thanksgiving with a meal of wild turkey, rabbit stew, sundry potato dishes, and apple pies. Vice President Gus Highland spoke about all the things they had to be thankful for: the efficiency of the stoves they'd purchased for the new homes; their very own post office up and running; the good progress being made on the livestock barn in spite of snow and cold; the hunting skills of the men who had taken turkey and rabbit for the dinner (a welcome break from venison, though the portions were skimpy); and the resourcefulness of the women who had cooked up a wonderful feast from diminishing cellar supplies. But everyone knew Gus was trying to lift their spirits and rally them together in the wake of President Gideon Noel's departure. Afterward, when Abraham told Elizabeth that he was disappointed the old and new villagers hadn't mixed at the gathering, she'd said, "No wonder, what with everybody taking sides over the squabble between Gideon and Walter."

"I'm not expecting anyone," said Abraham, setting down the harness piece and striding to the door. Swinging the door open, he exclaimed, "Why, John, Alva, what a surprise."

Elizabeth pulled a pot out of the warm reservoir water and grabbed her drying towel. "Well, hello brothers."

John walked in, and Alva propped his snowshoes outside the door, stomped his snow-matted shoes against the threshold, and followed John inside. He wasn't as tall as John, though he resembled him in some ways—he too sported an untamed beard, though his was more brown than gray and, like John, he favored the wool knickers and thick wool shirts of the lumberjack worker. But while John's quiet way bespoke dignified reserve, Alva's square, sharp-cornered face signaled tetchy sullenness.

"How's everything here?" John asked, looking from Abraham to Elizabeth.

"Oh, good enough," said Abraham. "We're keeping warm."

"Have a sit," Elizabeth said, motioning toward the table. "Got some water already warmed up for tea."

Abraham hesitated. Should he offer to take their coats? It was late, approaching seven o'clock, and most everybody was settled in their cabins at this hour, especially since it was biting cold outside. He contented himself with pushing aside his mending work and turning up the wick on the kerosene lamp. "What brings you out on this dark night?"

Alva hung his coat over a chair and, as he settled down into it, folded his hands on the table and turned to John.

Elizabeth fetched her tea kettle from the cupboard, scooped some of her chamomile into it, and poured the tea water.

John also shed his coat and nestled it over a chair. Easing his considerable frame into the chair, he tugged at his beard and glanced at Elizabeth and then Abraham. "Elvila and I were just visiting with Alva here and Ann. Have something we want to discuss with you."

"Oh?" Abraham lifted his brow and caught Elizabeth's eye as she took her place at the table. Abraham had never felt at ease with Elizabeth's brothers. They were so different from him—they showed no curiosity in the books and magazines stacked by his reading chair. Neither were they impressed with his command of the Bible and politics. Knowing this, Abraham's attempts at conversation with them were often halting and shaded with uncertainty.

John cleared his throat and inched up straight in his chair. Turning to Abraham, he spoke. "Like I was saying, the four of us were just visiting. Got to talking about our election. Wonder what you think about Mr. Mills declaring to run for president."

Abraham scratched behind his ear. "Well, it's his ideas behind our village. Seems to me he'd know how to make them work."

Elizabeth rose to fill everyone's teacups. "Must we talk about Mr. Mills?"

"I suppose you hear your fill, Sister," said John, taking a sip of his tea and lowering his cup back down.

He's got something up his sleeve, thought Abraham, wishing he'd just come out with it instead of shambling around. And Alva was leaving all the talking to John; he just sat there looking around the room like he'd never been there before, occasionally glancing at John as if to urge him on.

"Don't mind telling you some of us would rather not have Mr. Mills for president," said John.

"I know," Abraham said, welcoming John's admission. "Lots of folk think he went too hard on Gideon. But now the rules are clear. We shouldn't have a problem like that again, no matter who's president."

"Well, that's just the thing," John said. "Sometimes you can take rules too far."

A snort escaped from Alva as he thumped his clasped hands on the table. "Who wants Mills poking around their cupboards and cellar?"

"I'll grant it's a new way of living," Abraham said with a dip of his head. "But it's based on fairness and taking care of everybody's needs."

"Well, the thing is, Abraham," John said, wrapping his hands around his warm cup. "We were wondering if you'd consent to run for president."

Abraham yanked his head back in surprise. A rare stammer overtook him. "I, I hadn't thought of it."

John shifted his weight from one haunch to another. "Mr. Mills is always traveling. It'd be better to have a president who lives among us regular-like."

"It's true he has his lectures and such, but he's publicizing the village and seeking funds. I don't believe a president needs to be here all the time. There are other officers, too."

Alva rushed in, "And if his son gets elected vice president, it'll be only Mills' ways that we live by."

John reached his arm out toward Alva, restraining him. "What Alva means is we think it'd be better to have a president who understands the hardships of this country and who knows how we've managed all these years. You've seen cabins burn down, and you've helped rebuild them. You yourself hunt and trap, and Lizzie here knows more about doctoring than anybody else in the settlement. We need someone everyone can look up to."

Abraham sighed and crossed his arms. "Before the election I had a talk with Walter. Upon his advice, I decided not to take an officer's position, but to lend my support in other ways. And I've been content with that role."

"You ever think he wanted to keep you out of the way?" asked Alva.

John glared at Alva and then turned to Abraham. "You know I'm not much of one for politics, but I know displeasure when I see it. Mr. Mills doesn't have the trust of everyone in this village, and you do."

"Why, I don't know that, John," said Abraham. "Look at all the newcomers—Mrs. Clark and the Wrights and all the others. I haven't had many dealings with them. Who's to say if they trust me or not?"

"Mrs. Clark can't abide Mr. Mills," said Alva. "Don't you know that?"

"No, I know no such thing," said Abraham, stiffening and turning to Elizabeth.

Alva and John looked at Elizabeth.

Elizabeth glanced around the table, as if hoping someone else would pick up the thread, but all eyes rested on her. "It's true. Mrs. Clark worries about the Hueys. She doesn't think Mr. Mills appreciates their hardships."

Confound it, thought Abraham, why am I always the last to learn these things? And whose side is Elizabeth on anyway?

Alva chimed in, "And Essie told Beech her parents have their doubts about Mills, too."

"Well, besides you, that's just Mrs. Clark and the Wrights," said Abraham. "That doesn't account for everyone. Didn't you see how people flocked around Mr. Mills at the Thanksgiving dinner?"

Alva shook his head with disgust.

Before Alva could speak John warned him off with a raised hand, planted his forearms on the table, and leaned toward

Abraham. "It's your decision, Abraham. We're just telling you why we think you should. Will you give it some consideration?"

John pulled back from the table and planted his hands on his knees, preparing to rise. He studied Abraham.

Abraham welcomed the close of the conversation, for the longer it had gone on, the more it irritated him. He pressed his lips together, nodded, and said, "Yes, I'll give the matter some thought."

⁓

"I don't know what to do, Mother," Abraham said as he and Elizabeth crawled under the covers and nestled shoulder-to-shoulder.

"John and Alva have been with us from the beginning," said Elizabeth, tucking the quilt under her chin. "Seems to me their notions deserve some consideration."

"I suppose so," Abraham said, smoothing his feet over the foot warmer. "But I'm not sure they understand the ideas behind the product-sharing village."

"Ideas can't keep out the cold and feed the hungry. Doing the right thing is what's important."

"Well, I think the right thing is standing by the ideals of our village—seeing that everybody gets taken care of."

Elizabeth turned on her side, and her breath brushed at Abraham's cheek as she spoke. "Doesn't seem that's working if a good man like Gideon could get forced out."

"It's unfortunate, I'll warrant. Gideon was doing a fine job but putting new ideas into practice can sometimes be difficult."

Elizabeth let out a tiny snort. "You sure put a lot of faith in those ideas. They didn't work for Gideon. What makes you think they'll work for the rest of us?"

"I know the capitalist system isn't working. The way Chicago Lumbering runs this county and squeezes the mill workers and lumberjacks isn't working."

"I'm not talking about the Company. I'm talking about how we run our own affairs." Elizabeth cupped a hand over Abraham's shoulder. "Tell me this: If it'd fallen to you to deal with Gideon and Alberta's supplies, what would you have done?"

"I saw all those jars, and I knew the rules, but I didn't consider it my place to say anything to Gideon."

Not missing a beat, Elizabeth asked, "What if you were an officer, like the vice president? What would you've done when you saw that stock?"

"I'm not an officer, so it doesn't matter what I would have done."

"You afraid to tell me what you would've done?"

"No, I'm not," said Abraham, struggling to shake off the feeling he was a child caught at some wrongdoing.

"Well?"

"I suppose I would've had a talk with Gideon, told him it'd look bad if people found out he wasn't in strict accordance with the rules."

"And what would you have said to Alberta when she started blubbering about it?"

"Mother, you know I never took to that woman. She's not at all like you. Acted like the sky was falling at the smallest trifle."

"Not saying you have to take to her. Let's say you just told Gideon what you thought, and Alberta started fussing about being a good citizen and going on about all the bother over a few jars of jam."

"I suppose I'd try to reason with her. Tell her I know she prides herself on her cooking and that the best way to ward off any problems would be to just turn over most of the supplies to the community store so everybody could partake of her fine cooking."

"Well, there you go. That's not what Walter did. He just barged in there and accused Gideon of breaking the rules. And I doubt Gideon knew Alberta had put up such a store until that dinner gathering."

Abraham decided the conversation had gone far enough. "So? What's done is done."

"What's done did harm."

"There's nothing to do about it now."

"Yes, there is. You can run for president. All Walter cares about is that book of his. You know everybody in this settlement. You could do better."

Abraham sighed and drummed his fingers against his chest. It was true, he knew how to organize and inspire—and he enjoyed doing it. But it was all so complicated now. "I don't know, Mother. I just don't know. I wouldn't want to contribute to enmity with Walter."

"There's already enmity among us over this. Question is: Are we going to live in peace and harmony? Is everybody going to work together so we'll have enough food for all of us?"

"Yes, yes, I know. I need to think more on it. And pray."

"Well, I hope you won't be taking too long to decide."

"All right, Mother. We'll talk more about this later. I'd like to sleep now."

Elizabeth flattened her hand over Abraham's sternum and nestled her head against his shoulder. Soon her breathing elongated into that of the sleeper, but Abraham stared up into the dark, at the shadowy space above the rafters, and tried to imagine what would happen if he declared himself candidate for president. Would Walter campaign hard against him and force him to assert the differences between them? If Walter lost the election would he quit the village and take his financial support with him? And if Walter won, would he resent Abraham and exert his authority over him? Either way, it'd be hard for them to go on as comrades.

But the question was what was best for the colony. Abraham knew all the colony originals and their foibles and difficulties better than Walter. It was clear from what John and Alva had said that they and many others trusted him over Walter.

Still, his mind kept circling back to his concerns about Walter's comradeship and the financial support he'd lent—the village needed the money he brought in from outside. But would Walter be a good president, one that all the villagers could rally around?

Then there was the matter of outsiders, including the Manistique merchants they needed to conduct business with. He himself had engendered their rancor, whether deserved or not. And if he were president, they might not welcome the colony's business overtures. But Walter they admired: The local press had lauded him, and the bankers fawned over him.

Oh, what a spot he was in. Mounting a contest for presidency would heighten discord and intensify the dangerous division that had settled on the village. If only he could know in advance how an election might turn out. If his chances of prevailing were slim, well then, the decision would be easy. Still, if he prevailed, winning could have dire costs for the village.

Through a restless night, he fretted: How am I to decide?

REMARKABLE DEVELOPMENTS

DECEMBER 1894

Abraham and Elizabeth bid John and Elvila farewell and struck out for the next party on their visiting schedule. The matter of the presidency had come up during their call with John and Elvila, who made no secret of their wish for Abraham to declare soon and get on with his campaign. And Elizabeth, too, was vehement about which way she wanted the decision to go. In the past, Abraham had always relied on Elizabeth to intervene and smooth over any rifts between him and the Keplers, but now she'd taken their side and left him to work this out on his own. The Keplers were good-hearted and practical people, but he wished they'd just throw their support behind Mills and the whole village undertaking. When, as they took their leave, John had asked Abraham outright whether he'd be running, Abraham had responded, "Still have some considering to do. I'll let you know when I decide."

Elizabeth fell in beside Abraham on the snow-packed path and asked, "Well, when *are* you going to decide?"

Abraham squinted before the bright landscape. "After I discuss the matter with Walter."

"You're going to talk to *him* about it?"

"If I run, he ought to be the first to know."

Elizabeth swung around to face Abraham. "What do you think he'll say? Yes, Abraham, please run against me?"

"I'm not going to just declare it," Abraham said, guiding them wide around pine boughs caked with snow. "I'll ease into it—ask about his ideas for going forward. Anyway, my mind's made up."

"At least it's made up about something."

Abraham hated all this wrangling and badgering from Elizabeth. He stepped ahead of her on the narrow path. "I believe I'll walk over there right now and see if I can have a word with him."

Elizabeth spoke to his back. "You're not coming with me to Sarah and Eli's?"

"You want the matter settled, don't you?"

"Yes, but let's go see Sarah and Eli first."

"I'm not in the mood to listen to Sarah go on about Clifton's accident." Fact is, he'd heard plenty about it at John and Elvila's. They claimed that Walter Mills' son, Francis, had egged Clifton on to try the saw. And now all the Keplers were ranting about how they'd never forgive him for daring a youngster to play with a dangerous machine.

Elizabeth said, "Clifton loses a thumb and you're not in the mood to show compassion?"

"It's hard to show compassion when you're suffering a torrent of complaints."

"My sister has a terrible lot. How dare you talk about suffering."

"There's nothing more to discuss. I believe it's best if you go visit Sarah and Eli and I go talk with Walter."

"Oh, you cold-hearted man, you. Why can't you be more like Gideon? He knew how to stand up to Walter."

"That's enough." Barging ahead, Abraham said, "I'll not listen to any more of your argumentation."

"Suit yourself, you old fool," called Elizabeth.

I will, he thought, putting distance between himself and Elizabeth.

He might just spend the rest of the day at the Mills'. And, by God, he'd settle this today and be done with all the bickering. He'd thought about it for a full week, and all the fussing and agonizing hadn't done him—or anybody else—any good. He'd have a confidential chat with Walter and decide once and for all.

But as he approached the cabin that had once been his and Elizabeth's, his heart sank. Three sets of snowshoes leaned against the house beside the door. The Mills had visitors. Perhaps he could wait them out. Or, since it wasn't at all windy, and the sun's brightness moderated the freezing temperature, perhaps he'd invite Walter to join him for a walk on the perimeter road.

As he untied his snowshoes and leaned them against the porch, lively voices floated out from inside. Giving a quick knock, he stepped in. "Hello," he called out, and all eyes turned on him.

"Well, Abraham, come in, come in," said Walter, who sat in the place of honor, the rocker beside the stove. The others greeted him: Nettie, who sat on the other side of the stove; and, from around the table, Walter's son Francis; Miss Emolene Odell; Abraham's son Beech; and Essie Wright, the perky young woman whose company Beech had been keeping of late.

"Hello, Father," Beech said, "Essie and I missed you earlier."

"Your mother and I were out visiting."

"And how is Elizabeth?" asked Nettie.

"Why, fine, she's visiting her sister. Wanted to see how young Clifton is faring."

"Such a tragedy," said Francis, shaking his head. "Just got out of control with the boy treating that saw like it was a toy."

"Terrible shame," said Abraham, shedding his coat and taking up the empty chair beside Francis. "But not the first time that boy's done something foolish."

"Abraham," said Walter in his booming voice. "I wanted to wait until next month's meeting, but I got carried away in the moment. I've just been telling everyone here of a letter I've had from Dr. John Henry Randall."

"*The* John Henry Randall?" asked Abraham.

"Yes, *the* John Henry Randall," Walter smiled.

Francis eyed his father. "Father, just tell him."

Walter chuckled. "You must excuse my dramatics, Abraham. I'm pleased as can be: Dr. Randall is joining us in the spring."

"As a member?" asked Abraham.

"Yes," said Walter. "Him and his whole family—his wife, two sons, and three daughters."

"You know the man?" asked Abraham.

"Oh, yes. I had occasion to visit him last spring, before he undertook the march on Washington. He's disappointed with the results, but no noble undertaking is ever wasted."

"He delivered a message, that's for certain," said Abraham. "I say elected officials ignore it at their peril."

"Just think what he can do for the colony, him being as famous as he is," said Francis, his blue eyes gleaming. "He'll bring in more members. And investments, too."

"Do you think so?" asked Emolene, beaming at Francis.

"I do," Francis nodded.

Beech reached out and patted Essie's hand. "New members can do us a world of good."

Essie dropped her eyes to her lap.

"Yes," said Walter. "A propitious season is upon us, with the Randalls joining us and the colony's first wedding in the making."

"Wedding?" asked Abraham.

A hush fell over the room.

"Oh," said Nettie. "We assumed you knew."

"Uh, Father," said Beech. "We meant to tell you and Mother this morning, but you weren't home, and we got a little carried away with the announcement. Essie and I are getting married this summer."

Swallowing his rising confusion and consternation, Abraham said, "Well, congratulations, Son. I'm happy for both of you."

Abraham only half attended to the ensuing talk of wedding plans, preoccupied as he was with strategizing about a run for president, for the news about Dr. Randolph joining them compelled him to rethink the matter. Beech said something about getting the license when weather permitted . . . A wedding date, Nettie asked? . . . July 27, Essie said . . . Oh my, Abraham thought, how would Elizabeth, John, and Alva take the news of another famous person joining the colony? . . . Walter said, Ah, a high summer ceremony . . . I love weddings, remarked Nettie.

Catching Abraham's eye, Walter said, "I'd say the future looks bright for our village. Gus tells me they'll finish the livestock barn this week."

"Why, yes," said Abraham, snapping out of his reverie. "That's a relief. I was worried about which would come first, the next blizzard or the loft in that barn."

Walter slapped his palms on his thighs. "You needn't worry any longer. Our village is on the move. Say, Abraham," Walter continued, "why don't you join me at my desk, and we'll leave the young people to themselves."

"Oh," Nettie tittered. "Yes, you two run along and leave us young people, won't you?"

As Abraham followed Walter upstairs he thought, no, the time isn't right to discuss the matter of running for president. I need to give it more thought in view of the news about Dr. Randolph.

"Here, sit here," said Walter, insisting Abraham take his desk chair. Opening the top side drawer, he extracted a stack of papers and placed them before Abraham. "I've not told anyone," he said, patting the typed document with his plump fingers. "My attorney has finished the association incorporation papers."

Abraham scanned the first line: Hiawatha Village Association being now incorporated under the laws of the State of Michigan. "Is everything in order, then?"

"Yes, they're written as we directed. Would you like to study them yourself?"

"Why, yes," said Abraham. "I would."

Walter closed the file, nudged it toward Abraham, and straightened himself up. "We could circulate the document and get signatures between now and the time of the January meeting. It seems fitting to begin the year with the election of new officers *and* a signed incorporation agreement."

Oh, my, Abraham thought, this election decision just turned more complicated. He stared at Walter's desk—the engraved silver fountain pen in its wooden stand; the shiny white marble bookends bracing a tidy row of books, *The Product-Sharing Village* among them; the neat stack of scribed sheets set off at right angles on the side of the desk—and turned to look up at Walter's stately profile. "Yes, it would be fitting."

JANUARY 1895

On the afternoon of the third Saturday in January, beneath a sky thick with feathery snowflakes, the villagers of Hiawatha Colony assembled to vote for a new leader. As they converged on the community building, they shed their snowshoes, brushed the snow off their coats and hats, and gravitated toward the two blazing stoves. Abraham and Elizabeth, at Walter Mill's invitation, had arrived early to help the Mills' party stoke the stoves and ready the hall.

Walter spared no effort ensuring a welcoming atmosphere. As the hour of the meeting approached, the penetrating warmth of wood heat filled the expansive room and the new arrivals hesitated not at all to shed gloves, coats, and hats. Nettie and Emolene stood ready at the kettles, serving up coffee and cider. Walter, his son Francis, Abraham, and Elizabeth formed the welcoming line, meeting the villagers at the door and urging them to partake of refreshments.

"John, Elvila, welcome," said Abraham, reaching out to shake John's hand.

"Abraham," John nodded, shaking his hand.

John bent toward Elizabeth, "Sister, how are you?"

Elizabeth murmured, "Well as can be expected," and leaned in to embrace Elvila.

Abraham listened as John and Elvila moved on to greet Walter. Abraham knew John would maintain his dignity despite his disappointment, but he wanted to gauge the extent of his chagrin. "Yes, Mr. Mills," he heard John say, "it's a big day for all of us," and he contented himself that John had made some peace with the prospect of Mills as president.

By two o'clock some sixty adults had arrived. This being an official meeting of the Village Association, the children were left behind, some attended by aunts or grandmothers, others off sledding with cousins. Abraham and Elizabeth had dropped Goldie and Artie at the Hueys, since Mrs. Clark had offered to watch them and the Huey children. To Abraham's relief the opinionated Mrs. Clark had foregone the meeting: "Not many chances a woman gets to vote," she'd said, "but I have my reasons for sitting this one out." Abraham knew her reason, and he imagined some others also hoped the slate would change at the last minute, although he'd heard the young people and new members voice excitement at the prospect of a fresh beginning.

From the two-foot-high stage Vice President Gus Highland clapped his hands and called out, "Welcome all. Please gather round here."

Elizabeth followed John and Elvila to the side of the hall near the stage. Abraham cupped Elizabeth's elbow. "Shall we settle on the chairs in front?"

"No," she said, planting her feet. "Let's stay here."

Abraham did not press the matter, and Elizabeth inched closer to her brother, John. Ah well, Abraham thought, at least we have a good view of both the stage and the crowd gathered before it.

Gus brushed a hand over his rust-colored beard and spoke, "Shall we get our business underway?" Over the fall and winter months he'd nursed a beard, and between that and his checked flannel shirt, suspenders, and wool knickers, his transition from town mill worker to settlement member was pretty much complete. "A new year is upon us, and we have a slate of officers for the election. The first order of business is a call for any nominations from the floor."

Stillness overtook the room. Gus struck a pose of patience and for a long half-minute surveyed the audience for any sign of a nomination.

With a nod, Gus said, "I'll not waste any time then. I call on our candidate for president, Walter Thomas Mills, to come forward." He reached his hand side stage to Mr. Mills.

Mr. Mills strode up the stage steps and bowed to the crowd. Hearty clapping from Elonzo, Link, Lenniel, and the other Byers' sons and their wives, along with boisterous cheers from the Wright family and the other newcomers overcame the polite applause of the Kepler contingent.

"Ladies and gentlemen," began Mr. Mills. "Here we are in the heart of winter, but our hearts are not daunted. The Chicago

Lumbering Company has tried to foil our agriculture business, but they will not undo our hard-working spirit. We're almost thirty families strong, with many prospects for more members. In a few months none other than the esteemed Dr. John Henry Randall will join us—the man whose courage and conviction compelled him to command an army of unemployed to march on Washington. You see, word of our village has spread, and I'm certain others will follow the Randalls. By next fall I believe we'll be two hundred strong. We're learning how to live as a product-sharing village, and the wisdom of our ways is winning out over the selfishness and greed of unchecked capitalism. And now, I say to you, success is in our reach."

Mr. Mills smiled over the gathered. The crowd, taking his cue, cheered. Holding up his hands to cool the veneration lighting the faces of the young men and women in the front, he continued, "Today I stand before you as a candidate for president. If I should meet with your approval, I promise I will work tirelessly to secure more financial support, enough to get us on solid footing and improve our lumbering, agricultural, and sewing businesses. I'll publicize our experiment far and wide. I'll give my all to the Hiawatha Village Association."

Again, the crowd erupted into applause, led by the young people in the front.

Mr. Mills rocked back and forth on his heels, and his smile swelled. He reached into his vest pocket and pulled out a folded document. As the applause died down, he searched the crowd and boomed out, "I call on Abraham Byers to join me on the stage."

The crowd chanted, "Abraham, Abraham," and Abraham squeezed his way forward and stepped onto the stage beside Walter Mills.

Mr. Mills unfolded the papers, gave Abraham a glancing grin, and said, "I have here the incorporation agreement for our village. Allow me to read," he said, raising the document to chest level. "Hiawatha Village Association being now incorporated under the laws of the State of Michigan, Chapter 116, Section 3935, entitled 'Co-operative Associations,' and consisting of the following stockholders."

Mr. Mills looked up from the document. "You know what it says after that, for all of you are signers, and you've seen it with your own eyes. But I wish to recognize the very first signer. Do you know who that is?"

"Abraham Byers," yelled Francis Mills, and the crowd broke into raucous cheers.

Walter Mills clapped his hand over Abraham's shoulder and nodded at the crowd. When the applause quieted, he said, "Yes, our very own Abraham, and his lovely wife, Elizabeth, are first stockholders." Walter turned to face Abraham. "Abraham, I thank you and Elizabeth for all you've done to get our village off to such a propitious start."

Abraham welcomed the opportunity to implore all to overcome discord and serve each other and the Lord. He bowed his head once to Walter and then turned to the gathering. "The good Lord has watched over us. He has brought us to this beautiful land and guided us in forming this Christian community. He has tested our faith in ourselves and each other. And we've proven equal to the test. Strife is the way of the flesh, but by following the Lord God and His commandments we will vanquish greed and disunity. May the good Lord help us all live together in love and charity."

Abraham stepped down from the stage amidst respectful applause and made his way back to Elizabeth's side. John Kepler reached around behind Elizabeth and patted Abraham's shoulder, nodding approval. Well, thought Abraham, at least he's being gracious about the whole matter. He hoped all the Keplers would accept Mills as president and cooperate with the village's system. But he'd also intended his words for Walter, hoping he too would heed the call to live in brotherly love, and it occurred to him it was perhaps this prospect John had latched onto in indicating his own approval.

In the ensuing election the villagers unanimously elected Walter Thomas Mills as colony president. His son Francis was elected vice president. Claude Faust and Lenniel Byers continued as secretary and treasurer, respectively.

Gus Highland had decided not to run for re-election to the vice president post, explaining he was plenty busy with his building department position. But in private he'd told Abraham, "I refuse to serve as vice president to Mr. Mills. It would've been different if you'd run."

"Please, Gus, say no more of this," Abraham had replied. "We must all look to the future now—and not dwell on old grievances."

ONE LITTLE CHICKEN

FEBRUARY 1895

When the door flung open, Elizabeth, clutching her cleaning rag in both hands, swung around from the counter.

Elizabeth's sister, Sarah Huey, stood in the doorway, framed by the clear, cold February day. "Lizzie, I just don't know what to do."

Elizabeth took in Sarah's big, pleading eyes and knit-up brow. "Oh, dear. About what?"

Sarah closed the door, marched into the middle of the cabin, and flapped her hands. "That man. That Mills. He'll be the death of my Eli."

"What's he done now?" asked Elizabeth, wringing out her rag and draping it over the counter edge.

"I'm beside myself. I just don't know how much more of this I can take."

"Give me your coat." Elizabeth helped Sarah out of her coat and patted a chair at the table. "Sit."

Sarah's mouth and chin trembled. She sat and clasped a hand over her mouth.

Elizabeth settled into a chair across from Sarah and braced her forearms on the table. "Now, tell me what's got you upset."

"Eli needed some nourishment. You know how weak he is. Oh, my poor husband," she said, and the tears started. Through her sobs, she sputtered, "He's so poorly . . . He's dying . . . I just know it."

Elizabeth knew it, too. She studied her sister's eyes, deep pools of darkness in her wan complexion. Such tragedy on that family—both a husband and daughter stricken with the consumption and Clifton still healing from the loss of a thumb. "Now, Sarah, you've got to do what you can to nurse them along. You know I'll help."

"Oh," Sarah wailed. "I cashed Eli's pension check and bought a chicken to make soup. And that Mills says I should've turned the whole check over. That heartless, cruel man cut back our work credits."

"Oh, my," sighed Elizabeth. It wasn't enough that he'd hauled off Alberta's jam. Or driven Gideon Noel out of office. Now he was scrutinizing every penny brought in by every household.

"I hate that man," said Sarah. "He's killing my husband . . . I hate him."

Elizabeth walked to her shelf of linens and tugged out a handkerchief. Coming up behind Sarah, she handed her the handkerchief and smoothed a hand over her shaking shoulders. "There now," she said.

Sarah stilled her sobbing.

"Just let me think," said Elizabeth, keeping her voice soft, "how best to help."

Sarah sniffled and dabbed her tear-streaked cheeks. "He's trying to force us out. Just like he did the Noels."

"No," said Elizabeth, standing behind Sarah to conceal her own rising chagrin. She took in a deep breath and spoke, "No matter what, you'll not be leaving. I promise. I won't allow it."

"All our family's here. We've got no place to go," Sarah said.

It's not working, Elizabeth thought. The whole idea's a disaster. Why should Eli have to turn over his war check with no consideration for his health? It's just not right.

"Let me fix you a cup of tea." Elizabeth retrieved her tin of chamomile from the cupboard. "Don't you worry now. I'll have a talk with Abraham."

Elizabeth restrained herself the rest of the day, mulling over how to broach the matter with Abraham. She could have walked over to the barn and summoned him home from his chores, but she refused to stir questions among the others. She wanted this matter dealt with quietly, to keep it from getting around the whole village, like the problem with the Noels had. Once everyone heard about Walter raiding the Noel's blueberry preserves, Walter felt compelled to prove his rule about families not keeping large private stores. So she'd instructed Sarah to tell no one else of this and to ask Mrs. Clark, who'd been party to the conversation, to also refrain from spreading the news.

Elizabeth's mood only soured as the afternoon wore on. And looking around this sad excuse for a home didn't help, with its cramped quarters, draftiness, and barrenness. It had none of the touches they'd left behind: antler hooks for their clothes; her own quilted curtains; and beeswax seal around the door frames and windows. When she thought about Walter Mills roosting in the house Abraham and her brothers had built—the home she'd spent fifteen years nesting up—her vexation only increased. By God, she'd not put Abraham's dinner on the table until she'd said her piece.

When Abraham walked in and doffed his coat and hat, whistling like he had not a care in the world, she was ready for him.

She pointed to his seat at the table, "Abraham, come and sit."

That stopped his whistle. He turned from hanging his coat and scarf. "Is there something wrong, Mother?"

"There certainly is." Again, she motioned to his seat.

Abraham sat and folded his hands on the table, looking up at her.

She pulled out her chair and plopped down. "I've had a visit from Sarah. Walter reprimanded her for not turning over all of Eli's check."

"And why did she not?"

"Because they've had little meat on their table. You know Eli can't hunt, and Walter's keeping Edgar busy with papers and deeds. So she used some of it to buy a chicken in town. One little chicken."

"Dear, Lord. She knows the rules."

"I don't give a damn about the rules." Elizabeth saw Abraham wince at her words. If ever there was a time for swearing, this was it. "And you shouldn't either. Not when the health of our kin is threatened."

"I know what you're working up to, Mother."

"You're the only one who can get through to that man."

Abraham stiffened in his seat. "All of us, me included, agreed to abide by the rules of the product-sharing village."

"Don't you talk to me about rules."

"But we have them now, and we're all bound to them. I think it'd be best if you explained that to Sarah."

"I can't believe my ears. You're acting like Walter's rules are the Commandments from on high. Well, I'll not stand by and see him hurt my kin. You *will* talk to him about this matter."

Abraham pawed at his face with the back of his hand, like he was trying to figure out how to squirm out of a tight spot.

Elizabeth shook her finger at him. "Because if you prize Walter over me and my kin, you might as well pack up your bags and go live with him."

Abraham's eyes widened.

"I mean it. I'm at my wit's end. Something's got to change."

He bit at his lip and then nodded. "All right, Mother. I'll see what I can do."

"Good. You tell him to quit dividing us over his damn rules. Or he'll have a lot of angry people to answer to. Including me."

MERCY AND FORBEARANCE

FEBRUARY 1895

Walter and Abraham marched along the snow-packed perimeter road, sending the footfall of men's presence into the quiet, snow-laden woods—where fox and deer likely skittered away at their approach.

"Now look here, Walter," said Abraham, slowing his gait to match Mills' more leisurely pace. "You must take care to consider the well-being of the Hueys. Everyone knows death is knocking at their door."

"Oh, I comprehend that," Walter said, swinging his great head from side-to-side. "The family's misfortune weighs on me. I gave their circumstances careful consideration before taking action."

"Well, they—and Mrs. Clark and my Elizabeth—don't believe you're accounting for their misfortune."

"Then they don't understand all the factors I weighed. I mustn't appear to be making exceptions, for once that begins there's no good way to draw the line."

"But if drawing the line means visiting more sorrow on a family, when our vision is to take care of the old and ailing, then mightn't it be the wrong thing to do?"

"We've made provisions for them. Their medicine is supplied by the treasury. And Mrs. Clark helps Sarah nurse Eli and that sick girl of theirs."

"I tell you, sympathy is with them." Abraham tried to recall: How had Elizabeth put it? "You must avoid splitting our community for the sake of enforcing rules."

"And if I don't draw the line, those who believe all should be treated the same will call me lax and spineless."

Abraham couldn't help quickening his pace. "All the same, I think you need to find a better way to go about it."

"Our numbers are growing. I must enforce the rules. There's no way around that."

Confound it, thought Abraham. He's not taking my point. "Elizabeth says you need to draw the Hueys and Keplers into the fold.

And Mrs. Clark, too. Or their views toward you will harden into mistrust."

"I suppose you're right," said Walter, his breathing strained from the speeded-up gait. "You know them, and we must trust your fine wife's judgment in this matter."

"Why, I'm glad you understand," said Abraham, relaxing his forward-pitched stride into upright bearing. "Now, how might you bring them in?"

Mr. Mills trained his gaze straight ahead, puckering his brow in thoughtful contemplation.

"Hmm," began Mr. Mills, stopping and turning around to signal he wished to walk back.

Abraham turned and fell in alongside him.

Walter reached into his jacket for his handkerchief, swiped it under his dripping nose, and plunged it back into his pocket. "The building department will complete more of the village housing at the first thaw. The cabin next to yours has three rooms. Suppose we invited the Hueys to move into it when it's complete? They would be close to your Elizabeth and the Wright daughters, and Sarah could have the benefit of more assistance with Eli and the little girl."

"Elizabeth already expects to have them living next to us." Abraham feared this supposed concession would carry no weight with Elizabeth. "And they've got a much larger cabin now. They might not like moving into smaller quarters."

"I say, Abraham, can you think of another way to support them?"

"Well, you could apologize for the problem with the pension check and give them leave to keep part of it for the care of Eli and Evvie."

"No, Abraham," said Walter with nary a pause, "I can't do that. We've written our rules, and I must uphold them. Isn't it enough to move them to the village and help them pack and convey their goods?"

"Elizabeth says they're wary of you. I don't know how they'll take your gesture."

"Then you must intercede, Abraham. You must bring Elizabeth around to help convince them it is for their own good."

"I don't mind telling you, Elizabeth is going hard on me these days. I'm not sure I can recruit her to this cause."

"But you must." Walter thumped the air with a hand. "Don't you see how crucial this is? If order isn't upheld and our families not brought together in the village, we'll fail."

"Do you aim to get everybody into the village compound this season? Including yourself?"

"As many of us as we can. I've ordered the building department to procure supplies and move forward on village housing as soon as weather permits."

"Then what kind of concession will it appear if you want everybody moved to the village? The Hueys won't see it as any special consideration for them."

"They can be the first. And I understand Alva Kepler has been ailing these days. His family can be the next to move, and we'll help them resettle."

"I don't know," said Abraham, shaking his head. "They may not consider your offer a kind one."

"I can't help that." Walter swung around to face Abraham and scrunched his brow in appeal. "But I need your support now more than ever. We've come too far to turn our backs on our dream."

Abraham stopped and studied Walter's pleading eyes. "And what am I to tell Elizabeth and the Hueys? They're not disposed to trust you at this point."

"I fear that not everyone in our village grasps the goals we strive for. We must forge ahead and shape the colony into a true product-sharing village. Only by our success can we counter skepticism."

Abraham stiffened up. Walter just didn't seem to understand. "I'm sorry. I still have misgivings."

"You're my strong right arm, Abraham. Your help is crucial to our enterprise."

"I'm not sure I can undo the hard feelings you've roused."

"You're a preacher like none I've ever known. I've seen you stir the souls of men. Together we can make history. Don't you see that?"

"But at what cost? And do you imagine I've not tried in my way to bring some small justice to the working man?" But as God was his witness, he'd failed. And his failures dogged him still and tore at his very heart—for he knew he was right and that the corporations and politicians only cared about profiteering. He'd sought recompense for injured workers at the Furnace Company; instead, he'd brought the wrath of the company down on the men who'd joined his effort. All the sweat he'd poured into the '92 election was for naught. And even when he supported a strike against the Lumbering Company, the company used his allegiance to undermine the men and the strike. The capitalists had beaten him down. Had they won the battle? Or was forging a community under God's law his last chance to find some peace and justice in this crooked world?

Walter clapped both his hands on Abraham's shoulders. "Consider all that's at stake—we're poised to show the world there's a better way. I beseech you: Will you help bring the others into the fold?"

He wished for the success of their vision. And in Walter's steadfast eyes Abraham discerned the same gleaming certitude that had impressed him upon their first meeting. He recalled Walter's awe-inspiring lectures and the praise even the shilly-shallying reporters had heaped on him. With a sigh, he said, "I can try, but I cannot guarantee my pleas will meet with success. Meantime, you must do your part by showing the Hueys mercy and forbearance."

THE HUEYS MOVE

In the five weeks leading up to the Hueys' remove from their cabin, Elizabeth had visited her sister frequently, commiserating and helping her gather their belongings—first the summer clothes and canning supplies and then, when the worst of winter's chill passed, the heavy winter bedding. In the past week they'd turned their attention to packing the kitchen, leaving only the essentials for today. Now, with the last of their belongings loaded, Elizabeth joined the moving party in the back of the wagon, seated across from Sarah and Eli and beside Mrs. Clark.

Abraham and his son Elonzo jumped onto the wagon front, and Abraham swiveled around to face the party of four in the bed. "Everybody settled?"

Sarah and Eli stared across the wagon, ignoring Abraham. Mrs. Clark sat quietly, her head tilted back as if she preferred not to be bothered. Elizabeth nodded to Abraham.

Abraham turned to Elonzo and said, "Let's go."

Elizabeth, mindful of the kerosene lamp she clutched on her lap and the two trunks, rocker, and four chairs in the middle the wagon bed, spoke up. "But go easy."

Elonzo turned and checked the contents of the ample-bedded wagon. It was now the property of the Village Association but since it had belonged to Elonzo, he usually drove it. Earlier in the day, Elonzo had helped Edgar, the Hueys' eldest son, transport the three younger children to their new home, along with the family's clothing, kitchen supplies, table, and beds.

"Sure enough," said Elonzo, shaking the reins. Elizabeth wasn't close to Elonzo. He was Abraham's first son by Henrietta. When she'd married Abraham Elonzo was only ten, but she'd had little time to mother him for she was soon busy birthing and caring for the four sons she and Abraham had. Still, she considered Elonzo a decent man, though his eagerness to do Mills' bidding irked her.

The wagon trundled forward along the snowy, mud-rutted road, the horses' glossy backs steaming in the chill March air. Elizabeth, solemn in the face of Sarah's rare silence, caught her sister's eye across the wagon bed. Sarah smiled, tight-lipped, and, as the wagon reached a bend, turned her gaze back on their now deserted cabin.

Eli, who huddled beside Sarah, muffled a cough and pulled his woolen blanket tighter around his hunched shoulders. Sarah's eyes widened and latched onto her husband. His coughing turned to hacking, and he crumpled forward from the force of it. Sarah wrapped her arms around Eli, clutching him to her and rocking him.

On the driver's seat, Abraham and Elonzo sat facing forward, as if embarrassed by some intimacy not intended for their eyes.

Elizabeth, feeling helpless before Eli's misery, worried her hands on her lap. Finally, Eli's cough subsided, and he folded his arms over his racked chest and bowed his head in exhaustion.

Elizabeth could think of nothing to say. What words were there for this—a family leaving behind the cabin they'd called home for thirteen years? Walter and Abraham had said it would be best for them, that they would be nearer the others in the village and Sarah would have her own sister right next door. But Elizabeth couldn't shake the suspicion that Mills' motive for forcing the move had little to do with the Huey's well-being.

THE JOHN HENRY RANDALLS

APRIL 1895

Abraham burrowed his fists into his wool coat pockets and scuffed at the mat of last season's bedraggled grass. In front of him, eighty-some villagers mingled under the Hiawatha entry gate, their heads bobbing and weaving in lively conversation. Elizabeth stood beside him, mute and cross-armed.

When the wagon transporting the Randall family trundled into sight, the young people at the front of the crowd began to chant, "Sis, Boom, Bah! Hiawatha Colony! Sis, Boom, Bah!"

Jubilation infected the crowd, and the cheering spread to all its edges. Abraham self-consciously took up the chant and cast a sideways glance at Elizabeth; she kept on staring straight ahead with pursed lips. If he could have been certain no one would hear, he would've demanded, must you be so mule-faced? Instead, he turned away from her and angled for a view of the wagon.

Mud caked the wagon sides, no doubt acquired from crossing through the Sturgeon Hole Slough, and the four horses gleamed with sweat after their hilly journey from the Manistique train station. The wagon brimmed with its load of three trunks, suitcases, and nine people, including the seven members of the Randall family: a bespectacled John Henry Randall on the outside wagon seat; between him and the driver, his broad-faced wife, who clutched a black shawl tight about her shoulders; and in the wagon bed their two sons, awkward in suits they'd not yet grown into, and three daughters, their ages somewhere between fifteen and twenty, in comely long coats. Abraham and Elizabeth's son Lenniel accompanied the Randall party, sitting between two of the Randall daughters in the back of the wagon on a trunk. Abraham noticed Lenniel smiling, apparently relishing his position of prominence between two of the rosy-cheeked Randall daughters.

The crowd's chanting evoked good humor from everybody on the wagon: a close-mouthed grin from Dr. Randall; composed regard from Mrs. Randall; demure, eye-fluttering smiles from the young ladies; embarrassed chuckles from the gawky Randall boys; and head-held-high beams from Lenniel and the colony driver, Jonas Wright.

As the horses reached the colony entrance, Walter Mills stepped out and strode to the side of the horse team. Gripping the outside horse's bearing rein and holding his other hand before him, he looked up to Dr. Randall. "Greetings, Dr. Randall, our most hearty greetings."

"Thank you, and hello to all," called Dr. Randall, removing his hat and revealing a high forehead of receding gray-brown hair.

With a nod to Mrs. Randall Mills intoned, "My dear lady, I'm pleased to welcome you. And your children."

Mrs. Randall, a solid-limbed woman with tightly bound hair, nodded to Mills and scanned the crowd with a taut smile. "Thank you."

As Dr. and Mrs. Randall stood and stepped down from the wagon seat, cheers erupted from the crowd. The two Randall boys jumped over the wagon side and hustled to their parents' sides. Lenniel leaped off the wagon back, pulled down the wagon bed gate, and offered a hand to the ladies.

Walter hurried toward the Randalls, bowed to Mrs. Randall, and shook Dr. Randall's hand, all the time chattering away. Knowing Walter as he did, Abraham surmised his words were full of cheer and commendation.

Mills called, "Come one, come all," and led the crowd, with Dr. and Mrs. Randall at his side, along the path to the community building stocked with kettles of venison stew, biscuits, and fresh-baked squash pies.

Abraham and Elizabeth trailed along at the rear of the mostly young crowd. Abraham offered his arm, and Elizabeth accepted it, though as she did so she said, "I don't like this one bit. It's embarrassing."

Suffering blazes, since Walter had decided to install the Randalls in the Hueys cabin Abraham had endured nothing but peevishness and petulance from Elizabeth. He slowed his pace to open some distance from the jovial party and lowered his voice. "It's a matter of practicalities—and not the Randalls' fault. At least stay and meet them."

"Isn't that what I'm doing?" Elizabeth stiffened her grip on Abraham's arm. "All this fuss is unnecessary. And just rubs salt in the wound."

The crowd trooped into the community building, with Elizabeth and Abraham bringing up the rear. Mills escorted the Randalls onto the two-foot-high stage, and the colony members gathered around as the Randalls summoned their sons and daughters to join them.

Stepping to the front of the stage, Mills held his palms out to quiet the crowd. "It gives me great pleasure to introduce to you Dr. John Henry Randall, his capable wife, Charlotte, and their five lovely children." Mr. Mills motioned to the family members standing in a stiff line behind him on the stage.

The crowd broke into applause.

Mills beamed at Dr. and Mrs. Randall. Turning to the gathered and signaling for silence, he began. "The Randalls hardly need an introduction, but I will not be deprived of the opportunity to deliver one. As you know from the newspapers, last spring Dr. Randall joined Coxey's march to protest the blight of unemployment on our land. With the help of his able wife, who forged ahead and made advance arrangements, Dr. Randall helped bring a full army of unemployed men to the doorstep of our federal government. Think of it—marching all the way from Chicago to our capital."

Mr. Mills swept his hand toward Dr. and Mrs. Randall. "You have my great admiration for this feat."

Mills grinned as he waited for the cheering to subside. "Dr. Randall has found time for many noble political causes, including his work on behalf of the Greenback Party. He's a veteran of the War to Save the Union and a very learned man, having studied dentistry and practiced medicine. We're blessed to have his many skills brought to our cause."

Walter Mills turned and opened his arms to the Randalls. "We welcome all of you to Hiawatha Colony."

Dr. Randall stepped forward and grasped Walter Mills' hand. "Thank you, Mr. Mills." He faced the crowd. "We're so pleased to be joining you. I promise we'll do our utmost to be worthy of this wonderful welcome." John Randall glanced at his wife, whose smile had stiffened up like dried plaster. "Especially after we've rested from our journey."

"Yes, let's not wear our new members out too quickly," said Mills, turning to Mrs. Randall. "Please join us for some nourishment and then we'll have you and your belongings taken to your cabin."

The Randalls followed Walter Mills to the head of the line, where they spooned up stew and mounded fresh-baked biscuits onto their plates.

Lenniel took a place in line behind his parents. "Quite the excitement, isn't it?"

Abraham nestled up beside Elizabeth. "Oh, yes. Everyone seems pleased with the new arrivals."

Lenniel scanned the room. "I was hoping Alva or John would be here. Have you spoken with them yet, Father?"

"Well, no." Abraham raised his eyebrows at Elizabeth. "Maybe we'll call on them after we have some dinner."

Elizabeth turned and faced Lenniel, dismissing Abraham's remark. "I'm going to look in on Sarah and Eli."

Lenniel shot his mother a look of concern. "Are they still upset?"

Abraham glanced around, taking stock of the people near enough to overhear their conversation, and cleared his throat.

Elizabeth trained her eyes on Lenniel. "Of course they're still upset. And I don't blame them one bit."

Lenniel plunged his hands into his pockets. "I'm sorry to hear it, Mother. I wish there was something I could do."

"They should be allowed to keep their home," said Elizabeth.

"Now, Mother," said Abraham.

"Don't you 'now Mother' me," Elizabeth snapped. "You're not helping matters."

Abraham winced. "Best we not speak of this here."

Lenniel looked out over the gathering and turned to his mother. "Mother, I'd like to introduce you to Lottie Randall. I was telling her all about you on the ride here, and she wants to meet you."

Elizabeth glared at Abraham before responding to Lenniel. "I suppose so. Let me get some food in me first."

Confound it, thought Abraham, must she be so ornery? But he'd not express his feelings in front of their son. Elizabeth seemed intent on blaming the Randolphs for something they'd had no say in. And he hadn't the slightest idea of how to smooth things over. He felt like he was watching a runaway wagon careen down a hill.

COMINGS AND GOING

April 1895

After lingering over a plate of food, Elizabeth consented to meet the Randalls: first Mrs. Randall—"It's been such a long journey, Mrs. Byers; it's wonderful you've all readied a cabin for us"—then Lottie—"I'm delighted to meet you; I hope you'll teach me how to make that wonderful pie crust your son's been telling me about"—and Dr. Randall—"What remedy would you recommend for insect bites, Mrs. Byers? You must tell me what plants to acquire for my practice." Elizabeth had to force amiability into her manner, for she was in no mood to face the newcomers. After managing a round of polite conversation, she excused herself and told Abraham she was off to visit Sarah and Eli.

"You won't come with me to see John and Alva?" Abraham asked.

"Not on that devilish errand I won't," she said.

Elizabeth didn't have far to go, for the Hueys had moved to the cabin next to theirs, only a few buildings from the community hall.

"A lot of to-do. That's what it was," she told Sarah, Eli, and Lucinda Clark as she settled at the kitchen table with them. "And Mills carried on like it was St. Peter himself coming to live among us."

"Humph," said Sarah, "I have no stomach for that man's hoity-toity ways."

"Nothing but a showboater," sputtered Eli, suppressing a cough.

"Oh, dear," Sarah said, turning to her husband, "why don't you get some rest?"

"I'll just settle in the rocker," Eli said, waving her off. He rose from the table and shuffled to the rocker, the still-fresh floorboards creaking under his tall, gaunt frame.

Sarah and Lucinda watched Eli's every step, checking their conversation until he installed himself in the rocker and wrapped a blanket about his shoulders.

Lucinda leaned over her forearms toward Elizabeth. "I've made a decision."

Sarah closed her eyes hard and jerked her head to the side, as if struck by some pain.

"There, there," Lucinda said, patting Sarah's hand. "It might be the best thing I can do for you."

"What decision?" asked Elizabeth.

Lucinda straightened in her chair. "I'm leaving the colony."

"Oh, my," said Elizabeth, pulling her head back in surprise. "Does anyone else know?"

"No one outside of us. But I aim to tell Walter Mills myself."

Sarah pressed a hand to her cheek. "How I wish I could be there."

"No, it's best if I deliver the message alone. I wish to speak freely, without concern about embarrassing the man."

"You're courageous, Lucinda." Elizabeth shook her head. "I'm about out of patience myself at my husband—doing that man's bidding as he is."

"Someone needs to stand up to Mills and his pompous ways." Lucinda folded her hands on the table before her. "I'll tell him in no uncertain terms I do not share his ideals. When he can force a family with two ailing members out of their own home and turn around and give those Randalls the same home shortly thereafter—well, how dare he claim to treat us all as equals!"

Eli thumped his cane. "God bless you, Lucinda."

Sarah tugged the folds out of her rumpled dress sleeves. "The nerve of that man."

"I'm so outraged," said Elizabeth, "I'm about to tell Abraham to go live with Mills if he cares so much for his ideas."

"Well, I won't spare him my observations of his conduct," said Lucinda. "I believe he planned all along to put the Randalls in Eli and Sarah's home. If living in the village is so wonderful, why in the world couldn't we have stayed where we were, and the Randalls moved into this place?"

"That's just what I asked Abraham," said Elizabeth. "It makes no sense at all."

"It's to multiply our hardship," Sarah said.

Eli swung his cane around at the milled lumber walls of their new home. "Nothing but ramshackle."

Elizabeth said, "And now Mills wants Alva and John to leave their cabins."

"I believe he means to throw his weight around," said Lucinda. "I'll not countenance his whims any longer. I only hope my departure can make some impression on him and the others who abide his ways."

Elizabeth sighed. "I'll miss you, Lucinda, but Lord knows that man deserves a tongue lashing—and a shock to his system."

A DEVILISH ERRAND

APRIL 1895

As the welcoming party broke up, Abraham invited Lenniel to accompany him on his visits to Alva and John.

"No, with me being an officer," Lenniel said, "they might feel outnumbered. I'll leave it to you, Father."

"Your mother called it a 'devilish errand.'"

Lenniel chuckled in awkward amusement. "I don't envy you, I can say that."

Abraham set out on his walk through the woods, gloomy at the unpleasantness of the task before him. Yes, he'd agreed with Walter that he was the best man for the job—and that neither Alva nor John would welcome Walter in their homes—but he expected his entreaties to meet resistance.

Which one should he visit first, he pondered, training his gaze on the fir-needled trail as he neared the fork in the path. Alva. Yes, he'd call on Alva and Ann first. It was John who'd be more difficult to persuade. Perhaps if he could convince Alva, things would go down easier with John. And since Alva was recovering from the pneumonia and stayed close to home most days, he'd likely find him in—and not overly spirited.

As he neared Alva and Ann's cabin the forest thinned and opened onto a grassy clearing. It dawned on Abraham that he was empty-handed. Elizabeth always brings something, he thought. Looking around, he took out his pocketknife and cut some of the hardwood lilies and Dutchman's breeches at wood's edge and formed them into a rounded bouquet.

"Ann, Alva," he called as he nudged the door open.

Alva looked up from the stove, where he knelt stirring the fire, and brushed his sooty, thick-fingered hands on his wool trousers. "Hello, Abraham. Come from the party?"

"Yes, the Randalls are here, safe and sound." Abraham eased the door closed behind him. "Here, Ann, I picked a few flowers for you."

Ann sat at the table before a lump of dough, some of it formed into biscuit-sized rounds on her baking sheet. Standing up, she brushed a forearm against her brow, revealing a sinewy arm. With her usual matter-of-fact flatness, she said, "Well, how nice."

Abraham smiled up at her slender face as he handed her the flowers. Ann was only a few inches taller than Abraham, but her no-nonsense manner and near-constant motion made her a commanding presence.

"Your children seemed to enjoy the gathering," said Abraham.

Alva threw a log on the fire, clanked the stove door shut, and sat at the head of the table, not once looking at Abraham.

"You know young people," said Ann, arranging the flowers in a pitcher. "Always looking for a chance for each other's company."

"Where's Lizzy?" asked Alva.

"Oh," said Abraham. He'd not been invited to sit but summoned the pluck to do so anyway. "She's looking in on Sarah and Eli."

Alva watched his wife sit back down and pinch off a lump of dough. He asked, "Got something on your mind, Abraham?"

He won't make this easy, thought Abraham. "Well, you know village homes are being readied now for all of us."

Alva narrowed his eyes. "Excepting the Randalls."

Abraham studied his folded hands. "Yes, well, that's only temporary."

"I know what you're here for," said Alva.

"Yes, I expect you do." Abraham moistened his lips. "Well, are you willing to move into the village home that's been prepared for you?"

Alva glanced at his wife and swiped a hand under his nose. "Hate to give up our nice log home for a drafty shack."

"You know the plan is to face those houses with sturdy brick once we're able to manufacture them," said Abraham.

"When'll that be?"

"I can't say, Alva. It depends on the colony finances."

"I don't like this," said Alva, again looking to his wife. "Neither does my family."

"I know. I understand it's hard to give up a home." Abraham looked back and forth between Alva and Ann. "It still doesn't sit well with Elizabeth, us having left our cabin. But we're all bound to the village agreement. I believe in the long run this will work out for the good of us all."

Alva crossed his arms over this chest. "Some other highfalutin' folk going to take over our cabin?"

"No," said Abraham without hesitation. "No one else will be residing in this cabin."

Alva pursed his brow in thoughtfulness. "We have any choice in this?"

Abraham widened his nostrils. "I don't believe so, Alva."

Ann's hands froze, and she stared at her lump of dough. Alva hunched forward and dropped his folded hands between his knees.

"I know you've been ailing, Alva, and are not up to full strength," said Abraham, keeping his voice low. "We'll have some of the young people come around to help you organize and pack."

Neither Alva nor Ann spoke. The fire crackled in the stove. As Abraham stood, he could not help looking around at the walls made of solid logs he'd helped hew so many years ago. Alva and Ann had fashioned the cabin into a nice home, with a roomy kitchen and cozy parlor. I hope Walter is right, he thought, that all will end well, and these hardships will lead us to a better place.

Abraham walked to the door and gripped its handle. "I'm sorry," he said and slipped out.

Melancholy dogged Abraham on his walk to John's cabin, and the no-see-ums swarming about his head only magnified his perturbation. Yes, his meeting with Alva and Ann had gone as well as could be expected. And Walter would be relieved Alva had consented without too much grumbling. But it was a thankless task, pressing the Keplers to conform to the agreement to move to the village. And, if he considered Elizabeth's position, it was worse than thankless: It was downright disruptive, putting him and his own wife at odds.

I wish she'd understand it's for the greater good of the village, he thought. Here she is blaming Walter for alienating her brothers and sister, while she herself turns against me. By God, we've all signed on for this; it's past time to protest the terms. I for one won't turn away from our vision now. We're building a Christian community, and the Lord's way is not always the easiest path. I just need to help us all get over this hump.

Through the bare tree branches, Abraham could see smoke rising from the chimney of John and Elvila's cabin. Their home in the middle of a cleared stretch, silhouetted against the dusky sky, looked gloomy to him. Or perhaps he was only considering the task before him, for he knew John and Elvila cherished their cabin and its out-of-the-way location on the edge of the settlement.

"Hello," Abraham said as he poked his head in the door.

"Uncle Abe, dear me," said a sleepy-eyed Elvila, snapping alert in the rocker. "I wasn't expecting anyone, with the party and all."

"Is John about?" asked Abraham.

"No, he's off fishing."

"At Aldrich Lake?"

"Yup, should be back soon."

"Well, it's getting late," said Abraham. "I'll just head down that way and see if I can run into him."

Abraham struck out on the path, thinking he might as well get this over with once and for all. Halfway between the cabin and the lake, Abraham spied John trudging toward him. "Hello, John," he called, speeding up. "How was the fishing?"

John shifted his head from side-to-side, straining to see Abraham through the hardwood and fir trees lining the curving path. "Oh, Abraham," he said. "Caught a few bass."

Abraham closed the distance between himself and John to ten paces and asked, "Mind if I walk back to your cabin with you?"

"No," said John. "You come looking for me?"

"Yes, Elvila told me where you were." Abraham fell in alongside John on the trail.

"You meet those Randalls?"

"Yes, they arrived just hours ago. I only had a chance for a quick introduction. They're tired from their trip."

"What're they like?"

"They seem like decent folk. And it'll be good having a doctor and dentist among us."

"I suppose. Don't like the idea of somebody poking around in my mouth though."

"I'm sure he won't be forcing himself on anybody."

They plodded on, not speaking, as color leached out of the dimming forest, turning its green and brown tones to shades of gray.

Abraham broke the silence. "I've come on a particular errand, John."

"Oh, what's that?" John asked, staring stonily ahead.

"Housing is ready in the village for you. Will you and Elvila consent to move there?"

"No, Abraham. We will not."

"But Alva and Ann and all their children will be moving."

"I don't care what Alva or any of the others will be doing. I'm not moving."

Abraham righted himself from a stumble on the lumpy ground. "But, John, we need more land for crops. Here it is end of April. We must get as much land cultivated as soon as possible."

Still, John gazed ahead. "You can use the land around my cabin. But I'm not budging. Happen to like my home just where it is."

"You're going against the agreement, John, the one you consented to when you deeded your land and signed on as a member of the association."

"I see no reason to move into the village. You know I don't attend the meetings. The Village Association is doing just fine without me."

Abraham drew in and released a deep breath. "John, I'll not argue with you. I'll just ask once more: Will you, in accordance with colony rules, move to the village?"

"No, Abraham, I will not. And I'll thank you not to ask me again."

ONE LAST REQUEST

MAY 1895

Abraham steered clear of Walter for two full days while he pondered how to rectify John's refusal to move. But puzzle as he might, he could contrive no remedy. As he settled at the breakfast table that morning, he decided he mustn't leave the matter hanging any longer. He'd report back to Walter later today; it'd be a welcome relief to get it off his chest.

Elizabeth rounded up Goldie and Artie and plopped bowls of cornmeal porridge down before them. Upon lifting his spoon Abraham noticed that the usual dollop of molasses—a little indulgence of his—was missing from his bowl. He shot Elizabeth a questioning look.

Nestling into her chair across the table from him, she said, "Get your own molasses if you must."

Ornery as ever, thought Abraham, sinking his spoon into the bland porridge and swallowing it down. Elizabeth hadn't asked how his visits with Alva and John had gone, nor had he volunteered the news. She's likely heard from Sarah or John and Elvila themselves, he figured. Besides, why should he invite more rancor into his marriage? As things already stood, Elizabeth only grudgingly consented to cook for him.

Elizabeth reached over to Artie and tugged the folds out his bib. "Did you find any wintergreen leaves yesterday?"

So, it'd be the same thing all over again—her ignoring him at the table and chattering away with the children about some trifle or other. It'd gotten so bad Abraham had started working extra shifts with the livestock or visiting at the homes of his sons, which is what he did this overcast, breezy May day.

"Father," explained Lenniel, as they stood side by side on Lenniel's porch, "Walter *has* been expecting to hear from you."

"Suppose I'm being foolish," said Abraham, studying the various-sized clapboard houses lining the other side of the compound, "but I was hoping John would come around."

"He's a stubborn one, he is," said Lenniel.

"Yes, I believe the good Lord could come down to attest to the infallibility of our plan and John would stand before Him and say, 'Thank you, Jesus, but I don't care for it.'"

Lenniel chuckled. "Yes, that would be Uncle John."

"Well, I guess I better be getting over to Walter's."

It'd been easy for Abraham to avoid Walter since the Randalls had arrived, for Walter'd been spending most of his spare time over the last few days with the newcomers, no doubt getting re-acquainted with Dr. Randall and instructing the family on the village's ways. But, as Abraham well knew, Walter expected to hear how his efforts to persuade Alva and John had fared. No doubt word was circulating among the Kepler elders, but Abraham suspected none of them had ventured to deliver the bad news. In fact, they preferred to give Walter Mills wide berth.

It being late morning, Abraham surmised Walter would've finished directing the department heads on the day's work priorities and would, according to his custom, have retreated to his desk. Abraham strolled the short distance between Lenniel's home in the village compound to his old cabin, past the dozen-some men cultivating the potato, carrot, and turnip fields.

"Goodness, Abraham," said Nettie upon greeting Abraham at the door. "How is your Elizabeth? It has been *such* a long time since I've seen her."

"Fine, fine." Abraham was in no mood for Nettie's shameless prying. "Is Walter about?"

"Working in his study," she said.

"Well, I'll just go on up." Abraham stepped around Nettie and mounted the stairs to Walter's bedroom study—the very room that had once been his and Elizabeth's bedroom. Visiting his old home always stirred up a stew of sentiments: nostalgia for the cozy evenings he and Elizabeth had shared around the stove; pride over the fine workmanship of the window and door frames; and wonder mixed with discomposure at having the famous Walter Mills under this very roof.

"Good day, Abraham," said Walter, swiveling around in his desk chair and looping an arm over the chair back. "Fine planting weather we're having, don't you agree?"

"Why, yes, I see you've got the plows busy at the compound garden."

Walter nodded. "As I've learned well from you, we must get the crops in at the first blush of spring."

Abraham sat down in the red and gold-striped chair Walter kept by the window. "I've spoken with Alva and John."

Walter raised his eyebrows. "Yes?"

"Alva said they'll move, but John refuses."

"Oh, my," said Walter, leaning forward and bracing hands over knees. "This is not good news. Not good news at all."

"I pressed him, but he refused. And he asked me not to bring it up again."

"But we must get that land into production."

"He said we could use the land around his cabin."

"It's not just a matter of the land," said Walter, stroking his frizzy mutton chop. "It's how we're supposed to live, with all of us in the village."

Abraham nestled his back into the chair's bracing curve. "I don't mind telling you, that argument doesn't go down well when the Randalls are put up in the Huey cabin."

"But the Hueys' land isn't all cleared. It's Alva and John's land we need for planting."

"I don't know what to tell you," said Abraham, gripping the smooth upholstered arms of the chair. "John refuses to budge."

"I feared it might come to this. I asked my attorney in Chicago for an opinion on the matter." Walter drew a paper from the corner of his desk and, poking his glasses up on the bridge of his nose, read from it. "'In view of the terms of the incorporation agreement, I believe it is defensible to enforce a move to the compound.'"

"Enforce?" Abraham's mouth parched up: Elizabeth would not take well to this news. "And how do you suggest doing that?"

"We'll bring a wagon around and load up the family and their belongings." Walter returned the letter to its stack on his desk. "Now, John and Elvila should be informed in advance. How shall we manage that?"

Abraham brought a hand to his brow. "It pains me to think of the strife this will cause."

"We mustn't shirk our responsibility to the village. We must secure its future."

"This message will not sit well with John and Elvila," said Abraham, rubbing the stiffness at the back of his neck.

"They must be told. It wouldn't be right to force the action without their foreknowledge."

Abraham tried a different tactic. "Couldn't they and perhaps Alva and Ann stay in their cabins? All the new arrivals could take housing in the village, and building outside the compound could be prohibited going forward."

"I fear not, Abraham. As President, it's my duty to carry out our vision." Walter bent toward Abraham with the sureness of a sleuth who'd cornered his man. "And I must ask you to get behind it, too."

"Why, of course I'm behind it," Abraham said, perturbed at Walter's rebuke. "But not everybody else is, and that concerns me."

Walter eased back into his chair. "I know your intentions are honorable, and that you care about the future of the whole endeavor. This summer will be a critical season. We must act with dispatch to build the village and prepare for the winter."

Abraham stiffened at Walter's accusatory tone. "Anyone who's spent a winter here grasps the necessity of careful preparation."

"Then it's imperative we get everyone rallied around the cause."

"I'm not sure you're going about it the best way."

"My mind's made up," said Walter. "Now, which of us should tell John about the move?"

"I'm sorry, Walter, but I prefer not to convey this news."

Walter smoothed a hand over the lawyer's paper. "As your president, I'll ask you to shoulder this one last request. And then I'll manage the rest of the business myself."

Abraham knew this to be an order. He could only offer a grimaced nod.

Leaning over his clasped hands, Walter said, "And I advise you to see to it straight away."

Abraham could do naught but summon his resolve and hike to John and Elvila's cabin. He found John out front skinning a rabbit. "May I have a word with you, John?"

John put down his knife and wiped his blood-streaked hands with a rag. "You know you don't have to ask to speak to me, Abraham."

Abraham hitched his thumbs over his pants' pocket corners and adjusted his shoulders to sturdy wideness. "I'm sorry to be the one to tell you, but you and Elvila must move to the village."

John narrowed his eyes at Abraham. "Who says?"

"Walter, on the advice of his attorney."

John looked away and shook his head, as if a long-held suspicion had finally been confirmed. Turning back to him, he asked, "And you, Abraham, what do you have to say?"

"I know this is a great sacrifice for you," said Abraham, dipping his head, "but I believe you'll come to appreciate that it's for the good of all."

John took up his knife. "Then I have nothing more to say to you."

As Abraham tromped back through the woods, he fretted over Elizabeth's likely reaction. Should he tell her about the attorney's opinion or his talk with John? The last time they'd discussed the matter of everyone moving to the village, he'd alluded to the Village Association agreement. In view of that, perhaps he needn't make an issue of this business about the Chicago attorney. Maybe he should just let events take their course and wait for everyone to get over this unpleasant juncture. Once all the Keplers are living together in the village, he reasoned, Elizabeth can more easily visit with them, and maybe they'll all settle into each other's company. Yes, he decided, it'd be best not to say anything to her. He'd delivered Walter's message to John and now he'd wash his hands of the matter.

Over the next few days Abraham bided his time, staying away from home for long stretches at a time, visiting the cabins of his sons with more frequency than they or their wives were accustomed to. He realized the move would take place in a matter of days, but he preferred the unfettered ignorance of not knowing to the aggravation of anticipating its unwelcome undertaking.

SHOWDOWN

May 1895

After Elizabeth packed Goldie off to school and Artie to the children's room, she set about her chores, all the time agonizing over the unpleasantness between herself and Abraham. How she hated the atmosphere in their home, all clotted with ill will and stifling to the point of distraction. He could sashay in any time, she figured, since he doesn't keep predictable hours anymore. No, she opposed spending time with Abraham—she could hardly countenance his blind allegiance to Mr. Mills—so she resolved to spend some of the morning at the Huey household, as she'd done with fair regularity of late.

"We're up here," her sister Sarah called from the bedroom Lucinda Clark shared with the Hueys' nine-year-old daughter.

Elizabeth traipsed up the stairs to the small corner bedroom. Two narrow cots lined opposite walls, with a tall beech dresser separating them. Sarah perched on Lucinda's bed, with her back to the room's one window, watching Lucinda fold her powder-blue linen dress into a neat square and pat it into her traveling trunk.

Seating herself next to Sarah, Elizabeth looked up at Lucinda. "I hate to see you leave us. And I don't imagine it'll be easy for the children either."

The mention of any of the many trials dogging Sarah's family usually provoked her to tears. Now she tried to restrain herself, cupping a hand over her nose and mouth.

"I insist the whole family visit me in Peoria when everyone is fit enough to travel," said Lucinda, looking down on Sarah with puppy-soft eyes. "For I shall miss all of you."

"Oh," Sarah said, "how can we travel with Eli and Evvie ailing so?"

"Now, Sarah," said Lucinda, "you must think of the time when everyone will be well. You're a wonderful wife and mother, and the best of nurses."

Sarah sniffed back her tears and pressed her lips together in determination.

Elizabeth asked Lucinda, "How did your talk with Mr. Mills go?"

"I don't believe he comprehended my message."

Snapping her shoulders and head to statue-like stiffness, Sarah said, "He's an unfeeling monster—that's what he is."

Elizabeth asked, "What did he say about you leaving?"

"A great deal of tripe." The petite Lucinda braced her hands over her chest, imitating a puffed-up Mr. Mills. "'Oh, Mrs. Clark, I hate to see you leave us when we are on the verge of success . . . But you must do what your feelings dictate . . . No, Mrs. Clark, I do not see the injustice of carrying out village rules.'"

"Oh, my," said Elizabeth. "I wonder how he'll explain you leaving to the others."

"And the money she won't be donating," added Sarah.

"I expect he'll make light of it," said Lucinda, lifting a stack of white blouses from the dresser drawer and placing them in her trunk.

Elizabeth asked her, "Who's driving you to the train station?"

"Elonzo. But not until tomorrow. He said he'd be moving John and Elvila today."

Elizabeth widened her eyes. "Today?"

"Oh," said Sarah, a smug smile overtaking her milk-white cheeks, "Elvila told me John won't be allowing a move."

"There's no telling what that Mills will do," said Elizabeth, standing. "I'm going over to John and Elvila's right now. I've waited too long to speak my piece."

Elizabeth hurried through the woods, her forward pitch propelling her over the uneven ground and rattling her lean frame. This whole scheme has gone too far, she thought; I'll not stand for any more of this foolishness. The Hueys and Keplers must move so we can all live in the village? But the Randalls can take up the Hueys' cabin? No, I've had my fill of Mills' hypocrisy.

She hastened up the path to John and Elvila's home and flung the door open. John leaped up from his seat at the table, shotgun in hand, and Elvila stiffened with alarm.

"Oh, Lizzie," said John, "thought it'd be somebody else."

"I know," Elizabeth said, her wiry limbs atingle with outrage. "I heard they're wanting to move you today."

"They'll do no such thing." John sat down again, leaning his shotgun against his inner thigh and facing the door.

"No," said Elvila, folding her arms over her ample bosom, "I won't leave my home."

"Well, I'm here to lend my voice." Elizabeth marched up to the table and sat down beside Elvila.

The three of them, somber and sullen in their pact, settled around the table, forsaking talk as mere contrivance. Only the subdued whoosh of springtime breeze and the dee-dee-dee of chickadees in the boughs overhead reached through the cabin walls.

Soft footfalls approached. John grabbed his shotgun and jumped up. The door pushed open.

"John, Elvila?" Abraham called, easing in through the half-opened door and catching sight of Elizabeth. "Mother, I've been looking all over for you."

John lowered his shotgun but stood facing Abraham, his head stretched forward in an unspoken question.

Elizabeth regarded Abraham from her chair. "What for?"

"Well," said Abraham, "I, I don't want you in the middle of this."

Elizabeth's lower lip twitched. "Middle of what?"

Abraham glanced at John. "The move."

"There'll be no move," John said.

"I'll not argue with you, John," said Abraham, gripping the door's edge. "I only want Elizabeth to come away with me."

Elizabeth eyed Abraham, rumpling her chin into firmness. She already *was* smack dab in the middle of this, and that was just where she wanted to be.

"Lizzie," John said, easing down into his chair and facing her. "I don't want you mixed up in this. I can manage it myself."

Elizabeth swallowed hard. "I prefer to stay here with you."

"No, Lizzie," said Elvila, "you must do as John says."

Elizabeth looked at John.

"Go. It'll be easier that way," said John.

Elizabeth braced her hands on the table, pushed herself up, and turned to John and Elvila. "You know I stand with you."

John crinkled his cheek into a muted smile, and Elvila patted her hand.

Elizabeth marched toward Abraham, who backed out through the door and let her pass.

Without a word, Abraham closed the door and headed for the path across the clearing. Elizabeth followed three feet behind, lengthening the distance as they neared wood's edge.

"I'll keep my watch from here," she announced, stopping beside a stump.

Abraham swung around. "What's the sense in that?"

"I'm standing with my brother and Elvila. I won't back down."

"Mother, this has gone on too long—this strife between us."

"What's gone on too long is the foolishness of this village notion."

"You don't understand. It's for the good of all of us we're doing these things."

"I understand that Walter and the Randalls don't have to live in the village, but the Hueys and Keplers do."

Abraham glared at Elizabeth. "You're as stubborn as that brother of yours."

"You're as hardhearted as that Mills." A lump pushed up in Elizabeth's throat. She swallowed it down and plopped onto the stump, facing John and Elvila's cabin some two hundred feet away.

Abraham stood stock still beside Elizabeth. "I want you to come home with me."

"I'm staying right here."

"You shouldn't watch this."

"That's not for you to decide." Elizabeth trained her gaze on John and Elvila's cabin and hunched forward on the stump, her mind a hive of misery—about the whole village scheme, about how it was tearing up the lives of her kin, and about her own misery. Here she was in the midst of her sons and brothers and sister, with her husband of thirty-one years, and she'd never felt more alone. She could hardly bear Abraham's presence of late. Who was this man she called husband? He'd turned his back on her—and the spirit of togetherness that'd prompted them to start this settlement so many years ago. And now he'd abandoned her, her brother, and his own niece. No, she'd not budge, not if she had to sit there all day.

It was nary a half hour later when she caught sight of a wagon rounding the bend of the perimeter road. Elonzo Byers drove the wagon, Walter Mills sat at his side, and two of Mills' underlings, Charles Bernardo and Emil Forberg, held positions opposite each other in the wagon bed. Elonzo pulled the horses up in front of John and Elvila's cabin, and Walter Mills climbed down from the wagon seat, signaling the others to join him. The three gathered around him in a tight circle, and Mills spoke to them, gesticulating with his arms like a general assembling his troops.

As Elizabeth studied the scene Abraham stood at her side, glancing back and forth between her and the Mills' party. "Mother, please, let's go home now."

"You can go," she said. "I'm staying."

The front door of the cabin opened. John Kepler stepped out, closed the door behind him, and took up a position on the porch. He tucked his shotgun in the crook of his bent arm and planted his feet wide apart, straightening his tall frame up stiff as a post.

Mills stopped talking, and the foursome turned around and faced John.

With open palms, Mills commanded his party to hold back, and he advanced toward John.

John gripped his shotgun and raised it up, aiming it at Mills' footsteps.

Mills stopped, thirty feet shy of John.

Elizabeth couldn't hear the words John and Mills exchanged, but she saw Mills place his hand behind his back and flap it in some signal to the other men, who started walking down the road, as if to leave. What's going on, Elizabeth wondered. Are they backing down?

Mills took a step closer to John, who inched his shotgun up. As Mills stopped and raised his hands in a sign of surrender, John lowered the shotgun. Mills bounced his head in imploring jerks. John eyed him but did not speak.

The three men who had walked down the road turned and looped back toward the cabin, trotting toward it from the backside.

John can't see what they're up to, thought Elizabeth. They'll get in through the back door. I must warn him.

She stood and waved her arms at John.

But if John saw Elizabeth he made no sign of it. Mills, who blocked John's view, kept up his appeals.

Elizabeth lifted her skirt and, stepping high, started running toward John.

Abraham grabbed her arm, pulled her backside against his chest, and wrapped both his arms around her, pinning her arms to her sides. "No, Mother, don't. Don't get in the middle of this. John's got a shotgun."

"Let me go." She squirmed but couldn't break his hold.

The cabin door burst open and John swung around. Charles Bernardo, a brawny six-footer, stood in the doorway gripping Elvila by the upper arm.

John yelled, "Unhand her."

Mills ran up behind John, wrestled the down-turned shotgun away from him, and flung it aside.

Charles released Elvila and lunged for John, and Elonzo and Emil bolted out from inside the house. John stiffened his arms against Charles, struggling to cast him aside, but Elonzo and Emil pounced on him, seizing his long arms. The three men restrained John and dragged him in erratic jerks to the wagon.

Elizabeth stomped her heels against Abraham's boots, but he only clutched her harder.

"No," Elvila screamed at the men dragging her husband away. She rushed toward him.

Mills ran toward Elvila and shoved her back. She careened into the door frame, her head jerking like a rag doll's. As she righted herself, Mills grabbed her by the arm. She tried to wrench free, but he held her tight and yanked her to the wagon.

The other three men lifted the struggling John up onto the wagon bed. They forced him down onto the bed seat, roped his arms behind his back, and tied him to the wagon side.

"Dear God," said Abraham.

Elizabeth felt his grip on her loosen. She broke free and bounded forward.

"Let my husband go," Elvila wailed, flailing against Mills' hold on her. Charles jumped down from the wagon back, wrapped his arms around Elvila's waist, and helped Walter hoist her onto the wagon bed. Her dress hiked up to her knees, exposing her kicking legs. At the sight of Elvila maltreated and dishonored like that Elizabeth boiled over. "Stop," she screamed, bounding ahead.

Mills turned and saw her. He swept his arm at Elonzo and called, "Hurry."

Elonzo hopped down from the wagon bed and rushed to the wagon front, lurching over his bad leg. He clambered up to the driver's seat, shook the reins, and urged the horses forward.

"No," Elizabeth hollered. She'd gotten no closer than a hundred feet. Crumpling to her knees as the wagon trundled away, she exploded into sobs and shook her fists in the air.

She felt Abraham's arms encircling her quivering shoulders.

"It's not right, what they're doing," she cried, trying to break free from Abraham.

He held her tight, nestled his head against her shoulder blade, and rocked her in his arms. "Oh, Mother, I'm so sorry. Please, please, forgive me."

She felt her heart soften and allowed her tears to flow. This was what she'd longed for—the embrace of a loving husband.

SCENE OF A DISTURBANCE

MAY 1895

Abraham cradled Elizabeth in his arms until her tears and trembling subsided, and in those moments, he knew no one was more worthy of his respect than his dear, wise wife.

"Come now," said Abraham, turning her face to his and caressing her moist cheeks. "Let's see what we can do for John and Elvila."

Abraham helped Elizabeth to her feet. He tucked her hand around his forearm and folded his palm over it. Side by side they hiked through the soggy woods, under skies curdled with grey clouds. As they shuffled along, loamy scents of decomposing needles and fresh mushrooms rose from the forest floor.

"I should've never consented to move from our home," said Elizabeth, staring straight ahead. "That was the start of all this trouble."

"No, Mother, I was the one that urged that on you. And I'm ashamed now for everything I did that led to this."

Elizabeth said nothing, but Abraham felt her grip on his arm tighten.

When they reached their cabin, Abraham led Elizabeth to their bedroom. He sat on the bed and watched her pour a pitcher of water into the wash basin, splash her red cheeks, and cup water over her swollen eyes. She sat down at her dresser and let down her graying brown hair. When she lifted her brush Abraham went to her, took the brush, and stroked it through her glossy hair. She allowed him a good twenty strokes, took the brush, swirled her hair into a loose twist, and trussed it up at the back of her head.

"I'm ready now," she said.

They walked across the compound to the house that'd been prepared for John and Elvila. But it was empty—of people, of furniture, of any signs of life. They walked to the other side of the compound, to Alva and Ann Kepler's new home, and found Ann there by herself, sitting in a rocker amidst the clutter of their moved kitchen table and boxed-up supplies.

"We're looking for Elvila and John," Elizabeth said.

The rail-thin Ann glared at Abraham. "I'll not speak of them with Abraham here."

Ann's words took Abraham's breath away. He stepped forward and faced Ann. "I'm sorry for what's happened. I was wrong."

"We only want to help," said Elizabeth. "Where are they?"

Ann looked by turns at Elizabeth and Abraham. "I'll not say until you give me your word you won't interfere."

"You have my word," said Elizabeth. "I only want them back in their home."

With squinted eyes and clamped mouth, Ann studied Abraham.

He nodded, "I'm of the same mind."

"They've gone with Alva to get the sheriff," Ann said. "Frank Dodge is driving them in."

The Sheriff—Good Lord, the colony's problems will surely multiply. Where will it all end? But Frank's involvement didn't surprise Abraham; his property lay just outside the settlement, and he'd never taken to the colony.

Elizabeth nodded to Ann. "We saw with our own eyes what happened."

Ann smoothed her hands over her arms. The house was chill, and the stove untended. "Elvila's pretty bruised up."

"Mills sure got rough with her," said Elizabeth. "Couldn't believe my eyes."

"Frank says they can't get away with it. Or with taking our cabins apart."

Elizabeth leaned back on her heels as if buffeted by a gust. "Taking the cabins apart?"

Dear God, thought Abraham. He'd not bargained on that. But he held his tongue, knowing his words would count for naught.

Ann tightened her jaw and jutted out her chin. Blinking back tears, she blurted out, "Frank saw it. First thing this morning, before they moved John and Elvila, Mills and some of the others pried the logs on our cabin apart."

Just as dusk settled on the village Sheriff Carr and his under-sheriff drove their wagon into the middle of the village compound. They'd obviously stopped first at Mills' cabin, for Walter Mills sat on the wagon-bed bench, arms crossed, and head held high.

Abraham and Elizabeth watched the events from their porch. All the other village houses emptied too, and the families formed buzzing clutches in front of each other's homes, with the parties dividing into Mills' supporters and detractors. But Abraham and Elizabeth stood by themselves on their porch, for Abraham knew he wasn't welcome among the Kepler sympathizers—nor did he wish to commiserate with Walter's family or the newcomers who supported him.

Sheriff Carr and his undersheriff, all earnest and businesslike, stood near their wagon conferring. Motioning his undersheriff to stay put, Sheriff Carr marched up to Elonzo's house, knocked on the door, and disappeared inside. The undersheriff ambled to the wagon side and glanced at a silent Walter Mills, who surveyed the observers around the compound as if he were a bailiff watching over a rowdy courtroom.

Elizabeth leveled her gaze at Abraham. "Did you know they'd take the cabins apart?"

"I should've guessed," said Abraham, studying his feet. He was appalled but not surprised Walter had resorted to such extreme tactics. "Walter told me he wanted to get all that land in production right away."

Sheriff Carr emerged from Elonzo's cabin and escorted the other three members of the moving party—Elonzo Byers, Charles Bernardo, and Emil Forberg—to the wagon. Sheriff Carr stopped at the rear of the wagon and motioned the three forward. They climbed up into the wagon bed and sat down opposite Walter Mills.

The villagers came alive with chatter, as intent on accounting and reckoning as if they themselves were judge and jury. Sheriff Carr and his undersheriff strolled around to the wagon front and mounted the wagon seat, ignoring the villagers watching their every step. The sheriff pulled at the reins, steering the wagon out of the compound and down the road to Manistique.

Abraham surveyed the knots of observers and saw, in the eyes of the Kepler kin, accusation and anger. He muttered, to himself as much as to Elizabeth, "They blame me. They blame me for all this."

Elizabeth edged closer to Abraham. "Yes, they do. I should've tried harder to stop you. To stop all this. I knew all along it was wrong."

Abraham could no longer bear the burden of so many eyes on him. "Let's go in, Mother. I've had enough of this for one day."

⌒﹏◌

In the morning Abraham rode into town with a small party of villagers. Lenniel drove the wagon and carried a sack of food that Elonzo's wife had prepared for her husband. Walter's son, Francis Mills, transported a small suitcase Nettie had stocked with a clean shirt and suit for Walter. Charles' and Emil's wives had insisted on visiting their husbands and bringing them some proper court clothes.

Over the rollaways and across the slough, all their talk was of the arrests. Only Lucinda Clark, with her luggage and trunk in tow, refrained from joining the conversation; she sat upright in the wagon bed with an I-told-you-so look plastered on her face. Abraham had little to say about the matter himself, for he was still sorting out the mess created by Walter's insistence on forcing a move. One thing he intended to do in town was check the newspapers and assess the damage to the colony's reputation. He couldn't help fretting over what the arrests would mean for the association and everybody in it, including himself, who'd pledged their land and agreed to abide by its rules. What a kettle of fish— having their affairs scrutinized by the law and outsiders. He couldn't imagine a worse eventuality.

After the wagon party deposited Lucinda Clark at the train station and arranged their rendezvous time, Abraham walked to the Manistique *Pioneer*'s office and bought the new issue. Although not pleased with its write-up of events, he couldn't dispute the content:

> The Hiawatha Village Association was the scene of a disturbance yesterday, and a course of law is the result. Yesterday Judge Hill issued warrants for the arrest of Walter Thomas Mills, a man named Bernardo, and two Scandinavians, upon the charge of assault and battery on Mrs. John Kepler. Sheriff Carr and Undersheriff Fred Orr were dispatched to the scene of the disturbance last night. Alva Kepler and John Kepler, two members of the Village Association, swore out the warrant, claiming that they'd been forcibly ejected from their houses by the above parties, who wished them to take up residence in the colony village. The houses they lived in were on the land which these men signed over to the colony, and they preferred living there rather than moving to the colony quarters. There appear to be other matters connected with the row which may come out at the trial.

Abraham knew he should visit the jail to say a few words to his son, Elonzo. But he couldn't bring himself to do so for he was dead set against speaking with Walter: He'll just ask me to see to orders for the department heads or request that I testify on his behalf, and I don't have the stomach to entertain any more of the man's orders. Nor did he wish to give vent to the anger that'd taken hold of him: Walter's actions had, plain and simple, undermined the whole colony.

When Lenniel returned from his visit to the jail, Abraham asked him, "How's Elonzo holding up?"

"Well enough, I suppose." Lenniel leaned against the wagon beside his father and plunged his hands into his pockets. "Walter's been assuring him they'll all be exonerated."

"This has got to be hard on Elonzo. He's such a gentle soul. Is there anything he wants me to do?"

"He just asked us to pray for guidance for him."

"When will the trial be?"

"Day after tomorrow. The attorney asked for their release, but the judge wouldn't let them out on bail."

Abraham snorted. "Well, why not?"

"Judge Hill doesn't want to take a chance on any more damage to property until the matter gets sorted out."

⁓~◦◦

Abraham and Elizabeth traveled to Manistique two days later for the trial. They, like several others in the village, had been subpoenaed. Abraham hoped he'd not have to testify, for he dreaded the prospect of having his complicity trotted out before the townspeople and his own fellows.

Walter's Aunt Nettie had given Abraham the association papers, according to instructions from Walter, and Abraham carried them in his satchel. This, perhaps, was Walter's way of trying to drag him into the morass. Well, if called to the stand he'd not refer to the documents, but he'd hand them over if Walter wished to read from them.

The morning of the trial word spread around town that Judge Hill had scheduled Walter Thomas Mills first on the docket. Even during the behind-closed-doors jury selection, townspeople crammed the courtroom so full that latecomers were relegated to the back, where they stood jostling each other as they angled for a good view and waited for the proceedings to get underway.

"All rise," called the bailiff as the side door swung open and the elderly Judge Hill strode in, his black gown flapping about his stooped frame. As they stood Abraham nudged closer to Elizabeth. He felt lonely and chastened amid inquiring glances from Manistique residents and accusatory glares from many of their own kin.

After making quick work of the preliminaries, Judge Hill announced, "Counselor Dunton, you may call your first witness."

Prosecuting Attorney Dunton requested that John Kepler take the stand, and the judge swore him in.

"Mr. Kepler," intoned Dunton from the prosecutor's table, his straight-fitting suit emphasizing his lanky torso, "will you describe the events that took place at your home on the date of May sixth?"

John clasped his hands on his lap and bowed his head. With his bulky frame all hunched over in the witness box, he resembled a bear stuffed into a small cage. "Yes, sir. Four men came to our cabin in a wagon and forced me and my wife out of our home."

"And are any of this party in the courtroom today? Can you name them?" Dunton turned toward the defendant's table.

John followed Dunton's gaze to where Mills sat beside his attorney. "Yes, sir, it was him—Walter Mills." Looking down at his hands, he continued, "The others were Charles Bernardo, Emil Forberg, and Elonzo Byers."

"And did any of these men assault your wife?"

Attorney Walsh sprang up from the defendant's table. "Objection. That's leading the witness."

Judge Hill flapped his hand in mild exasperation and turned to Dunton. "Counsel, will you rephrase your question?"

Dunton tucked one side of his mouth into the hollow of his cheek in a half-hearted attempt to hide a smirk. "Mr. Kepler, please tell us in your own words what happened to your wife on the occasion of your removal from the cabin."

"Well," said John, pausing and clearing his throat, "My wife got upset when I was being dragged away from our cabin and she tried to get to me, but Mr. Mills shoved her away and she fell hard against the cabin. I saw it because I was trying to break out of the hold the other men had on me. Then Mr. Mills grabbed her by the arm and yanked her to the wagon. He and the other men forced her up onto the wagon bed. She was mighty upset by then. And crying from the pain." John looked at his wife in the front row. "And she's not the crying type."

Titters escaped from a bevy of young women at the back of the courtroom.

"Order," commanded the judge, peering at the group. "If you don't respect these proceedings, I'll close this court to spectators."

The onlookers kept quiet for the next few hours, through the cross-examination of John and during Elvila's testimony, too.

But a buzz of excitement skittered over the crowd when the defense called Walter Thomas Mills to the stand.

"Mr. Mills," began Defending Attorney Walsh, "what is your position in the Hiawatha Village Association?"

"I'm the association president," said Mills, his head tilted back, and his trunk held straight and square. No one could mistake his stance: He was not ashamed of his actions. In fact, he exuded the confidence of a winning general.

"Can you describe for the court what the nature of this association is?"

"Certainly," said Mr. Mills with a measured nod. "The association is an incorporated entity. Fifty individuals have signed on as official members."

"And what does membership entail?"

"The association is the umbrella organization for the village. It governs the financial dealings of the village and sets forth rules for its unique operations. It's fashioned in the likeness of my book, *The Product-Sharing Village.*"

"And do the rules of the association speak to the housing arrangements for the village?"

"Indeed, they do. The rules stipulate that all members of the association are to come together in the housing compound as housing is made available for them."

Walsh put hand to chin and paused with weighty consideration. Taking his hand away, he said, "Now tell us, Mr. Mills, have John and Elvila Kepler signed on as members of this association?"

"Yes, sir. Both have signed the association membership roll."

"And were they aware that they were expected to move to the village compound?"

"Oh, yes. It was in writing when they signed. And Abraham Byers assured me he advised John of this requirement."

"Objection," Dunton called, rising from the prosecutor's table. "That's hearsay, Your Honor."

Judge Hill agreed: Yes, it was hearsay. But this did Abraham no good. He was called next to testify.

Defending Attorney Walsh studied Abraham from under bunched-up eyebrows. "Mr. Byers, did you, on the second of May, talk with John Kepler about the village compound?"

"Yes, sir, I did," said Abraham, tucking his fingers under his thighs on the smooth seat of the witness box.

"And what was the nature of that discussion?"

"Well, I told him a house was ready for him in the compound and asked if he would move into it."

"Did you advise him he was required to move to the village?"

"Well, I mostly asked him if he would move."

Walsh snapped his head into angled severity. "I didn't ask what you mostly did, Mr. Byers. Did you advise John Kepler that he was required to move to the village?"

Abraham moistened his lips and avoided Elizabeth's eye. "Yes, sir, I did."

That'd been the worst the attorney had forced out of him. Yes, he was also asked to recount what he'd observed on the day of the move, but that wasn't in dispute. Even those in the back of the courtroom had gasped at the sight of the incandescent bruises purpling Elvila's arms. And neither did Mills dispute the claim that he'd ordered and enforced the removal of John and Elvila from their cabin. No, it was the insinuation of Abraham's involvement in the whole ordeal that pained him the most, for he knew in his heart that he bore some responsibility for this outcome.

The attorneys exhausted their list of witnesses late in the afternoon. Judge Hill ordered the jury to get on with its deliberations in the case of the People vs. Walter Thomas Mills, whereupon the onlookers filed out of the courtroom to relieve and refresh themselves during the recess. A mere half hour later, the bailiff called to the crowd milling in the hall, "Court in session . . . five minutes to session."

Abraham and Elizabeth shuffled back into the courtroom and took up their seat in the witness row. The time of judgment is upon us, thought Abraham, hoping with all his might the village would be allowed the freedom to settle its own affairs, even if Walter had done wrong. Perhaps if the jury found Mills guilty, the judge would reprimand him for the means he'd employed to enforce the rules. Yes, that would be just and fair. And then perhaps he could work with Walter and the Keplers to find some middle ground, some way for the village to continue on its path and bring everyone together again. Abraham watched the jury emerge from the side room and walk to their seats. He studied their expressions, but they all kept their eyes cast down and revealed not a hint of either self-satisfaction or regret.

"All rise," announced the bailiff. The judge strode to his seat, and the courtroom rustled with the shuffle of feet and the settling of bodies as the lawyers, jury, defendants, and onlookers seated themselves.

Judge Hill turned to the jury foreman. "Has the jury reached a verdict?"

"Yes, Your Honor."

"Please tell the court," said the judge.

"The jury finds Walter Thomas Mills guilty as charged of assault and battery upon the person of Mrs. John Kepler."

Exclamations burst from the back of the court, "Yes," "Enough is enough," and "Tis just," as if several in the crowd had all along hungered for Mills' comeuppance. Abraham twisted around and gazed wide-eyed at the outraged townspeople and Kepler kin. Elizabeth gave him a corner-of-the-eye glance, as if to take measure of his reaction.

"Order," called Judge Hill, bringing his mallet down twice. "Mr. Mills, will you please rise."

Walter Thomas Mills rose from his seat and looked to the judge, his jaw stiff and eyes steely.

"Mr. Mills," intoned the judge, "I sentence you to pay a fine of $50 and costs of $20 within one hour or serve 90 days in jail." Judge Hill thumped his mallet. "This court is recessed until the trials of Charles Bernardo, Emil Forberg, and Elonzo Byers in the morning."

Abraham and Elizabeth squeezed out of the courtroom into the hall of people milling and buzzing with news of Mills' guilty verdict.

I must do what's right, thought Abraham, turning to Elizabeth. "Let's go to John and Elvila."

Elizabeth looked him full in the face. "They'll not want to speak with you. They've lost trust in you."

Abraham's eyes pleaded with his wife. "I know, Mother. I must apologize."

"They'll expect more than an apology."

A child tapped Abraham's arm. "My father gave me a leather case just like that one."

Abraham looked down on a freckled, blond-haired boy who stood beside him, about eye level with the satchel Abraham carried. "And who is your father?"

"I am," boomed a voice from behind the boy.

Abraham looked over his shoulder. There stood his old nemesis, Artin Quick, manager at the Chicago Lumbering Company and head of its Soo Shipping Line office, patting his son on the head.

Elizabeth twisted around for a look.

Abraham turned to Quick. "And might I ask how you acquired that satchel, Mr. Quick?"

Quick rolled his eyes from one side to the other, as if exasperated by the inquiry. "I bought it from a relation of yours."

Abraham studied Quick's ruddy complexion and plump cheeks. He looks like greed itself, thought Abraham. "And what relation is that?"

"A nephew of yours, I believe. Joseph Booth."

Oh, dear God, thought Abraham. My great-nephew stole from me. Why? Why would he do this? But the satchel, the very satchel his father fashioned for him was found again. "Then I'll ask you to return it, for that satchel was stolen from me."

"No, Mr. Byers, I purchased that satchel."

"And did you ask Joseph to acquire it for you?"

"I'd advise you to check your insinuation."

Elizabeth tugged at Abraham's sleeve. "What's this all about?"

But Abraham persisted in his inquiries. "That satchel belongs to me. It's a keepsake from my father."

Quick reached down for his son's shoulder and urged him ahead. "Mr. Booth informed me it had at one time belonged to you." Quick took a step away from Abraham before turning around and saying, "He sold it to raise money and get away from you and your stifling ways. Judging by today's verdict, he figured you right."

All the injustices Quick had committed rushed through Abraham's mind: docking Beech's pay when he drove Gus to the doctor; lying about Abraham's role in the failed mill workers' strike; and sabotaging the shipment of their crops. "I leave it to the Lord Almighty to judge the both of us, sir."

With a huff rank with superiority, Quick hurried away.

Abraham's head swirled. Betrayed by his great-nephew! And now his own kin judging him as an accomplice to Walter Mills. What would become of the colony? What of the trust his relations and flock had once placed in him? How could he live among them after taking them down this path?

He hustled Elizabeth out of the court building, even as she cast inquiring looks upon him. "Mother, I just don't know what to do."

"About what?" she asked.

"Everything, everything," he said, gripping her by the elbow and steering her across the street and away from the dispersing crowd. "The village and where we go from here. Our flock and our relations. Do you know Joseph stole that satchel from me?"

"I always said he was trouble." Elizabeth shook her head. "And ever since the day Florence left, I've regretted how we pushed her out—the both of us."

"Oh, Mother, what am I to do? I've lost the trust of our kin."

"Yes, you must choose sides now. It's either Mills and his ways or your kin and the order the jury imposed."

"It should be some comfort to John and Elvila that the judge found Mills guilty."

"John isn't a vindictive man. He cares little about Mills' guilt or punishment. He only wants to stay in his home."

"Why, yes, Mother. I've amends to make. I surely do." But could he manage such amends *and* preserve something of his and Walter's vision?

AMENDS

May 1895

Two days later Abraham visited Walter in his study with the latest news. Leaning over Walter's shoulder, he pointed to the column in Manistique's *Semi-Weekly Pioneer.* "Here, Walter. They put it right on the front page."

As Walter hunched over the newspaper atop his desk and studied it, Abraham reread the report over his shoulder:

> Cases were called yesterday against Emil Forberg, Charles Bernando, and Elonzo Byers. This time Justice Hill heard the cases without a jury being called. No defense was made. The prosecution examined a few witnesses and the Justice fined each of them in various sums, with the usual imprisonment in case of a failure to pay. It is rumored that more arrests will be made. The officers are breaking up the outlawry of Mills, and his gang will learn that Schoolcraft County will not tolerate such crimes.

"More arrests," Walter huffed, shoving the newspaper aside. "I don't know what grounds they have for more arrests."

Abraham stepped to the red and gold-striped chair in front of Walter's desk and sat down. "I'm afraid the court has made it clear: We cannot use force to impose association rules."

Walter leaned back in his desk chair. "Abraham, outsiders are trying to bring us down. This language— 'outlawry,' 'Mills and his gang'—is nothing short of incendiary."

Abraham nodded. He didn't wish to draw out this discussion, but he thought it best to build to the right moment to apprise Walter of the recent turn of events.

Slapping his hands against his knee tops Walter declared, "Never have I heard such distorted drivel. I will ask my attorney to prepare an appeal of our cases."

Abraham took in a deep breath and clenched the smooth arms of the chair. "It's not just outsiders, Walter. Some of our own have turned against the cause. I believe we must grapple with this internal strife."

Walter tilted his head with wariness. "A grand movement such as ours cannot be accomplished without strife. You better than any of the others should understand this."

"Our cause cannot succeed with discord ripping at its members. Something must be done about this."

"Fine," Walter said, stiffening his arms against his knees. "Once we win the appeal, John and Alva will be compelled to honor the rules, and we can go forward in accordance with them."

"No, Walter. I believe we must straightaway resolve the grievances of John and Alva."

Mills' nostrils flared. "Have I heard you right? Are you urging surrender of our cause?"

"I'm urging the rebuilding of Alva and John's cabins so the families can take them up again."

Mills leaned forward in his chair and planted his forearms on his desk, smug as pie. "I can't order that on my own. It must come from a vote of the officers, just as the order to remove them did."

Abraham relaxed the clench of his fingers on the chair arms. "I've already spoken with all the officers. They're in favor of such a decision."

Walter furrowed his brow and eyed Abraham for a moment, as if seeing him anew. "You've gone behind my back, Abraham. I wouldn't have expected this of you."

Leaning in, Abraham stared into Walter's eyes. "I feel strongly about this matter. These are my kin. I'll not have more bitterness visited on this family settlement."

"I thought it was Hiawatha Colony."

"It was the Byers' Settlement before it was Hiawatha Colony, and I was its pastor. I'll not betray the trust of my flock any longer."

"You're interfering with the rules and order of the Association."

"I don't care for rules that don't serve the people. And I advise you to ward off any future arrests. The judge has sent a signal. I believe if you persist in enforcing rules this way, he'll issue more warrants."

Mills thumped a fist on his desk. "This is outrageous. You're tying my hands. You're undoing my authority as president."

"Many times, you've asked for my help in matters of the colony. I'm now offering it with a free conscience." Abraham stood, took a step toward the door, and turned to Walter. "And there's one more action I've urged on the other officers—a return of the deeds to any landowners who wish to resign the Association."

Never had Abraham observed Walter at a loss for words.

Abraham quit Walter's study, for there was nothing more he wished to say. Besides, he had other business to attend to. Over the last two days he'd refrained from revealing his behind-the-scenes maneuvers to Elizabeth. He hurried home, full of excitement to share his news.

He found Elizabeth standing over her boiling tub and stirring the laundry. The steam rising from the vat warmed the room and steamed the windows. It made him feel cozy and safe.

"Mother," he said, "I've just come from discussing some matters with Walter."

"Oh," said Elizabeth, glancing up. "What matters?"

"I've urged him to have John and Alva's cabins rebuilt and to allow them to move back into them."

Elizabeth pulled her stirring stick out of the tub and straightened up. "Will he allow it?"

"He has no choice. I've discussed the matter with the other officers, and they'll outvote him if he goes against it."

Elizabeth blinked back her surprise. "Oh, my heavens."

"And the officers will also vote to allow any who wish to have their land deeded back to be allowed to do so."

"Do John and Alva know yet?"

"I was hoping you'd go with me to tell them. Will you?"

The hint of a smile crept over Elizabeth's face. "Yes, Husband, I believe I will. Soon as I finish here."

Abraham pulled a chair out at the table and sat. "Do you know what Lenniel told me?"

"What's that?"

"That Walter and his wife are divorcing."

"Humph," said Elizabeth, wiping the sweat from her brow with her forearm. "Not surprised."

"What do you think of all this, Mother?"

Elizabeth plunged her stick back into the laundry vat. "Maybe next time you'll listen to me before you go off half-cocked."

After Mills, Forberg, Bernardo, and Elonzo Byers were found guilty of assault, Hiawatha Colony members rebuilt the cabins of John and Alva Kepler and voted to return the plots of John Kepler, Alva Kepler, and Emily Rose to them. Late in 1895, Mills, his family members, and many others departed, leaving only about fifteen families to winter over that season, at which time colony rules were essentially abandoned. David Byers, Abraham and Elizabeth's youngest son, was elected president of the Hiawatha Association and spent the next five years sorting out association business affairs and parceling out the land. Some colony land was sold to satisfy mortgage claims, and many original landowners, including Abraham Byers, Link Byers, Edgar Huey, and Elonzo Byers, recovered only portions of their original tracts.

In September 1895 Lenniel Byers married Lottie Randall, daughter of John Henry Randall, and in 1896 they moved to Chicago with the rest of the Randall family, where Lenniel obtained work as a conductor for the Chicago Street Railway.

All of Sarah and Eli Huey's land was returned to them in January 1897, but the family's trials continued. Daughter Eva had succumbed to tuberculosis in July 1896, and Eli died in June 1897. Son Edgar left Hiawatha after his father's death and joined another cooperative colony in the state of Washington. Shortly afterward, Sarah sold their Hiawatha land and moved her other children, Vincent, Clifton, and Pearl, to Washington, where they joined Edgar. A few years later Edgar died of tuberculosis.

Link and Elonzo Byers sold their land and left the settlement in spring of 1898. Beech Byers and his new wife, Essie Wright, remained in Hiawatha for a few years and lived with Elizabeth and Abraham. After Beech and Essie departed for Washington state, Lenniel and his wife, Lottie, returned from Chicago and took up residence with Abraham and Elizabeth. Descendants of Lenniel and Lottie Byers still live on the acreage homesteaded by Abraham and Elizabeth.

In the years following the demise of Hiawatha Colony, Walter Thomas Mills tried to launch other cooperative villages but never met with success. He continued his political work on behalf of socialist and labor movement causes, traveling and lecturing all around the United States, Great Britain, Australia, and New Zealand. Reputed to be a philanderer, he married three times and divorced twice.

The Alva Kepler family eventually moved west. Their cabin, which had been torn down and then rebuilt after the trial, was later acquired by the Schoolcraft Historical Society and moved to Manistique in 1978, where it now stands as a museum and memorial to the Byers' Settlement and Hiawatha Colony.

The graves of those few original settlers who lived out their years on settlement lands can be found in Hiawatha Cemetery, which Abraham founded in 1887. Abraham and Elizabeth Byers are buried there, side-by-side, as are John and Elvila Kepler.

ABOUT THE AUTHOR

Maryka Biaggio, Ph.D., is a former psychology professor turned novelist who specializes in historical fiction based on real people. She enjoys the challenge of starting with actual historical figures and dramatizing their lives—figuring out what motivated them to behave as they did, studying how the cultural and historical context may have influenced them, and recreating some sense of their emotional world through dialogue and action. Doubleday published her debut novel, PARLOR GAMES, in January 2013. She lives in Portland, Oregon, that edgy green gem of the Pacific Northwest. You can visit her web page at marykabiaggio.com.

AUTHOR'S NOTES AND ACKNOWLEDGMENTS

Elizabeth Kepler Byers and Abraham Byers, matriarch and patriarch of the Byers Settlement, are my great-great-great grandparents. I first learned of Hiawatha Colony in the 1990s when my mother, Phyllis Weber Biaggio, gave me her copy of *Utopia in Upper Michigan*, a study of the colony by Olive M. Anderson (1982, Northern Michigan University Press, Marquette, MI). The story stayed with me, and I began work on *Eden Waits* in 2005.

I made extensive use of Olive Anderson's scholarly book, *Utopia in Upper Michigan,* in my research. Ms. Anderson interviewed descendants of colony members and mined historical records and newspaper reports. She died in 2003, but years earlier she donated her primary research materials to the Marquette County Historical Society.

I'm grateful to Rosemary Michelin, librarian of 26 years at the Marquette County Historical Society, for answering sundry questions and guiding me through relevant research materials, including Olive Anderson's archives. I also found valuable material about life in the Upper Peninsula during the 1890s in William S. Crowe's book *Lumberjack: Inside an Era in the Upper Peninsula of Michigan* (2002, North Country Publishing, Skandia, MI). Searches of period newspapers at the Manistique Public Library yielded facts and stories about key events in the colony. Walter Thomas Mills' 1894 book, *The Product-Sharing Village* (Civic Letters Co., Oak Park, IL) provided information about the principles underlying colony operations.

Many details about individuals are derived from my and others' genealogical research. Monisa Wisener of the Randolph County Historical Society in Indiana provided information about the Byers and Keplers. Josie Berard of Tabernash, Colorado, a descendant of Beech and Essie Byers, generously shared her genealogy records. My uncle, Gerald Weber, kindly took me on a tour of the Hiawatha Cemetery and Byers' Settlement grounds. Another uncle, Richard "Buddy" Weber, and aunt, Dolores Hawthorne, provided pictures of Abraham, Elizabeth, and other principles of the colony, bringing these people to life for me. And my mother, Phyllis Weber Biaggio, who has the best and longest memory of anyone I've ever known, was always quick with tales of ancestors or information about wild fruits, woodsy smells, and olden times in the Upper Peninsula.

This novelized account of the colony obviously enlarges on known events. My aim was not to create a factual rendering; inconsistencies abound even in first-person accounts of the colony. I tried, however, to bring authenticity to the novel, to follow the general outline of the story, and to accurately represent key events and issues surrounding this utopian experiment. At times during the story I take liberties with these materials or modify the timeline of events for the sake of narrative pacing. But all original content cited in this novel, either word-for-word or in paraphrased form, is credited in the narrative or in these acknowledgements.

Have I invented day-to-day happenings and conversations in this telling? Yes, because I hoped to capture some sense of the dreams, drama, and heartache of those who lived in the settlement and colony. I hope my readers will forgive these liberties and set aside their reservations long enough to enjoy this rendering of Hiawatha Colony and the lives of Abraham and Elizabeth Byers. Then they may imagine for themselves: What was it like to live this history?

Maryka Biaggio, Ph.D.
Portland, OR
June 2019

Made in the USA
Columbia, SC
04 September 2019